MURDER ON
FIFTH AVENUE

Berkley Prime Crime titles by Victoria Thompson

MURDER ON FIFTH AVENUE

A Gaslight Mystery

Victoria Thompson

BERKLEY PRIME CRIME, NEW YORK

THE BERKLEY PUBLISHING GROUP
Published by the Penguin Group
Penguin Group (USA) Inc.
375 Hudson Street, New York, New York 10014, USA
Penguin Group (Canada), 90 Eglinton Avenue East, Suite 700, Toronto, Ontario M4P 2Y3, Canada
(a division of Pearson Penguin Canada Inc.) • Penguin Books Ltd., 80 Strand, London WC2R 0RL,
England • Penguin Group Ireland, 25 St. Stephen's Green, Dublin 2, Ireland (a division of Penguin
Books Ltd.) • Penguin Group (Australia), 250 Camberwell Road, Camberwell, Victoria 3124, Australia
(a division of Pearson Australia Group Pty. Ltd.) • Penguin Books India Pvt. Ltd., 11 Community
Centre, Panchsheel Park, New Delhi—110 017, India • Penguin Group (NZ), 67 Apollo Drive,
Rosedale, Auckland 0632, New Zealand (a division of Pearson New Zealand Ltd.) • Penguin Books
(South Africa) (Pty.) Ltd., 24 Sturdee Avenue, Rosebank, Johannesburg 2196, South Africa

Penguin Books Ltd., Registered Offices: 80 Strand, London WC2R 0RL, England

This book is an original publication of The Berkley Publishing Group.

This is a work of fiction. Names, characters, places, and incidents either are the product of the author's
imagination or are used fictitiously, and any resemblance to actual persons, living or dead, business
establishments, events, or locales is entirely coincidental. The publisher does not have any control over
and does not assume any responsibility for author or third-party websites or their content.

FIRST EDITION: May 2012

Library of Congress Cataloging-in-Publication Data

Thompson, Victoria (Victoria E.)
Murder on Fifth Avenue / Victoria Thompson.—1st ed.
p. cm.— (A gaslight mystery)
ISBN 978-0-425-24741-9 (hardcover)
1. Malloy, Frank (Fictitious character)—Fiction. 2. Police—New York (State)—New York—
Fiction. 3. Brandt, Sarah (Fictitious character)—Fiction. 4. Midwives—New York (State)—
New York—Fiction. 5. Murder—Investigation—Fiction. 6. Rich people—Fiction. 7. Fifth
Avenue (New York, N.Y.)—Fiction. I. Title.
PS3570.H6442M867 2012
813'.54—dc22
2011052355

PRINTED IN THE UNITED STATES OF AMERICA

10 9 8 7 6 5 4 3 2

ALWAYS LEARNING   **PEARSON**

To my daughter Ellen,
for introducing me to Fifth Avenue

MURDER ON
FIFTH AVENUE

I

"**D**ETECTIVE SERGEANT MALLOY?"

Frank hated answering stupid questions from goo-goos when he was in the middle of an investigation. He looked up from interviewing one of the employees of the warehouse that had been robbed last night. This brand-new police officer didn't even look old enough to shave. "What?"

"I have a message for you from the chief." The way he was puffing, he must've run all the way from Police Headquarters to deliver it.

"Which chief?"

"Chief O'Brien."

Frank straightened. He didn't dare ignore a message from the chief of detectives. The young man held out a piece of paper, and Frank snatched it from him. Unfolding it, he read the message. *Felix Decker requests your presence at the Knickerbocker Club immediately.* O'Brien had given the address and signed it.

Frank swore. Felix Decker might not be the richest, most powerful man in the city, but he was rich and powerful enough, and he knew all the men who were richer and more powerful than he was. He also knew the chief of detectives, the chief of police, and the mayor. Most of all, he knew Frank. And Frank knew Felix Decker's daughter, Sarah Brandt, which was the real reason Decker knew Frank would jump when Decker called.

"What am I supposed to do about this?" Frank gestured to include the warehouse where he'd spent most of the day investigating the robbery.

"The chief said he'd send somebody else to take over."

Of course he would. He'd send another detective who would gladly take over and get the reward for solving this case. As soon as Frank had located the thieves and negotiated with them, he would have split the reward with them and returned the merchandise. That's how business was done in New York City, and everybody knew it. Another detective would be more than happy to take over his case.

Frank swore again.

FRANK HUNKERED INSIDE HIS OVERCOAT AGAINST WINTER'S late afternoon chill as he stopped on the sidewalk outside the Knickerbocker Club to catch his breath. The trip from the riverfront warehouse uptown involved more walking than Frank normally liked to do, but the jam of wagons in the city streets made it by far the fastest mode of crosstown transportation. Then he had boarded the Sixth Avenue Elevated Train, the only truly fast mode of transportation in the city, squeezing into a packed car for the trip uptown. Another brisk walk over to Fifth Avenue, and here he was.

New York had hundreds of men's clubs, few more exclusive than the Knickerbocker. Micks need not apply, nor much of anyone else, as far as he knew. Except for a few of the Jewish upper crust, membership was restricted to descendants of the original Dutch and English settlers of the city. Knickerbockers. Some said the nickname *Knickerbocker* came from the knee-length pants the early colonists wore. Others said from a story by Washington Irving. What did he care? Even though they allowed Jews to belong, he'd bet a year's pay no Irish Catholic had ever crossed the threshold.

So why in God's name had Decker set their meeting here and not at his office? Unfortunately, the only way to find out was to go inside.

He climbed the front steps and gave the imposing brass knocker a serious thump. The door swung wide, and he exchanged glances with a man got up for a fancy dress ball in his cutaway and stiff white shirt. Fortunately, Frank had been around enough rich people to know the fellow who answered the door was a servant, no matter how he might be dressed.

Frank opened his mouth to quickly explain his presence here before the butler could slam the door in his face—it had happened before—but the fellow said, "Mr. Malloy, Mr. Decker is expecting you," before he could speak.

He stepped back to allow Frank to enter and took his hat and coat, then led him down a short hallway. Thick carpets muffled their footsteps, and Frank inhaled the scent of expensive cigars and old leather. Dark paneling covered the walls, and decorative light fixtures muted the glare of the electric lights. Nothing but the best. As they reached a small sitting room, he caught sight of Felix Decker, who was apparently trying to pace a hole in the expensive carpeting.

"Mr. Malloy has arrived," the butler said, then took his leave.

The tall elegant man stopped instantly and strode forward, offering Frank his hand. "Thank you for coming so quickly, Mr. Malloy."

As if he could have refused. Frank simply nodded as he returned Decker's firm handshake.

"Please, sit down." Decker indicated the chesterfield sofa. A liberal amount of silver threaded Decker's fair hair, and his blue eyes held the wisdom and cynicism of age, although today they were troubled in a way Frank had never seen before. Decker took the closest chair and rubbed his hands together as if uncertain exactly what to do with them.

Felix Decker was upset. Frank didn't think Felix Decker ever got upset.

"Have you been here before?" Decker asked.

"No." Frank didn't bother to explain his theory that he was the first Irish Catholic to ever enter the club by the front door.

"We aren't a particularly old club," Decker said. "We formed back in seventy-one, when some Union Club members felt the membership requirements there had become too liberal."

Frank had no trouble believing that at all.

"I tell you this so you'll understand the men with whom you'll be dealing."

Frank didn't think Felix Decker was going to propose him for membership, so he couldn't imagine needing to have any contact with the other members at all. "Dealing?"

"Yes, you see, one of our members was found dead here this afternoon."

"Dead or murdered?" Simply finding somebody dead wouldn't prompt anybody to send for a police detective.

Decker drew a deep breath. "At first we assumed he had simply passed away from natural causes. A bad heart, perhaps. He seemed to be dozing peacefully in his chair, but when one of the waiters accidentally bumped the chair and he didn't react . . . Well, he was quite cold, so they knew he had been dead for a while."

"But now you don't think he just passed away."

"No. You see, we sent for an undertaker. He was the one who noticed the bloodstain on the chair and then on Devries's clothing. He quickly determined that he had been stabbed in the back."

"So somebody here stabbed him?"

"Certainly not. At least we are fairly confident it couldn't have happened here without Devries raising some kind of alarm, so it must have happened prior to his arrival. As far as I can ascertain, he appeared here sometime in the midafternoon and went to the library to read the newspapers. He complained to one of the staff of not feeling well. He asked for some brandy but only drank a small amount, and then he fell asleep, or so everyone thought."

This wasn't making sense. If a man got stabbed, why wouldn't he get medical attention? Or at least stay at home and tend to his wound? Why would he go out to his club, of all things? "Was it possible he didn't know he'd been stabbed?"

"The wound is small, according to the undertaker, and it had bled very little. I can't imagine he would have been traveling around the city if he'd suspected he was mortally wounded."

"Did the undertaker think this small wound could have killed him?"

Decker pressed his lips together, as if he had tasted something unpleasant. "Mr. Robinson, the undertaker, suggested as much. He said he has seen similar things before in his line of work. Most of the bleeding occurs inside the body, apparently."

Frank supposed such a thing could happen. He'd seen someone die from being stabbed with a hat pin, of all things. "Did Robinson refuse to take the body?"

"Oh, no, not at all. I gather he was perfectly willing to be discreet, but he felt the club should know, in case we wanted to deal with the matter ourselves."

So they were back to dealing again. This, Frank assumed, was to be his part in it. "What did you decide?"

Now Decker looked positively gray around the gills. Plainly, he wasn't used to discussing such unpleasantries, at least not within the walls of his beloved Knickerbocker. "We called together all the board members who happened to be on the premises this afternoon. I'm sure you understand we want the club's reputation protected at all costs."

"Then tell the undertaker to pack up the body."

"Please do not judge us so harshly." He was angry now, and Frank didn't blame him. "If Devries did indeed die by the hand of another, we would also like to see justice done."

Frank leaned back on the surprisingly uncomfortable sofa and studied Decker for a long moment. He didn't like this one bit, probably because he didn't believe Decker's protests about wanting justice. "Are you saying you want me to find out who killed this Devries character?"

"Find out, yes. That's exactly what we want you to do."

"And then what?"

"What do you mean?"

"You know what I mean. Usually, when I solve a murder, I arrest the killer, and he goes to trial, and then, if he's found guilty, he goes to prison or gets executed." Of course, it wasn't always so neat, but he didn't need to mention that to Decker. "Is that what you want?"

"It all depends."

Ah, now we're getting down to it. "On what?"

"On who is responsible for Devries's death. You must realize this is why I summoned you, out of all the detectives in New York, Mr. Malloy, because I know you can be trusted."

Frank didn't know how trustworthy he was, but he knew Decker rarely called him *mister*. He must be feeling desperate.

"What you mean is I know how to keep a secret."

"I would have said you know how to be discreet."

He was right about that. Frank nodded.

"You will make your report to me, when you have all the facts, and then I will take the matter to our board to decide."

Now this was something Frank could understand. The rich looked out for each other. He assumed it was much like the police department, where you watched out for your own and stood up for them when they were in trouble. Frank couldn't imagine why rich people would need that kind of help, but he knew it was available to them.

"Just so I'm clear, what happens if I find out one of your club members is the killer?"

"Then you would not need to take any action at all. We would take care of the matter among ourselves."

Frank doubted the club had an electric chair on the premises to *take care* of murderous members or even a cell or two for confining the drunk and disorderly ones. "You'd let a killer go free?"

"Malloy, you know as well as I do your chief would never allow you to arrest any member of this club, no matter what he had done. If you did, he would be freed with an apology from the mayor within hours, and you would lose your job."

Frank did know this. He'd just wanted to find out what Decker had in mind. "Then why call me in at all?"

"If Devries's killer is someone you can bring to justice, you may do so with our blessing. If the killer is someone whom the law cannot touch, then we will take care of the matter ourselves. That is all you need to know. Now, are you willing to assist us?"

Did he really have a choice? Decker and his kind were more than capable of taking care of *him* if he refused. "Devries's family and the other members of your club aren't going to want an Irish cop nosing around in their business." That was the real problem with calling Frank in on this, and Decker should've known it.

"They will when I introduce you, and if anyone fails to cooperate with your investigation, you are to notify me immediately."

Frank wanted to refuse. He wanted to have a good reason to refuse, but investigating crimes was his job, and pleasing men like Felix Decker was the job of everyone in the city, if they knew what was good for them.

Besides, what would he say to Sarah Brandt if he refused to help her father?

Frank managed not to sigh in defeat. "Is the body still here?"

THE KNICKERBOCKER LIBRARY HELD FEW ACTUAL BOOKS, just those on the set of shelves along one wall, and they looked as if they had never been opened. Newspapers lay stacked on just about every other available surface, however. A quick glance told Frank they seemed to have a copy of every rag and scandal sheet in the city, in addition to the *World*, the *Herald*, and the *Times*. Since most of the papers published two editions a day, simply purchasing all of them must be a full-time job for someone.

The fellow who had answered the door had let them into the library. "I made sure no one else came in after Mr. Robinson left," he told Decker.

"Good, good." Decker turned to Frank. "Hartley here is the one who realized Mr. Devries was dead."

Mr. Devries still sat propped in a wingback chair beside the fireplace, where the undertaker must have left him. The fire had burned down, but the room was still warm. Clearly the Knickerbocker Club had central heating.

In life, Devries had been a substantial man, not fat but large boned. Of medium height, he wore a suit that had been tailor-made to fit his frame to best advantage. His dark hair showed only a touch of gray and had been tamed this morning with a liberal dose of hair tonic. His well-tended hands lay slightly clenched in his lap, as if silently resisting a final spasm of pain. He sat slumped to one side. His eyes were closed, and his mouth open.

"Is that how you found him?"

Hartley shook his head. "Not exactly. Mr. Robinson had brought a stretcher, and his two helpers were moving Mr. Devries from the chair when they noticed the bloodstain on the chair back. Mr. Robinson quickly realized it had come from Mr. Devries, so he told his assistants to put Mr. Devries back as they'd found him, and he asked me to summon someone in authority. Mr. Decker was the highest-ranking club officer present, so I informed him of Mr. Robinson's request."

Frank looked closely at the dead man to see if anything seemed out of place. "Do you remember *exactly* how he was sitting when you found him?"

"Much like this, except perhaps a bit straighter in the chair. His head was resting against the wing of the chair, and his eyes were closed, as if he had dozed off."

Frank glanced around. "Mr. Decker said someone brought him brandy."

"I did, but he only took a sip or two. I removed the snifter when Mr. Robinson arrived."

"I'll need to see the glass and the bottle you poured it from."

"The glass had been washed."

Frank bit back his irritation. "The bottle, then." He didn't think the man had been poisoned, but he wanted to be thorough. He turned to Decker. "I'll need to call the medical examiner to take the body. They'll have to do an autopsy to be sure what killed him."

"Is that really necessary?" Decker asked with obvious distaste.

"Unless you want me harassing a bunch of rich people when the man really did die of a heart attack."

Irritation registered on Decker's face, but no trace of it was evident in his voice. "Hartley, show Mr. Malloy where the telephone is."

DOC HAYNES BROUGHT TWO ASSISTANTS WITH HIM, TOO. As soon as they moved the body to the stretcher, Frank saw the bloodstain on the chair back.

"He didn't bleed much," Frank observed.

"Let's take a look," Doc Haynes said.

He had the two orderlies roll Devries over and lift his suit coat. The undertaker had obviously already made a similar examination. Devries's shirttail was still out in the back. They pushed up the suit coat, vest, shirt, and undershirt, all of which bore evidence of the blood that had stained the chair. The stain on the undershirt was the largest. They grew progressively smaller until the one on the chair was only the size of a coin.

Haynes traced the tiny wound with his finger. If they hadn't been looking for it, Frank would've missed it entirely. "A wound like this wouldn't bleed much, and his clothes absorbed most of it, as you can see."

"Could a wound that small have killed him?"

"Depends on what caused it. How long the weapon was, I mean. A stiletto makes a hole like this. So does an ice pick."

"Or a hat pin."

"You have a lot of experience getting stabbed with hat pins?" Haynes asked with amusement.

"If you mean for getting fresh with women on streetcars, no," Frank said with a grin. "But I had a case once where a fellow got killed by one."

"Oh, yeah, I remember it now. So you understand, it's possible. Just depends how far the weapon went in and what it hit. Right here, now . . ." Haynes pointed to the spot in the middle of the right side of Devries's back where the dried blood was starting to flake. "There's probably a kidney an inch or two behind this hole. A knife or other sharp object stuck into a kidney, well, it would be just a matter of time until he bled to death internally unless he got help. Even if he did get help, probably. I doubt a surgeon would cut him open for something that small, at least not right away."

"And later would be too late."

"Yeah, by the time he started feeling sick, he'd probably be back at home. Or at his club."

Frank didn't return his grin. "Don't forget to test the brandy, just to be sure."

"Don't worry. We'll get him packed up and be on our way. I'll send you word when I'm finished with the autopsy."

Frank left Haynes and his helpers to their work and went in search of Decker. He found him in what was apparently the main room of the club, a large open area furnished with groupings of chairs and sofas. Decker was the only one there.

"Where is everybody?"

Decker rose as Frank approached. "I sent them home when we realized there was a question about Devries's death."

Frank resisted the urge to swear at Felix Decker. "I'll need to know who was here, in case they know anything," he replied, pleased to note that the fury roiling inside of him wasn't evident in his voice.

"Hartley will make a list for you, but I already told you, he wasn't attacked by anyone here at the club."

"You're probably right, but Devries might've said something about being attacked earlier today."

"I didn't think of that, but I suppose he might have. I'll have Hartley ask all the members who were present if they spoke with Devries. Would that be satisfactory?"

Frank supposed it would have to be. "I need to go see his family. Has anybody notified them yet?"

Decker's composure slipped a bit. "No, I . . . I was waiting until I had something more to tell them besides that he was . . . deceased."

"Are you going to tell them yourself?"

"I feel it's my duty, yes."

"Then I'll go with you. I need to see their reaction."

"You can't think anyone in his family is responsible!"

Frank gripped the back of the chair, glanced at the mantel clock, then back at his host. "First you tell me his friends couldn't have done it. Now you tell me his family couldn't have done it. Do you think some stranger just came up to him on the street and stuck a knife in his back for no reason?"

Color flooded Decker's face as he obviously fought for composure as well. Frank knew he wasn't used to being challenged by the help. "That would, of course, be my preference, but I suppose it's too much to ask. I'll have Hartley summon a cab for us."

T HEY COULD HAVE WALKED TO DEVRIES'S HOUSE MUCH more quickly than the cab carried them through the clogged streets, but Frank supposed men like Felix Decker didn't walk in the city. Frank could think of no appropriate small talk to break the tense silence, and apparently, Decker couldn't either.

Devries had lived only a few blocks from the Deckers' residence on the Upper West Side, a place Frank had visited only once and not at Felix Decker's invitation. The houses on these streets had been built to impress but not intimidate, the way the mansions on Fifth Avenue had. He'd been in enough of them to know what to expect, and he wasn't surprised by anything he saw here.

A maid answered the door and her face lit with recognition. "Mr. Decker, I'm sorry, but Mr. Devries is not at home."

"I know he's not. Is Mrs. Devries here? I need to speak with her immediately."

"Oh, dear, yes, of course. Please come in and I'll see if Mrs. Devries can receive you."

Frank watched alarm alter her features as she sensed the urgency and tried to decide how best to treat these unexpected visitors. She probably feared offending Decker if she showed them to the inevitably small, uncomfortable room near the front door where such guests usually waited while it was determined if they were welcome or not.

"We can wait in the front parlor," Decker said, as if sensing her dilemma.

"Yes, sir," she said with obvious relief, and led them upstairs into an oppressively overstuffed room obviously reserved for formal company. No fire had been lit, but Frank decided, despite the abundance of knickknacks cluttering every tabletop, velvets, and doilies, it would have been cold in any case. Nothing about it was comfortable.

"Sir, should I . . . ?"

"Yes?"

"I mean, do you want to see just Mrs. Devries, or should I ask Mr. Paul to join you?"

"Please ask Paul to join us, too, if he's at home."

When the maid had closed the door behind herself, Decker turned to Frank. "I suppose I should have asked your permission to include Paul. That's Devries's son."

Frank ignored the sarcasm. "If the wife is going to get hysterical, having the son here is a good idea."

Decker made a rude noise, but Frank didn't know what in particular had annoyed him, so he pretended not to notice his displeasure. Instead he glanced around at the enormous furniture upholstered in dark blue plush overwhelming the space. A large painting of a sour-looking gentleman hung above the fireplace in a hideous gilt frame, and dark landscapes depicting fox hunts adorned the others. Heavy drapes hung at the windows, trailing onto the floor and tied back with gold cords. No ray of sunlight had managed to enter the room.

Mrs. Devries didn't keep them waiting long. He figured he had Decker to thank for that.

The wisp of a woman, dressed in a gown more suited to someone half her age, paused in the doorway and struck a pose, her finger to her chin as she gazed first at Decker and then at him. She wasn't exactly what he was expecting. Her fair hair had been elaborately arranged but appeared stiff as straw. Like her face, it seemed a bit the worse for wear. After a moment, she tipped her head quizzically to one side and offered the hand not clutching a lacy handkerchief to Decker.

"Felix, what on earth brings you here at this ungodly hour? I hope the girl told you Chilton isn't at home, and I have no idea when he'll return. He never confides in me, you know. You have no idea how I suffer."

Decker took her hand in both of his. "Lucretia, I know very well how you suffer. You tell me every time I set eyes on you. Please, come in and sit down. Is Paul here?"

"I'm sure I don't know. Paul never confides in me either. I'm always the last to know everything that goes on in my own house."

This was going to be horrible, Frank decided. The wife would dissolve into hysterics and he wouldn't be able to get a thing out of her. Then her doctor would come and give her laudanum, and he'd never be allowed back in the house again.

Mrs. Devries jabbered on about something or other that had caused her distress as Decker escorted her to a sofa. He had no sooner seated her than a young man appeared, still smoothing his suit coat as he strode into the room. "Mr. Decker, what a pleasant surprise."

Paul Devries resembled his mother. A small man with delicate features and her fair coloring, he seemed nervous and uncertain as he ran a hand over his thinning hair. Frank wondered if this was his usual temperament or if Decker's arrival had upset him.

"I'm very sorry to burst in on you like this, but I'm afraid I have some bad news."

Something that might have been alarm flickered over Paul Devries's face but was gone before Frank could be sure.

"I'm sure I don't want to hear bad news, whatever it might be," Mrs. Devries was saying. "I have a very nervous disposition, you know. I cannot abide unpleasantness."

"You will have to abide this, I'm afraid," Decker said, plainly unmoved by her protests. "Chilton is dead."

Both mother and son stared at him in what appeared to be genuine shock.

"Dead?" Paul echoed, as if he'd never heard the word before.

"That's impossible," his mother said. "He was perfectly fine when he left the house this morning."

"What time was that?" Frank asked from where he stood beside the cold fireplace.

Both Devrieses looked at him in surprise.

"I'm very sorry. I should have introduced you," Decker said. "Lucretia, Paul, this is Detective Sergeant Malloy of the New York City Police Department."

If anything, they looked even more surprised.

Paul blinked first. "Police? Why are the police here?"

"Because it appears your father was murdered."

Frank braced himself for screaming, but to his surprise, the widow seemed more annoyed than upset.

"What on earth are you talking about, Felix? None of this makes any sense at all!"

"I'm afraid I've made a botch of this, although I'm sure you can understand I have never had occasion to notify a family that one of their members has been . . . killed."

"Perhaps you should start at the beginning," Paul said,

moving somewhat awkwardly to the nearest chair and lowering himself into it.

To Frank's surprise, Decker looked over at him, as if to get his approval. Frank nodded, then watched carefully for their reactions.

"Chilly came to the Knickerbocker this afternoon."

"As was his habit," Mrs. Devries said. "But surely you know that."

"Yes, well, in any case, he went to the library to read the newspapers. The staff noticed he seemed to have dozed off, but eventually, when he did not respond to a disturbance, they realized he had passed away."

"In his sleep? Just like that?" Mrs. Devries said.

"That hardly sounds like murder," Paul said with a trace of outrage.

"We sent for an undertaker, and when he moved the body, he discovered some blood. The source of the blood was a wound on Chilly's back. Someone had stabbed him."

"Are you saying someone at the club stabbed him?" Mrs. Devries asked. "How could such a thing happen?"

"We believe someone stabbed him before he arrived at the club."

"Are you saying my father was fatally stabbed, and yet he walked away, went to his club, and sat down to read the newspapers without saying a word to anyone?"

"The wound itself is quite small and on his back, and it bled very little. He probably had no idea how seriously he had been injured. It may even have been an accident," Decker added, with a glance at Frank, who chose not to contradict him. Maybe it *had* been an accident.

"How could such a small injury have killed him, then?" Mrs. Devries seemed offended at the thought.

"I am sure the medical examiner will be able to explain that after the autopsy."

Paul jumped to his feet. "Good God, they're not doing an autopsy!"

"I'm afraid they must. We have to be sure what killed him, you see."

"So there is still some doubt?" Mrs. Devries said. "He may not have been murdered at all?"

"I suppose it's possible," Decker said.

Frank caught his imploring glance and took a seat near Paul Devries. When Frank sat down, Paul resumed his seat as well. "When did you last see your husband, Mrs. Devries?"

She widened her eyes at him, then looked him over with disdain. "Felix, really, is this necessary?"

"I'm afraid it is. If someone murdered Chilly, you want them found, don't you?"

Mrs. Devries seemed to consider her answer carefully, but before she replied, her son said, "Of course we do. I saw my father this morning, before he left the house. He was perfectly fine, and I saw no one attack him."

"It must have happened after he left home. There can be no other explanation," his mother confirmed. "No one here would have stabbed him, I can assure you of that."

Frank looked from mother to son and back again. Had either of them realized they had not expressed the least bit of anguish or grief at hearing the head of their family was dead? "As Mr. Decker said, it may have been an accident, but we need to be sure. Who else lives here?"

"The servants, of course, and my wife," Paul said.

"Your wife?"

Paul bristled. "You can't think *she* stabbed my father in the back."

Frank had to admit it sounded unlikely, but he hadn't met her yet, so he would reserve judgment. "Any other family members?"

"My two daughters are married, so of course they don't live here."

"Can you tell me what time Mr. Devries left the house today?"

"I certainly cannot," his wife said. "Mr. Devries comes and goes as he pleases without consulting me."

"Do you know what his plans were for the day?"

Mrs. Devries glared at him. "I told you, Mr. Devries does as he pleases."

Frank was starting to wish she'd gotten hysterical.

"Roderick will know. That's his valet," Paul said.

"I'll need to talk with him and with your other servants, too," Frank said.

"Is this necessary? I don't want the household upset," Mrs. Devries said. "My nerves won't stand it."

"Mother, there's no help for it. With Papa dead—"

"Dead?" a new voice said.

They all looked up. A young woman had entered the room. She wore a simple gown, and her rich, dark hair had been brushed into an ordinary bun, but her unadorned beauty far outshone Mrs. Devries's frippery. This must be the other Mrs. Devries.

The men rose instantly to their feet.

"Who's dead?" she asked.

"Oh, Garnet," Mrs. Devries said, her voice rising into a wail. "Mr. Decker has come to tell us poor Papa is dead." The tears Frank had expected earlier began to flow, making him wonder if she'd just been waiting for the right audience.

Paul immediately went to comfort his mother, leaving his

wife to her own devices. She looked at Felix Decker. "Is it true? Is the old man really dead?"

"Yes, I'm sorry to say."

Frank watched the emotions flicker across her face too rapidly for him to identify, and then to his surprise, she broke into a dazzling smile. "He's dead," she said with what could only be called exultation, and she began to laugh.

2

Now this was an interesting reaction to news of a family member's death. It also drew Paul's attention away from his mother. For a few seconds they all stared at Garnet Devries. She must be hysterical, but the only cure Frank knew was to slap her, and slapping Garnet Devries would not improve his chances of interviewing the rest of the family more thoroughly. Fortunately, Felix Decker had no such concerns.

He grabbed her by the shoulders and gave her a shake that snapped her head back. Her laughter ceased at once, and she gazed up at him in surprise for a moment before she went limp. Decker caught her before she could fall, and Paul rushed over. Together they got her into a chair. Her color was high, and her eyes glittered from some inner fire.

"Get her some brandy," Decker told Paul.

"Good heavens, not brandy," Mrs. Devries said. "Sherry should do the trick."

Paul went to a sideboard and found whatever he had decided to give his wife. He brought it back in a crystal tumbler. Frank expected him to put the glass to her lips, but he merely held it out to her at arm's length. She didn't even notice it.

Decker took the glass and put it to her lips. She wrapped her hands over his while she sipped, coughed a bit, then sipped again before looking up at him. "Thank you, Mr. Decker. I don't know what came over me."

"It's the shock, I'm sure," Decker said.

It might be more than that. Frank had never seen anyone laugh when they found out a loved one was dead.

"The shock, of course," Mrs. Devries said. Frank noticed she'd forgotten she was supposed to be crying. "I feel rather faint myself. Poor Chilly. And what an undignified way to go. Stabbed, you say? I can hardly credit it."

Garnet's head came up. "Stabbed? What do you mean, *stabbed*?"

"They think someone stabbed Father."

"Stabbed him where?" she asked.

"In the back, apparently," Paul said.

She sighed. "No, I mean where was he when it happened?"

Paul and his mother exchanged a glance, then looked at Decker, who turned to Frank.

"We don't know when or where it happened. The wound was small. He probably didn't know he was seriously hurt, but he died later from the injury."

"Who are you?" she asked, and Frank noticed the abrupt question didn't sound rude coming from her.

"Frank Malloy."

"He's a policeman," Paul added.

Garnet looked Frank over but showed none of the disdain

her mother-in-law had exhibited. "He doesn't look like a policeman. Where's his uniform?"

"I'm a detective sergeant with the city police."

"Mr. Malloy is investigating Chilly's death," Decker added.

She considered this information. "If you don't know when or where he was stabbed, how are you going to investigate?"

"It won't be easy," Frank admitted with a small smile.

To his amazement, she smiled back. For a second he was afraid she might start laughing again, but she didn't. "I think you like things that aren't easy, Mr. Malloy."

Frank wasn't sure what he should say to that. Luckily, Decker saved him from having to think of something. "Perhaps you could arrange for Mr. Malloy to question Roderick and the other servants, Lucretia."

"Must he do it now? They'll be no good to anyone for the rest of the day if he upsets them."

"They'll be upset when they hear about Chilly anyway," Decker said. "Might as well get it all over with at once."

"I'll ring for the maid." Paul moved to the bell rope.

"I'll need a room where I can see them alone," Frank said.

"The receiving room should do nicely." Mrs. Devries rose. "I think I shall retire. All of this excitement is bad for my nerves. My doctor told me I should never become upset, you know. It's the very worst thing when you have bad nerves."

"I'm sorry to have distressed you, Lucretia," Decker said, "but someone had to tell you about Chilly. I thought it would be easier from me than from a stranger."

Paul stepped forward. "You were very kind to come yourself, wasn't he, Mother? I know the truth of it hasn't really sunk in for me yet. There's so much to do, isn't there? A funeral and . . . and . . ." He gestured vaguely.

"We'll need mourning clothes, I suppose," his mother said. "I detest wearing black, but there's no help for it, is there?"

"No, Mother Devries, there's no help for it." Garnet sighed again and turned as the maid came in.

Frank waited as Paul told her that Mr. Malloy would like to speak with Roderick in the receiving room, and then he would like to see some of the other servants, too. Roderick would take care of all that. Her eyes were like saucers at the strange request, but, of course, she couldn't question him. She'd have to wait for the gossip to make its way through the household.

"Are you going to tell this Roderick that Mr. Devries is dead?" he asked Paul.

The young man blanched. "Oh, uh, well, you can tell him, can't you? I'm not good at that sort of thing, you know."

Nobody was good at that sort of thing, but Frank just nodded. He hoped this Roderick wasn't too fond of his master. He'd certainly resent having to find out about his death from a policeman, in any case.

Decker was expressing his condolences to Mrs. Devries, who managed to look stricken even though she obviously didn't give a fig. She, in turn, thanked him for his concern and promised to let him know immediately if he could do anything to assist her. Frank figured she would think of a lot of ways he could do that. Mrs. Devries and Paul didn't seem like the kind of people who could accomplish much on their own.

Garnet, however, was another matter entirely. She apparently had more brains than the other two put together. How had she ended up married to an idiot like Paul Devries? Frank would never understand the rich, who seemed to sell their daughters off to the highest bidder with no thought to whether they would be happy or not.

Then again, both of Felix Decker's daughters had run off with men of their own choosing and neither of those marriages had ended so well, either.

Decker shook her hand and moved toward the door. "I'm sure Elizabeth will call on you as soon as she hears the news."

Frank wished he could talk to Decker's wife, Elizabeth, before she made that call. She had once assisted him on an investigation, and surely she could learn some useful information on this one if he told her what to ask. Unfortunately, Decker had no idea his wife had been involved in a murder case, and Frank wasn't going to be the one to tell him.

Paul rang for the maid again to show him out.

"Mr. Malloy can walk out with me and wait downstairs for the valet," Decker said.

Frank thanked them for their help, although they hadn't helped him at all, and followed Decker out. He had the feeling Decker wanted a minute alone with him, but when they reached the front hallway, a man who could only be the valet Roderick was already waiting.

Decker took his hat from the maid and turned to Frank. "I'll look forward to hearing from you."

Frank figured he would.

SARAH BRANDT WAS ENJOYING A RARE DAY AT HOME. AS A midwife, she had to be available night or day to go on a delivery, but no babies had seen fit to enter the world today, leaving her free to enjoy her foster daughter, Catherine. Her mother had also stopped by for a visit, although Sarah knew she had mostly come to see Catherine, who filled her need to have a grandchild.

They were all in the child's bedroom, sipping make-believe tea from a tiny china set, when the front doorbell rang.

Catherine's bottom lip immediately popped into a pout.

"I'll answer it." Her nursemaid, Maeve, jumped up from her place on the floor. "Maybe it's not a birth. Maybe it's Mr. Malloy," she added with a wicked grin. Catherine clapped her hands and Sarah smiled. The child adored Frank Malloy.

"Have you seen Mr. Malloy lately?" Mrs. Decker asked from where she sat on Catherine's bed.

Sarah wasn't fooled by her mother's seemingly innocent question. "No, not lately." She pushed herself up from the floor. Whoever was at the door would probably want to see her even if they didn't need her for a delivery.

A man's voice rumbled below.

"Heavens, that sounds like your father," Mrs. Decker said.

"What would he be doing here?" Sarah couldn't remember the last time her father had been to her modest home. Surely not since her husband, Tom, died, over four years ago.

"Maybe he's looking for me. Oh, dear, I hope nothing bad has happened. Sarah, you really should get a telephone. You have no idea how convenient they are."

"And you have no idea how expensive they are, Mother." Sarah left the room with her mother and Catherine close behind. From the stair landing she caught Maeve looking up, her expression mirroring her own astonishment.

"Father, what a nice surprise."

"I hope it is." He blinked. "Elizabeth, I didn't know you were here."

"You didn't? We thought you might have come looking for me."

"No, I . . . I needed to speak with Sarah, but I'm glad you're here. It will save me having to tell it twice."

Sarah felt a tug as Catherine peered from behind her skirts. "Darling, you remember Mr. Decker, don't you?"

The child nodded.

"I'm very pleased to see you again, Catherine," he said. "I believe you've grown since I saw you last."

Catherine looked up at Sarah.

"I believe she has." Sarah couldn't blame Catherine for not answering. Her father spent his life intimidating his own business associates. Even when he was trying to be charming, he could seem frightening to a child.

"Should I take Catherine upstairs, Mrs. Brandt?" Maeve asked.

"Yes, please."

"We won't be long, I'm sure," Mrs. Decker said with a smile that held all the warmth her husband's did not. "Then I'll be back to finish our tea party."

Sarah saw her father's eyebrows rise, but he said nothing as his wife stroked Catherine's smooth cheek before Maeve took the child's hand and led her back up the stairs.

"Let's go into the kitchen. I'll make some coffee." Sarah led them to the kitchen, her home's main gathering place. Her front room had long since been converted into an office for her late husband's medical practice and where she still consulted with her own patients.

"I hope you aren't here to tell us something horrible," her mother said as her parents took seats at the well-worn kitchen table. Sarah doubted her father had sat in many kitchens in his life, but she offered no apologies. She started making the coffee.

"Chilton Devries died."

"Good heavens! Was it an accident?"

"No, I believe it was on purpose."

Sarah looked up. *"On purpose?"*

"Your Mr. Malloy believes he was murdered."

Sarah didn't bother to point out that he wasn't *her* Mr. Malloy. "Is Mr. Malloy investigating?"

"I called him in, yes."

Any reply she made would be wrong, so she busied herself with filling the coffeepot.

"You were very wise to choose Mr. Malloy, my dear," her mother said. "Now tell us everything."

While her father explained, Sarah set the pot on the stove to boil, then took a seat at the table.

"So then Mr. Malloy and I called on the Devrieses to break the news."

"Dear heaven," her mother said. "I suppose Lucretia became hysterical."

"Oddly enough, no. She merely seemed put out."

Sarah frowned. "Put out? You mean she was annoyed that her husband had died?"

"Yes, and not nearly as grief-stricken as I hope you would be if I died," he added to his wife.

"I would be inconsolable," she replied.

"I'm glad to hear it."

"I'm trying to remember who the Devrieses are," Sarah said.

"You remember their son, Paul, I'm sure. You're of an age, I believe. Mousey little boy with yellow hair. Never had much to say for himself."

"Which hardly makes him memorable, but I think I may have danced with him a time or two when we were growing up. Is he married?"

Her mother nodded. "Yes, but I don't think his wife is anyone you'd know. I don't think I even know where she came from. I can't seem recall her name, either."

"Garnet," her father said. "She started laughing when she heard Devries was dead."

Elizabeth Decker's eyebrows rose. "Laughing?"

"I'm sure it was hysteria. The shock."

"I'm sure." She didn't sound it.

"Why did you feel you needed to make a special trip here to tell me all this?" Sarah asked.

To her surprise, her father didn't answer right away. He glanced from her mother to his well-tended hands. He finally looked up, and Sarah had never seen her father look so uncertain before. "I know you have assisted Mr. Malloy with his investigations in the past."

"Felix—"

Without turning away, he raised a hand to silence her mother. "I have not always approved of your involvement with him. You have, at times, even put yourself in danger."

Sarah felt her hackles rising. She had fought against his will her entire life, even estranging herself from both her parents for years. She wasn't going to submit now. "Father, I'm a grown woman and—"

"I know, I know. I don't want to argue with you, Sarah. Just hear me out. I don't believe you have any reason to involve yourself in this investigation. You hardly know the Devries family, but I was hoping you would accompany your mother when she makes a condolence call tomorrow."

Both women gaped at him. Sarah found her tongue first. "A condolence call?"

He turned to his wife. "I'm afraid I already promised Lucretia you would call."

"Of course I will. She may be insufferable, but we've known them all our lives. But why do you want Sarah to go with me?"

Sarah caught his glance. "Because something is very strange

in that house, and I doubt Mr. Malloy has the slightest chance of finding out what it is."

Roderick was a man of middle years, and Frank could see he took his position as valet to the master of the house very seriously. His suit and shirt were impeccable. His neatly parted dark hair, lightly touched with gray, lay smoothly against his head. His suspicious glare also said he didn't appreciate being called away from his duties by the likes of Frank Malloy.

"Mary Catherine said you wanted to speak with me," Roderick said when Mr. Decker had taken his leave.

"Yes." Frank led him into the ugly little receiving room and closed the door. "Would you like to sit down?"

Roderick stiffened, not giving an inch. "I don't think that . . ."

"Mr. Devries is dead."

Frank's words had the desired effect. Roderick blinked a few times, and the color drained from his face, along with all resistance. Frank took his arm and put him into one of the wooden chairs that formed practically the only furnishings in the room.

He looked up, his face slack. "Dead? But how . . . ?"

"We think he was murdered." Frank sat down across from him and waited. The man who had risen to the exalted position of valet had been serving wealthy people most of his life. He'd overheard every intimate detail of their lives. Frank hoped Roderick would blurt out his opinion of someone's guilt, but the silence grew deafening. He was far too well trained for that. He wouldn't be where he was if he hadn't learned to keep the family's secrets to himself.

"How? When?" he finally asked. To his credit, he was the only one in the house so far who had reacted as if he cared what had happened to the dead man.

"We don't know exactly. That's why I need to talk to everyone who might've seen him today. I'm trying to figure out where he was and who he might've been with."

Roderick stiffened again and color flooded back to his face. "I'm sure I have no idea where he was after he left the house today."

"He didn't mention where he was going? Maybe he had a business meeting or an appointment with somebody."

"Mr. Devries kept his own counsel. He wasn't one to confide in his servants."

Frank nodded as if he understood perfectly the habits of wealthy men. "You knew him better than anyone, though. Did he seem anxious or worried about anything?"

"I'm sure I couldn't say."

"Don't know or just couldn't say?"

Roderick blinked again. "I don't know what you mean."

"Yes, you do. Look, Roderick, here's what happened. Somebody stabbed Devries in the back."

The valet gasped.

"But he didn't die right away. We don't know what he got stabbed with, but the wound was small, and he must not have known how badly he was hurt. He went on about his business for a while, and when he got to his club this afternoon, he sat down in a chair and died. So now we need to figure out where he was today so we can figure out who could've stabbed him."

"No one here would have harmed Mr. Devries."

"I didn't say anybody did. I asked you to tell me where else he might've been today."

Roderick's dark eyes narrowed. "You said he was injured a long time before he died."

"That's right."

"How long?"

"I don't know for sure."

"Could it have been . . . early this morning?"

"Maybe. What happened early this morning?"

"I don't know. I mean, Mr. Devries wasn't here."

"Where was he?"

"He . . . He spent the night elsewhere."

Frank leaned forward in his chair. "Do you know where?"

"As I said, Mr. Devries keeps his own counsel . . . or, at least, he did."

"But you're pretty sure you know where he was."

Roderick's lips tightened as if he were trying to hold back what he wanted to say. "He owns a house down on Mercer Street, near Washington Square."

"And you think he was there last night?"

"He stays there frequently." Roderick sighed. "I don't suppose it matters now, but . . . someone else lives there."

"Who?"

"His mistress."

"I CAN HARDLY BELIEVE IT," ELIZABETH DECKER SAID TO Sarah as they stood together in the entryway, having just seen Felix Decker out. "Your father has given both of us permission to investigate Chilly Devries's murder."

"I believe he actually *ordered* me to do it, but I don't think he has the slightest expectation that you will do anything except escort me."

"You may be right, but I feel obligated to misunderstand him if it serves my interests."

"Until he finds out and locks you in the cellar."

"Then we'll have to make sure he doesn't find out."

"Did Mr. Decker leave?" Maeve called from the top of the stairs.

"Yes, dear," Mrs. Decker replied. "Could you get the tea things ready again? I'll be right up." She turned back to Sarah. "I'll stop by for you in the morning, and we can make our plans on the way over to Lucretia's house. This evening, I'll try to find out what else your father knows."

"Wouldn't it make more sense for me to come to you in the morning?"

"Probably, but we'll need to plan what we're going to ask her, and I don't want to take the chance that your father will stay at home tomorrow. We couldn't possibly speak freely if he's around."

"I can't wait to meet this Garnet Devries. She sounds like an interesting woman."

"I hope so. Her mother-in-law is an insufferable bore. One of those women whose only concern is herself. She'll thoroughly enjoy being a widow, I'm afraid."

"What do you mean?"

"I mean she'll get attention from her friends; she'll have her husband's money to spend, but she won't have to put up with him anymore."

"Was Mr. Devries a bore, too?"

"No worse than many of the men your father knows, I suppose. I've often wondered how they amuse themselves at that club of theirs since none of them has the slightest idea how to have a good time."

Sarah bit back a smile. "What I don't understand is why Father is so interested in Mr. Devries's death."

"Because it happened at the Knickerbocker, of course. He's the club secretary, I believe. Or treasurer. Something like that. He feels responsible, I'm sure. What concerns me is that he has involved Mr. Malloy."

Sarah frowned. "Of course he would involve Malloy. He wants the murder solved, and he knows Malloy is the man to do it."

"Does he?"

"Of course he does. Malloy is the best detective in New York."

Her mother arched an eyebrow. "Is he now? But that isn't what I meant. I meant, does your father really want the murder solved? I'm guessing he doesn't know that himself yet, although I'll grant you he knows Malloy has the skill to discover the killer. The question is what your father will do with the information once he learns it."

"Father doesn't have to do anything with it. The police will arrest the killer and bring him to trial."

Mrs. Decker shook her head. "Sarah, where did you get an idea like that?"

"Because it's the law!"

"If your father doesn't want the killer arrested, he won't be. You should know that as well as I."

"All right, I do, but if Father doesn't want the killer arrested, why did he involve Malloy at all?"

"That is what concerns me. If he wanted the crime ignored, he could have done that without anyone's help. Instead, he called in the one man he is sure can solve it."

"Perhaps you aren't giving Father enough credit. Perhaps he simply wants to see justice done."

"And perhaps your father has another goal entirely."

"Such as?"

"Such as putting Frank Malloy to some sort of test. Now if you'll excuse me, I have a tea party to attend."

FRANK STARED AT RODERICK. "HIS MISTRESS?"

Roderick shrugged.

Frank retrieved a small notebook and pencil from his pocket. "Where is this house again?"

Roderick gave him the address. "The young lady who lives there is Miss Norah English. I doubt that's her real name, but that's what she calls herself."

"How do you know all this?"

Roderick seemed to find the question somewhat insulting. "I have been Mr. Devries's valet for thirty-two years. I know everything about him."

So much for his claim that Devries kept his own counsel. "When did he get home this morning?"

"He came in around nine, I believe. He wanted a bath and a shave. He always does when he returns from visiting Miss English."

"Did you help him with his bath?"

He acted insulted again. "I always help him."

"I'm just trying to find out if you noticed a wound on his back."

Roderick frowned. "Where would it have been located?"

Frank half turned and reached around to touch his thumb to the approximate spot on his own back. "Like I said, it was small."

"I didn't notice anything, but . . ."

"But what?"

"He might have put some sticking plaster on it, mightn't he? To keep it from bleeding? That could be why I didn't notice."

Roderick seemed very eager to implicate the mistress. "Is this Miss English the kind of girl who might stick a knife into Mr. Devries?"

"She's the kind of girl who might do anything."

Frank considered this information for a long moment. "Does Mrs. Devries know about Miss English?"

"Ladies of Mrs. Devries's station make a point of ignoring women like Miss English."

"So you think she knows but has decided not to make a fuss."

"I believe that would be an accurate assumption, yes."

"Do Mr. and Mrs. Devries get along?"

"What do you mean by that?"

"I mean, do they fight?"

"Certainly not."

"At least not where the help can hear."

Roderick winced. "The staff can hear everything. They simply don't speak to each other as a general rule. At least, Mr. Devries tries to avoid speaking with her whenever possible."

"Is it usually possible?"

"Mrs. Devries occasionally attempts to have a conversation with her husband."

"Did she attempt to have a conversation with him this morning?"

Roderick hesitated, and Frank figured he was trying to decide whether to lie or not. "I believe she did," he said finally.

"Did anyone else have a conversation with him?"

Roderick rubbed his palms along his thighs, as if to dry them. "Mr. Paul Devries sought him out as well, I believe."

"Any idea what they talked about?"

"No."

Roderick had just told him the staff heard everything, but Frank let the lie pass for now. Paul Devries would probably admit it himself. He didn't look like a very good liar. "Mr. Devries had a busy morning. Did he meet with anybody else? Any visitors, maybe?"

"No one came to the house. This house, I mean. The only other people he would have seen are the other staff members, but none of them had a reason to attack Mr. Devries, and if one of them had, he surely would have raised an alarm."

Just like he would've raised an alarm if somebody had stabbed him at the club. "What about his daughter-in-law?"

An emotion flickered across Roderick's face too quickly for Frank to identify. "Why do you ask about her?"

"I'm just being thorough. Perhaps she noticed something. Did she see Mr. Devries that morning?"

"I have no idea. She may have."

Another lie. Frank was sure of it. He wanted to ask if Garnet Devries was the kind of girl who might stick a knife in Mr. Devries, but Roderick would probably lie about that, too, if he didn't die of shock at the suggestion. "Did Mr. Devries get along with his daughter-in-law?"

"I'm sure they had a very cordial relationship."

"I thought you knew everything about him."

Roderick flushed again. "They were always civil to each other in my presence."

Civil. An interesting description. In his experience, people who were civil to each other were trying to hide stronger emotions, and Garnet Devries had seemed to enjoy the news that her father-in-law was dead.

He wondered how good a liar she would be.

"Let me get this straight now. Mr. Devries spent last night at his mistress's house. He came home around nine o'clock this morning, had a bath and a shave, argued with his son—"

"I never said they argued!"

"Then argued with his wife, then was civil to his daughter-in-law, and then what? He left the house?"

Roderick's face was scarlet. "Yes, he left the house."

"What time?"

"Around eleven."

"How long would it take him to get to the Knickerbocker Club from here?" Frank knew how long it had taken him in the cab Decker had chosen, but he wanted to find out how Devries had traveled.

"Ten or fifteen minutes if he walked."

"Would he have walked?"

"He didn't go straight to the club."

Frank knew that. He hadn't arrived at the club until much later. "Where did he go?"

"He had an appointment."

"With who?"

Roderick's lips tightened again. He either didn't want to say or he wanted to say it too much. "With the person who probably killed him."

3

FRANK KNEW BETTER THAN TO JUMP TO ANY CONCLUSIONS.
"You think the person Mr. Devries saw after he left the house
today is the one who killed him?"

"Well, I wouldn't go that far, but I do know that Mr.
Devries was not looking forward to the interview."

"Did he tell you that?"

"Not in so many words, but as I said, I know . . . *knew* Mr.
Devries very well. I could read his moods."

"And what was his mood today?"

"He seemed preoccupied."

"Worried?"

"That would be too strong a word, I believe. He was antic-
ipating his meeting with Mr. Angotti with some concern."

"*Who?*"

"Mr. Salvatore Angotti. He is a foreigner. Italian, if I recall."

Frank just barely managed to keep his mouth from dropping

open in surprise. An Italian. Doc Haynes thought Devries had been stabbed with a thin-bladed knife, like the kind Italians had brought with them to America. A stiletto. "What business would Mr. Devries have with an Italian?"

Roderick shrugged. "I have no idea. That is something you will have to discuss with Mr. Angotti."

Frank leaned back in his chair and considered this information. "Do you usually keep track of Mr. Devries's business appointments?"

"Certainly not, but I would inquire about his plans for the day in order to select the proper attire. This morning, he said, *Roderick, I'm sure whatever I wear will impress Salvatore Angotti.*"

"Do you know this Angotti?"

Once again Roderick stiffened. "No one with a name like Angotti would ever visit Mr. Devries at his home."

This was undoubtedly true. "Had you heard of him before today?"

"I do not believe I have, no. And I'm afraid I was unable to conceal my surprise that Mr. Devries would be meeting with someone like that. He must have noticed, because he said, *Angotti is a very unpleasant man, Roderick. I shall be glad to see the last of him.*"

"What did he mean by that?"

"I assumed he was hoping to never have to meet with the man again."

"And you don't have any idea who he is or how Mr. Devries knew him?"

"None at all."

"Who would?"

"Someone at Mr. Devries's offices may know this Angotti person. If anyone stabbed Mr. Devries, I'm sure he's the one."

And Frank was sure Felix Decker would be very pleased if he could put the blame for Devries's murder on an Italian.

SARAH SAT AT HER KITCHEN TABLE, SAVORING THE LAST hour of the day. With Catherine safely tucked in for the night, she had just filled Maeve in on what she knew about Chilton Devries's death and her plans to visit the widow tomorrow with her mother.

A knock at the door made them both sigh. "I knew this was too good to last." Sarah rose and motioned for Maeve to stay put.

"Maybe it's not a baby."

"This late? What else could it be?"

What else indeed?

"Malloy," she said with a welcoming smile when she'd opened the door. She'd long since stopped feeling guilty for the rush of joy she experienced whenever she saw him. His visits didn't always make her happy, but he certainly made her life more interesting.

"I'm sorry to call so late," he said, stepping into the entryway.

She closed the door and took his hat and coat. He looked tired. "You know you're always welcome, but you're especially welcome this evening. I need to find out what you'd like me to ask Mrs. Devries tomorrow." She managed not to laugh out loud at his expression.

"How—Your father . . . ?"

"He stopped by to see me after he left you. Come into the kitchen. Have you eaten?"

"The Devrieses' cook took pity on me. I could use some coffee if you have any, though."

"How is Brian doing in school?"

"He's learning to sign new words every day. I can't keep up with him." Sarah could see his pride in his deaf son's progress shinning in his eyes.

"Hello, Mr. Malloy," Maeve said as they entered the kitchen. "We're so glad you came. We've been sitting here trying to figure out what Mrs. Brandt and Mrs. Decker should do tomorrow when they visit Mrs. Devries."

Malloy's expression grew even more amazed, and he plunked down in one of the kitchen chairs as if he'd been punched. "What did your father say to you?"

Sarah found a cup in the cupboard and filled it from the remains of the pot she'd made earlier for her parents. "You probably think he forbade me to get involved in investigating Mr. Devries's murder and that I plan to visit the widow tomorrow out of spite."

He glanced at Maeve, who was grinning. "Are you telling me he *didn't* forbid you to get involved?"

Sarah set the cup on the table in front of him. "Not only did he not forbid me, he asked me go along with my mother on her condolence call to see what I could find out about the Devries family."

"Why would he do a thing like that?"

Sarah took a seat. "I hope you won't be insulted, but he said he thought something odd was going on in that house, and he didn't think you would be able to find out what it is."

"He's right about that."

"Which part?"

"Both parts."

"Oh, dear. I just hope *you* didn't come here tonight to forbid me from getting involved, because I couldn't possibly disobey my father."

That bit of nonsense made Malloy smile, as she had known it would. "As a matter of fact, I came here to ask if you could possibly go with your mother or at least ask her to see what she could find out about the family."

"I'm starting to think I must be dreaming, Maeve. Malloy and my father are *both* asking me to help in a murder investigation."

Maeve grinned. "It does seem strange."

Sarah turned back to Malloy. "I guess this means you really weren't able to find out anything useful."

Malloy sighed. "I spent all this time since your father left the Devrieses' house questioning the servants. All I found out is that nobody in that house would have hurt Devries and that he had an appointment this afternoon with some mysterious Italian fellow nobody there has ever seen."

"Italian?" Maeve said. "They use those stilettos, don't they? Isn't that what stabbed Mr. Devries?"

"Could be. It makes sense, at least. But I don't know who this Italian is or why he was meeting with Devries. Devries might not have even met with him after all. He could be completely innocent."

Maeve frowned. "Whether he met with him or not, they'll try to blame him."

"Of course they will," Sarah said. "We've seen firsthand how much people distrust the Italians. That's why it's important for Mr. Malloy to find out the truth."

Sarah turned to Malloy, expecting a confirmation. Instead he said, "So your mother is going to call on Mrs. Devries tomorrow?"

"Yes, and my father asked me to accompany her so I could ask some nosy questions and find out why none of his family members seemed the least bit grief-stricken that Mr. Devries is dead."

"Did he tell you the daughter-in-law actually laughed when she heard the news?"

"That could have been shock," Sarah said.

"You didn't see her. I wanted to ask her some questions, but I knew the family would never allow it."

"Just tell me what to ask."

Malloy frowned and sipped his coffee. "I'm not sure you'll get much out of her if the widow and the son are there."

"I may have to make a return visit, then. I'm sure Mrs. Devries will want to receive my mother herself tomorrow, and if the daughter-in-law has something unflattering to say about the dead man, Mrs. Devries will never leave us alone with her."

Maeve leaned forward in her chair. "Do you have any idea what might be going on? Didn't you find out anything at all from the servants?"

"I found out the dead man's valet is loyal to him, even though he didn't particularly care for the man. The rest of the servants don't want to be accused of gossiping about the master of the house, so they weren't very helpful. I got the feeling they could have told me a lot if they'd dared, though."

"About what?"

"I'm not sure. I do know that Mr. and Mrs. Devries barely spoke to each other, and Mr. Devries has a mistress that he keeps in a house on Mercer Street."

Sarah should have been shocked, but she knew many rich men kept mistresses. "That's interesting."

"Even more interesting, he spent the night there last night and came home around nine o'clock this morning."

"Why is that interesting?" Maeve asked.

"You mean except for the scandalous excitement such news might cause?" Sarah asked with a grin.

"The medical examiner told me that Devries might've been stabbed hours before he died. I don't know how many hours exactly, but it's possible he got into an argument with his mistress, and she stuck a hat pin in his back."

Sarah knew how lethal a well-placed hat pin could be. She'd seen for herself how the six-inch shaft could pierce a heart with a lucky thrust. "Father said Mr. Devries was stabbed in the back."

"The medical examiner thinks the blade went into his kidney, and he slowly bled to death."

Maeve curled her lip. "That's a lot of blood. Wouldn't somebody have noticed he was bleeding? Wouldn't *he* have noticed?"

"The bleeding was inside his body. The little that he bled outside mostly got soaked up by his undershirt."

"I can't understand why he allowed someone to injure him so badly and then never even mentioned it to anyone."

"He probably didn't know how badly he was hurt. He might've thought somebody just punched him or hit him. If it was somebody in his family—"

"Or his mistress," Maeve added.

"Or his mistress," Malloy continued, "he probably wouldn't imagine they were trying to kill him. He argued with his wife and son that morning. If one of them hit him, he wouldn't call for help or raise any kind of alarm."

Maeve straightened in her chair. "Why ever not?"

Malloy deferred to Sarah with a nod, picking up his cup again. "He wouldn't want the servants to know his wife or his son had struck him. Rich people like to pretend they're better than other people."

Maeve nodded. "I should've figured that out myself."

"Yes, you should," Malloy said.

"He must've been pretty mean to his daughter-in-law, then," Maeve said.

"Why do you say that?" Sarah asked.

"I can't imagine laughing when I heard somebody died unless I really hated him."

"His wife and son didn't act like they even cared," Malloy said.

"Father said Mrs. Devries seemed to be *put out* by the news."

"I guess that's pretty close to how she reacted," Malloy said. "She sure wasn't happy about having to wear black now that she's a widow."

"Some women just don't look good in black," Sarah said, earning a scowl for her sarcasm.

"Have you met the mistress yet?" Maeve asked.

"No. It was too late to call on her when I finished up with the servants. That's what I'll be doing tomorrow, that and trying to find this Salvatore Angotti."

"The Italian," Maeve said.

"What kind of business would Mr. Devries have with an Italian?" Sarah asked.

"The valet didn't know, and he made it clear Devries didn't socialize with people like that."

"Of course not, but . . . I wonder if my father would know this . . . What was his name again?"

"Angotti. How would your father know somebody like that?"

"If Devries did, maybe he's involved in some business in the city."

Malloy's expression told her how unlikely he thought this was.

Sarah shrugged. "Maybe he owns a restaurant or something. What other explanation can you think of for why Devries would be meeting with him?"

"Maybe Mr. Devries wanted him to kill someone for him," Maeve said.

They gaped at her.

"Don't look at me like that. You know about the Black Hand. That's what they do, isn't it?"

Sarah knew it very well. They'd encountered the secret group before. "The Black Hand usually only preys on other Italians, though."

"Things are changing," Malloy said. "Maeve may be right, but even if she is, you aren't going to even mention Angotti's name to anybody at the Devrieses' house or anywhere else. All you have to do is find out what you can about his family. I'll take care of the rest."

"What do you want us to find out exactly?" Sarah asked.

"Why he was arguing with his wife and son on the morning he died, but most of all, why Garnet Devries laughed when she heard he was dead."

FRANK WONDERED IF ANYONE HAD TOLD MISS NORAH English that her protector was dead. He couldn't imagine the Devries family thinking of it or doing it if they had. They might not even know she existed. Did Felix Decker know about Miss English? And if so, would he have taken it upon himself to inform her? Frank couldn't imagine that either. So the chances were good he would be the one to break the news and find out just what Miss English thought of Devries.

Although the city had been bustling busily for several hours, Frank's visit was still extremely early for a social call.

The window shades on the small house on Mercer Street had not yet been raised, giving the impression the house was still asleep.

A maid answered his thundering knock. The stout woman, past middle-aged, seemed harried and not at all pleased to see him. She adjusted her cap, cheeks red from exertion. Or something. She looked him over with a critical—and disapproving—eye. "Who're you?"

"Detective Sergeant Frank Malloy with the New York City Police. I need to see Miss English right away."

Her eyes widened when he said *police*, but then her face settled back into a scowl. "Miss English ain't receiving visitors."

"I'm not a visitor. This is police business. Tell her I need to speak to her about Mr. Devries."

"You can't scare me. I know the police don't have no business with Mr. Devries."

"They do if he's been murdered."

Her red face went slack. "The devil, you say!"

Frank slapped the partially opened door and gave it a shove, sending her staggering back, then stepped into the tiny foyer. "Go tell Miss English I need to see her."

"She ain't even awake yet!"

"Then wake her up and get her down here."

He could see she was starting to realize the ramifications to her and her mistress. "I ain't gonna tell her he's dead."

"Please don't. Just tell her there's been some trouble. I'll be happy to break the news to her myself."

"Dear God in heaven, what'll become of us now?" she muttered.

Frank had no answer for that.

She shut the door behind him. "You can wait in the parlor."

She nodded toward the doorway to his left and trudged off to the back of the house.

Frank removed his hat and coat and hung them on the coat tree by the door. Then he took the opportunity to look around. Devries hadn't spent a lot of money fixing up the house. Judging from the style and condition of the furnishings, they were leftover from a previous resident who had died of old age. The wallpaper in the hallway and the parlor had faded until the original design was little more than a suggestion. The sofa sagged more than a bit. Only the draperies appeared to be new, probably because the old ones had disintegrated from dry rot.

Miss English had made an effort at personalizing the place with some cheap knickknacks, notable for their tackiness, that cluttered the mantel and a tabletop. Frank had plenty of time to admire them. Miss English did not appear for almost an hour.

He wasn't sure what he'd been expecting, but Norah English looked much too young and innocent to be anyone's mistress. A plump girl with apple cheeks, she wore her dark brown hair in an elaborate style that explained why she had taken so long to get dressed. Her dress had probably cost a small fortune, but it didn't flatter her at all. The multitude of ruffles and flounces only made her look plumper. Or maybe that's what Devries liked.

"Lizzie said you're with the police," she said, her brow furrowed with either uncertainty or concern. "I don't know why you're here. I haven't done anything wrong."

Frank could've argued with her, but he said, "Maybe you should sit down. I have some bad news for you."

"I don't think I should talk to you. Mr. Devries doesn't like me to talk to strange men. If you have bad news for me, you should tell him. Mr. Devries is my protector. He'll tell me anything he thinks I need to know." She folded her hands in front of her and nodded once, as if satisfied at the way she had handled this difficult situation.

He should be kind to this girl who would need all the kindness she could get. "Miss English, I'm very sorry to inform you that Mr. Chilton Devries died yesterday."

She stared at him for a long moment, blinking furiously. "That's impossible," she finally said. "Mr. Devries was here yesterday morning, and he was perfectly fine then."

"I'm sure he was. He was perfectly fine until yesterday afternoon when he died at his club."

"He . . . he *died*?" The color drained from her apple cheeks. "You're sure?"

"I'm afraid so, Miss English. Would you like to sit down?"

She didn't reply. She just kept staring at him. At first he didn't know where the sound was coming from, and then he realized she was making it, a high-pitched keening just short of a wail. Then she swayed, and he caught her and managed to get her to one of the armchairs before her knees gave way.

"What've you done to her?" the maid Lizzie demanded, appearing in the doorway like an avenging angel. "Miss Norah, are you all right?"

Miss English just kept wailing, rocking from side to side in her chair.

"Do you have any brandy?" The maid ignored him. Instead, she strode over to Miss English and slapped her in the face.

Miss English instantly stopped keening. "Chilton is dead," Miss English said, without so much as a complaint about getting slapped. "What'll become of us, Lizzie? What will we do?"

"We'll manage. We always do." Lizzie turned to Frank. "You can leave now. You've done enough damage for one day."

"I need to ask Miss English some questions first."

"What kind of questions?"

"That's none of your business," Frank said.

"Everything about Miss Norah is my business."

He considered reminding her she was just the maid, but the way she'd slapped the girl made him wonder. "Fine. You'll hear the questions when I ask them, then. Miss English?"

The girl looked up at him, rubbing her cheek absently. Her eyes were moist, but he didn't think she was crying over Devries. "Yes?"

"Can you tell me what happened with Mr. Devries yesterday morning?"

"What do you mean?"

"Can you just tell me what he did and what he said from the time he woke up until he left here? I know he'd spent the night."

The color rose in her face and her expression hardened. "You don't have any right to judge me."

"I'm not judging you. I know how hard it can be for a young woman alone."

"What does it matter what he did here anyway?" Lizzie asked. "You said he died at his club in the afternoon."

Frank ignored her. "Did you have an argument with Mr. Devries?" he asked the girl.

Her eyes widened. "Do you think it was my fault? That he died, I mean? Is that why? He got upset and had a heart attack or apoplexy or something?"

"So you did have an argument that morning."

"They just had words," Lizzie said. "Mr. Devries, he never wanted Lizzie to leave the house, but she's a young girl. She needs to have some fun once in a while, doesn't she? He never would take her anywhere, either. That's all. He wasn't even mad. Besides, he was fine when he left here."

Frank kept his gaze on the girl, but she kept glancing from him to the maid. "That's right. He never got mad at me, you know. He was always very nice, wasn't he, Lizzie?"

"That's right, miss. Always."

"Did you hit him?" Frank asked.

The girl blinked. "What?"

Lizzie was beet red now. "Of course she never hit him! What kind of a girl do you think she is?"

Frank knew exactly what kind of a girl she was. "Sometimes people get so angry they do foolish things. I was just wondering if Miss English had ever hit Mr. Devries in frustration."

"I—"

"Don't say a word!" Lizzie snapped, then turned to Frank. "I told you to get out of here. You can't come in here and bully us."

Of course he could, but that would be a waste of time. The girl wasn't going to admit anything now. "Mr. Devries didn't have a heart attack."

"How did he die, then?" the girl asked.

He couldn't tell her the truth, not if he ever expected to find out if she'd done it. "We don't know yet."

"Why not?"

"The medical examiner is doing an autopsy to find out what killed him."

"Then why are you bothering us?" Lizzie asked. "Miss English has enough problems without the likes of you getting her all upset."

"Miss English, do you know a man named Salvatore Angotti?"

The girl's eyes widened again.

"Of course she don't. How would she know somebody like that? A foreigner, of all people. Miss English don't know people like that."

Except Frank would've bet a month's pay she knew him very well or had at least heard his name before. He needed to get Miss English alone, without the meddling older woman. But since she was here, he would have to give up for now. He looked around the sad little room. "Do you own the house, Miss English?"

"I—"

"What business is it of yours?" Lizzie asked.

"Just curious. I hope she got him to give her a financial settlement at least. The family won't waste any time putting her out if she doesn't own it."

Fear flashed across the girl's face. "How long do you think I have?"

So she didn't own the house. "That depends on whether someone in the family knows about you or not. It might take some time for them to find out if they don't. If I were you, I'd start making other plans, though. You can't stay here forever."

The girl's eyes filled with tears, and Frank had to look away. He saw plenty of human misery every day. This girl's situation wasn't even particularly bleak. She'd probably find another protector, and next time she'd be smarter and ask for the house. In any case, he could do nothing for her. He gave her his card. "I may be back again if I have more questions."

"More questions about what?" she asked.

Frank didn't answer. He just walked out of the room with Lizzie on his heels. As if suddenly remembering her duties, she helped Frank on with his coat and handed him his hat.

"How did he die?" she asked in a whisper.

"I told you, I don't know yet."

"But you think somebody did him in, don't you? Was it poison?"

"Maybe. Any idea who might've wanted him dead?"

"Anybody that knew him, I'd guess."

Not a very nice epitaph. "Do you know this Salvatore Angotti?"

"How would I?" She was lying. Frank was sure of it. "But if Devries was poisoned, I'd say he done it. You can't trust those foreigners."

Frank figured that's what everyone would tell him.

MIRACULOUSLY, NO ONE SUMMONED SARAH TO A BIRTH the next day, so she was ready when her mother's carriage stopped in front of her house on Bank Street that afternoon. Sarah kissed Catherine good-bye and promised that Mrs. Decker would come in to see her when they returned.

Her mother smiled a greeting when Sarah climbed into the carriage. She wore a dove gray suit beneath her fur-lined cape. "I could hardly sleep last night," she confessed as Sarah settled on the seat beside her.

"Did you find out anything new from Father last night?"

"No, he went back to the club and didn't come in until late. He felt he should be there in case any of the members wanted to know what had happened to poor Chilton. Then he went back today. Why are mourning calls made in the afternoon? This has been the slowest day of my life."

Sarah smiled. "I don't know who created the rules for proper behavior, but I imagine women decided that having mourning callers in the morning didn't give them enough time to dress properly or something."

"Don't make fun, Sarah. These things are very important to many people."

"I'm not making fun, Mother, but I must say, I'm thankful I don't have to worry about these things much anymore. By the way, Malloy came by last night."

"He did? I'm so sorry I missed him. Did you tell him about our plans?"

"Yes, and he was just as shocked as we were that Father wanted me to go with you."

"I'm sure he was. Oh, dear, I suppose he came to warn you *not* to get involved. I know how he feels about you putting yourself in danger."

"That's what I expected, too, but no, he also asked me to go with you today. So we have his blessing, too."

Mrs. Decker frowned. "I'm not sure I like this. Having permission takes away a lot of the excitement, doesn't it?"

"*Mother.*"

"Well, it does. So tell me what Mr. Malloy had to say so we can plan what we're going to do when we get to Lucretia's house."

City traffic slowed their progress to a crawl, so Sarah had plenty of time to relay what Malloy had shared with her. By the time they were escorted into the Devrieses' parlor, they both felt confident of their mission.

"Elizabeth, thank you so much for coming," Lucretia Devries said, ensconced in an overstuffed chair, her feet resting demurely on a needlepoint footstool. She offered a limp hand, wrist to ankle encased in the unrelieved black taffeta of a recent widow.

"I'm so very sorry to hear about Chilton," Elizabeth said, taking the offered hand.

"Oh, yes, such a terrible shock. I don't know what I would

do without Paul. Children can be such a comfort during a time like this."

"I'm sure they can. Lucretia, you remember my daughter, Sarah Brandt, don't you?"

Sarah watched the older woman's gaze sharpen as she turned, perhaps remembering Sarah's rebellious elopement and the resulting rift with her family. "My condolences, Mrs. Devries."

"Thank you, my dear. Please, sit down. I've rung for some tea. You must be frozen. How troublesome to have to bury Chilton when the weather is so bad."

Sarah seated herself on a sofa across from Mrs. Devries. "I'm sure he never thought of the inconvenience when he died," her mother said with a perfectly straight face as she joined her.

"How like him."

Sarah coughed to cover a laugh.

"Oh, dear, I hope you're not ill. I'm very susceptible to illness."

"Oh, no, not at all," Sarah said.

"I don't believe I've met your daughter-in-law, Lucretia," Mrs. Decker said. "Will she be joining us?"

"I'm sure I don't know. I sent the maid to tell her we have visitors, but that girl does only what she wants."

"How long have she and Paul been married now?"

"Almost two years, and no sign of a child yet. Young women today have no sense of responsibility. I was already expecting my second child when I'd been married for two years."

"I'm sure you're anxious for more grandchildren," Mrs. Decker said.

"I don't care a thing about grandchildren, but one has a duty to carry on the family name, doesn't one?"

The parlor door opened, breaking the awkward silence, and

a beautiful young woman stepped in, also swathed in the unrelieved black of full mourning.

"Oh, here she is at last," Mrs. Devries said, as if they had been waiting hours. "My daughter-in-law, Garnet. Mrs. Decker and her daughter, Mrs. Brandt."

Sarah and her mother made the proper replies to Garnet Devries's polite greeting, then they offered their condolences on her recent loss, to which she merely murmured a stiff, "Thank you," before taking a seat on the chair farthest from her mother-in-law.

"Oh, yes," Mrs. Devries said. "I know Garnet will feel Chilly's loss more than any of us. He was so very fond of her, you know."

Sarah turned in time to catch an expression of the fiercest hatred twisting Garnet's lovely features.

If looks really could kill, the Devrieses would be planning two funerals this week.

4

FRANK HAD GOTTEN THE ADDRESS OF CHILTON DEVRIES'S office from Felix Decker yesterday, and he found the building without too much trouble. Devries, it seemed, owned a good chunk of New York City real estate and kept his family in style by collecting rents from the thousands of people who had no choice but to live in the run-down hovels men like Devries provided for them. As an elevator operator guided the car to the top floor of the tall building, Frank wondered idly if Devries owned the building where he lived with his mother and his son.

An attractive young female sat at the desk in the reception area, a rare sight but growing more common by the day as women learned typewriting and other office skills. Frank recognized the type—plump and wholesome. Devries knew what he liked. She looked as if she'd been crying, but she smiled bravely as Frank approached her desk.

"May I help you?"

Frank introduced himself, making her smile vanish. "I need to speak to whoever is in charge now that Mr. Devries is"—he caught himself when he saw she was tearing up again—"gone."

"I suppose Mr. Watkins could help you." She disappeared into one of the offices that opened off the reception area and returned to escort him in.

Mr. Watkins greeted him with suspicion. An older man with graying hair and a solid gold watch chain stretched across his slight paunch, he looked like someone perfectly capable of assuming whatever responsibility would fall to him now that Devries was dead. He invited Frank to take a seat on one of the chairs situated conveniently in front of his desk.

"I'm very sorry about Mr. Devries," Frank said. "Have you worked for him for a long time?"

"Twenty-seven years in March." Watkins leaned back in his impressively large chair and peered at Frank thoughtfully. "Why are you here, Mr. Malloy?"

"Because we believe Mr. Devries's death was not natural, and I need to find out who might have wanted to murder him."

"Good God, you must be insane. Who would want to kill Mr. Devries?"

Frank remembered Lizzie the maid's theory, but he didn't voice it. "A man as rich and powerful as Mr. Devries must have made some enemies along the way."

"Mr. Devries inherited most of his real estate holdings from his father, and I and my staff have added to them quietly and without drawing undue attention to Mr. Devries and his family. I assure you, no one has any reason to bear him a grudge."

"What about his tenants? Has he evicted anybody lately?"

"Mr. Devries has never evicted anyone. We have staff who handle those duties. In fact, Mr. Devries spent little time here, and I assure you, I know of no one who wished him ill because of his business interests."

Frank pretended to consider this for a few minutes. "What do you know about Salvatore Angotti?"

"Who?"

"Salvatore Angotti. Don't you know him?"

"Never heard of him."

Frank believed him. "He doesn't work for the company, then?"

"Certainly not. Although . . . as I said, we have staff members who handle difficult tasks for us. I don't know everyone who works at that level."

"Who does?"

"I'll summon him. Miss Shively?" he called.

The girl came to the door.

"Will you ask Mr. Pitt to come to my office immediately, please?"

"Yes, sir."

"Who would keep track of Mr. Devries's appointments?" Frank asked when the girl had gone.

Watkins frowned. "As I said, Mr. Devries didn't spend much time here, and when he did . . . Well, he has never taken much interest in the company."

"What did he take an interest in?"

"I'm sure I don't know. My responsibility is to make sure the company runs smoothly and continues to be successful."

"To make a lot of money, you mean."

Like most people who had money, Watkins didn't like to talk about it. "That would be the result of success, yes."

"And is the company successful?"

"I can assure you it is."

"Then Mr. Devries didn't have any reason to be upset with anybody here?"

Mr. Watkins appeared to be offended. "Certainly not!"

"And you hadn't had words with him about anything?"

Mr. Watkins' cheeks were growing red. "I haven't seen Mr. Devries in several weeks."

"Was that unusual?"

"Not at all."

Frank nodded, considering. "Do you know about the woman who lives in the house on Mercer Street?"

This time Watkins stiffened slightly. "Which house on Mercer Street?"

"I think you know which one. The one where Miss English lives."

"Is that her name?"

"So she says. I take it Mr. Devries didn't deed it to her."

Watkins sniffed derisively. "I'm surprised he didn't make her pay rent."

For the second time today, Frank had to keep his jaw from dropping open. "What will happen to her now?"

"I couldn't say. That will be up to . . ."

"To who?"

Mr. Watkins frowned. "I was going to say to the family, but . . ."

"I can see how awkward it would be for you to raise the subject. But surely, you can talk to his son. He's a man of the world."

Plainly, Mr. Watkins did not agree. "I suppose . . ."

"You don't need to be in a hurry about it. I'm sure the girl would appreciate having some time to make other arrangements."

"Girl? Why do you call her a girl?"

"Because she's not any older than Miss Shively out there."

This news seemed to disturb Mr. Watkins even more, but

Frank didn't have an opportunity to discuss it with him any further because another man came into the office. He stopped when he saw Frank.

"Excuse me, Mr. Watkins, I—"

"Come in, Pitt." Watkins introduced him to Frank. Pitt was about Frank's age, early thirties, and his pale skin, thinning hair, and slight build marked him as a man who spent his days in an office. "Mr. Malloy needs to know if we have anyone working for us by the name of . . . What was it again?"

"Salvatore Angotti."

Pitt's pale eyebrows rose. "Is Mr. Angotti in some sort of trouble?"

At last, someone who knew this Italian. "No," Frank lied, managing to keep his excitement from showing. "I just need to ask him some questions."

"Does this man work for us?" Watkins asked, obviously not pleased by the thought.

"Oh, no. Or at least, he isn't on our payroll."

"Who is he, then?" Watkins asked.

"He assists us with . . . difficult cases. When someone refuses to move out, for instance. We rarely have that situation," Pitt hastened to explain to Frank. "Most people, when they can't pay the rent, they stay as long as they possibly can, until they can't put us off any longer, and when we come back the next day, they've vanished. They're embarrassed, you see. Or afraid we'll get the law on them or something. Many of them are from countries where the authorities are worse than the criminals."

Frank had often thought that was true in New York City, too, but he didn't say so. "Sometimes they don't vanish, though."

"Yes, and then . . . Well, it's foolish to put our employees in danger. People like that can be unpredictable and . . . well, dangerous."

"And that's when Mr. Angotti helps you."

"Yes. Mr. Angotti enjoys . . . respect," he said, choosing the word with obvious care. "When people learn he is involved, they usually behave reasonably."

Frank nodded, comprehending the situation only too well. "Why would Mr. Devries have gone to see this Angotti?"

Pitt suddenly looked very uncomfortable, and he glanced at Watkins as if for guidance.

"What is it, Pitt?" Watkins asked.

"I . . . I had no idea Mr. Devries knew Mr. Angotti."

"And yet he did," Frank said.

Pitt's gaze shifted to Frank but didn't quite meet his before it darted away again. "I can't imagine how he would. Mr. Angotti . . . Well, he isn't the kind of person a man like Mr. Devries would know, is he?"

"I don't know what kind of people Mr. Devries might know," Frank said, "but he did know Angotti. Did you introduce them?"

The color drained from Pitt's face. "Certainly not! Mr. Devries would never ask me for an introduction to anyone."

But Frank would have sworn that Devries had done just that, however much Pitt didn't want to admit it. The question was, did he not want to admit it in front of Watkins or in front of Frank?

"There you have it, Mr. Malloy," Watkins was saying. "You must be mistaken about this Angotti fellow knowing Mr. Devries."

"How can I get in touch with this Angotti?" Frank asked Pitt.

Pitt's hands were shaking now. He clasped them tightly together to hide it. "Why would you want to do that?"

"What do you care?"

Pitt glanced at Watkins again but received no assistance from that quarter. "I wouldn't want Mr. Angotti to become offended. He might . . . He might begin to work against us in the community."

"You mean he might burn down your buildings?" Frank asked.

Pitt blinked several times. "I just meant he might refuse to help us in the future."

"I'm sure if you continue to pay for his services, he will continue to help," Watkins said. "Those people all have their price."

Pitt flushed. "May I go now, Mr. Watkins? I'm very busy."

"Yes, yes, of course. Thank you for your assistance."

Frank didn't thank him because he hadn't been that helpful. He hadn't even told Frank where to find Angotti.

Which gave him a good excuse to see Pitt again before he left.

SARAH WATCHED IN FASCINATION AS GARNET DEVRIES'S expression smoothed out again, all trace of the emotion that had caused her to glare so murderously at her mother-in-law vanquished. Whatever she felt about her in-laws, her face now revealed none of it. She turned a bland smile to Sarah.

"I don't think we've met before, Mrs. Brandt."

"No, we haven't. I don't move in the same social circles as my mother."

"Sarah hasn't been in society for years now," Mrs. Devries said. "Ever since she married."

Sarah didn't even glance at Mrs. Devries, not wanting to give the impression she was ashamed of not wasting her life as a society matron. "I married a physician, and I've been very happy in my new life."

"I know your parents were disappointed that you refused to return home after your husband died," Mrs. Devries said.

Sarah sensed her mother stiffen beside her at the implied criticism of Sarah's choice. "We would have loved having Sarah return to our home when Dr. Brandt died, but I must admit, I'm very proud of the way she has managed on her own. I could never have done such a thing at her age."

Sarah could hardly believe her mother was defending her. She felt a warm glow to know after so many years that her mother admired her.

"How *do* you manage?" Garnet asked, leaning forward. "To support yourself, I mean."

Sensing her question was more than idle curiosity, Sarah said, "I'm a midwife."

Surprise and something else flickered across Garnet's face and then was gone. "How interesting."

"I should hate it myself," Mrs. Devries said. "I can't think of anything more unpleasant than listening to women screaming in agony all the time."

Sarah bit back the words she wanted to say. Arguing with Mrs. Devries would be pointless, and she didn't want to distress her mother by debating with her friend.

"I'd like to hear about it," Garnet said. "Perhaps—"

"You wouldn't like to hear about it at all," Mrs. Devries said. "You can find out everything you need to know when you have your own children. Until then, the less you hear about it, the better."

Once again, Garnet glared at her mother-in-law, but Mrs. Devries wasn't paying attention.

"What a lovely gown, Elizabeth," Mrs. Devries said. "Who

made it for you? All my mourning clothes are sadly out of fashion, and I'm going to need something new."

For a few minutes the two women discussed the relative merits of dressmakers as Sarah surreptitiously studied Garnet. She had folded her hands in her lap and again smoothed all trace of emotion from her face. Sarah thought this would be a useful skill to acquire if she had to live with Mrs. Devries.

Sarah's mother asked about the funeral arrangements, and Mrs. Devries explained they had to wait until the police returned the body. She had no idea how long that would take.

"I suppose Paul will be taking his father's position in the company," Sarah said, hoping to find out something useful to help Malloy.

"Oh, heavens, no," Mrs. Devries replied.

"Paul has no head for business," Garnet said.

Mrs. Devries flushed. "That isn't the reason at all."

Garnet frowned with apparent confusion. "Isn't it? I've heard Father Devries say so a hundred times."

Mrs. Devries flushed scarlet. "Silly girl! I don't know what you're talking about. Oh, no, Paul simply has no interest in commerce. His tastes are too refined for that. Putting him in an office would be a waste of his talents."

"What talents are those, Mother Devries?"

This time Mrs. Devries glared at Garnet, who seemed as unconcerned as her mother-in-law had been at her evil looks.

"Where are you from originally?" Sarah's mother asked Garnet with a hint of desperation in her apparent eagerness to change the subject. "I don't know that I ever heard how you and Paul came to meet."

"She's from Virginia." Mrs. Devries waved her hand dismissively.

"We moved here when I was still in school," Garnet said. "My father was in the importing business."

"He tried to join the Knickerbocker." The glow of satisfaction in Mrs. Devries's eyes indicated he had failed. "That was how he met Chilly."

"And when he met me," Garnet said, "he decided I would be perfect for . . . Paul."

Sarah felt a chill at the tone of her voice, but her expression betrayed nothing. Garnet could have been carved from stone.

Mrs. Devries nodded a bit too enthusiastically. "That's right, although Paul could have married anyone at all. Such an accomplished young man and so handsome. Many girls were bitterly disappointed when he married Garnet, I can assure you."

"One certainly was," Garnet said and smiled at Sarah. "Do you have an office, Mrs. Brandt? Do women come to see you?"

"Some of my patients do, although they prefer I go to them. But I have an office in my home on Bank Street. I should be happy if you called on me sometime."

"There's no point in that," Mrs. Devries said. "She'll never have any use for a midwife. She's barren."

Sarah's mother gasped in shock at the casual cruelty of the remark. Sarah quickly said, "I meant a social call. I'm sure my mother would say that I have neglected my old friends dreadfully, and I would be happy to make a new one."

"Oh, yes," Elizabeth Decker said. "I would love for Sarah to have more friends. She spends entirely too much time working."

"And taking care of my daughter."

Mrs. Devries frowned. "I didn't know you had a child."

"Sarah has adopted a little girl from a settlement house," her mother said.

"How very noble of her," Mrs. Devries said without much conviction.

"I'm sure she brings you a lot of joy," Garnet said.

"Yes, she does. I'd love for you to meet her." Sarah didn't think she could be any clearer that she wanted Garnet Devries to visit her.

"Garnet won't be meeting anyone for a while," Mrs. Devries said. "Not while we're in mourning, at any rate." If she saw the flash of irritation that crossed Garnet's face, she gave no indication. Instead she asked Sarah's mother her opinion of hymns they might sing at Mr. Devries's funeral, effectively turning the topic to something she could control.

After a few more minutes of polite conversation, Sarah and her mother took their leave. Sarah didn't think she imagined the warmth in Garnet's parting words, spoken so softly no one else could hear them.

"I hope to see you very soon, Mrs. Brandt."

How interesting that Garnet was as anxious to see Sarah as she was to see her.

When she and her mother were safely ensconced in the Decker family carriage, where no one could overhear them, Sarah said, "I don't think we learned anything helpful."

"No, Lucretia is much too clever for that, but you made a friend of the younger Mrs. Devries."

"I hope so. She wants to visit me. Do you think she could just be lonely?"

Her mother sniffed. "Living in that house? Of course she's lonely, but I thought it was more than that. She seemed drawn to you."

"Maybe she thinks I can help her have a child."

"Can you?"

Sarah frowned. "Some midwives claim they can, but there's really nothing I can do. Nothing *anyone* can do except pray."

"What do these other midwives do, then, if they claim they can help?"

"Oh, they make up foul-tasting potions or teas and have women drink them. Or they tell them to put charms under their mattresses and things like that."

"But if nothing really works—"

"A certain number of women will conceive after doing what a midwife told them to do, even if it's nothing more than coincidence. I'm sure the herbs or the charms had nothing to do with it, but who can say? People believe what they want to believe, don't they?"

"I suppose you're right. I've seen people given up for dead get well and people die from something very minor. Perhaps if Garnet Devries believes you can help her conceive, she will."

"Maybe, but . . ."

"But what?" her mother asked.

"I wonder if that's really why she wants to see me."

FRANK HAD TO PRETEND TO LEAVE THE OFFICE BUILDING to escape Mr. Watkins' scrutiny, but as soon as he reached the lobby, he claimed to have forgotten something. The elevator operator was only too glad to take him to the floor where Mr. Pitt worked when Frank explained he needed to ask him one more question.

Frank followed the operator's instructions and easily found Pitt's office, a small room lined with shelves crammed full of ledgers.

Pitt was not happy to see him. "What do you want?"

Frank just smiled, watching Pitt mop his damp forehead with a snowy white handkerchief.

"I can send for Mr. Watkins," Pitt said, as if it were a threat.

"Go ahead. I'm sure he'll be interested to find out you introduced Mr. Devries to the man who killed him."

All the remaining color drained out of Pitt's sweaty face. "I didn't introduce them!"

"Brought them together, then. Why did Mr. Devries want to meet this Angotti?"

Pitt jumped out of his chair and closed the door of his office after checking the corridor for possible eavesdroppers. "You can't tell anyone I was involved with this."

"I won't need to tell anybody anything if you answer my questions."

"But I don't know a thing about Mr. Devries's death."

"Just tell me what you do know, but maybe you better sit down first. You don't look very good."

Pitt sank back into his chair and mopped his forehead again. His handkerchief was getting a little limp. "Please, I told you—"

"When did Devries ask you to introduce him to Angotti?"

"He didn't."

Frank took a step toward him, and the man squeaked in terror and threw up his hands as if to ward off a blow. "He didn't ask me to introduce them! I already told you that. He just . . ." He lowered his hands a bit and peered at Frank as if to judge his intent.

Frank waited, making no further threatening moves.

Pitt drew a deep breath. "He asked if I knew someone who could help him with a particular matter."

"What kind of matter?"

"He didn't actually say, but . . . Well, he led me to believe it might involve violence. He asked me who I used to handle the troublesome tenants. That was the word he used, *troublesome*."

"So you told him about Angotti."

"Yes, but I made sure Mr. Devries understood that Mr. Angotti doesn't actually do the work himself. He has men under him. They are the ones who . . ." He gestured vaguely.

"Who handle the troublesome tenants."

Pitt swallowed. "Yes."

"So did you set up a meeting or what?"

"I . . . Yes, I arranged for Mr. Devries to meet with Mr. Angotti in a restaurant in Little Italy."

"Were you there?"

"Of course not. I merely delivered the invitation to Mr. Angotti."

"When did they meet?"

"About a month ago, I think. At least that was when their meeting was scheduled. I have no way of knowing if it even took place."

Frank considered this information, giving Pitt an opportunity to remember anything else that might be helpful.

After a moment, Pitt said, "Did Angotti really kill Mr. Devries?"

"I don't know yet, but they had an appointment on the day he died. I need to see Angotti."

The prospect seemed to alarm Pitt. "You shouldn't go alone."

"Do you see Angotti alone?"

"Yes, but . . . I have business for him." Pitt wiped his forehead again.

Frank wondered if Pitt sweated like this when he went to see Angotti. "Can you arrange for me to meet with Angotti?"

"I . . . I wouldn't like to get involved in something like that."

Frank could easily understand his reluctance. "Then tell me where to find him."

"You won't mention my name?"

"Why would I?"

Pitt snatched a scrap of paper from his desk and picked up the pen he had discarded when Frank had burst into his office a few minutes ago. He dipped it carefully into the inkwell and scratched out an address.

Frank took the still-wet message. He recognized the neighborhood, which wasn't too far from Police Headquarters. "Do you think Mr. Devries wanted Angotti to kill someone for him?"

Pitt's shock was almost comic. "I . . . I have no idea! I can't imagine Mr. Devries wanting someone killed at all."

"And now Mr. Devries himself is dead."

Pitt had nothing to say to that.

FRANK DIDN'T HAVE TOO MUCH TROUBLE LOCATING OFFIcer Gino Donatelli. As one of the few Italians in the New York City Police Department, he worked mostly in Little Italy, and everyone there knew him well. Frank distributed pennies to some street urchins and sat down in a café to wait, although the other patrons eyed him suspiciously over their pastries. The place smelled pleasantly of anise and baking bread.

Before he'd finished his first cup of coffee, Donatelli appeared.

The handsome youth grinned broadly when he spotted Frank sitting at a table with his back to the wall. "I heard you were looking for me," he said, taking a seat.

Before Frank could answer, the owner of the restaurant had brought Donatelli something that looked like coffee but in a tiny cup. The two exchanged some pleasantries in Italian before the owner slipped away again.

"Aren't you old enough to drink a full cup of coffee?" Frank asked, eyeing the miniature cup.

"This is espresso. Extra-strong Italian coffee. You're only supposed to drink a little. Want to try some?" Donatelli raised a hand to catch the owner's eye.

"No, I'm fine." Frank thought he'd feel silly drinking out of a cup that small, no matter what was in it.

Donatelli grinned again and took a sip of the mysterious brew. "How can I help you, Detective Sergeant?"

"What do you know about Salvatore Angotti?"

Gino's grin vanished, and he glanced around anxiously. "Don't say that name too loud around here. Why do you want to know about him?"

Frank leaned forward and spoke softly. "A man died yesterday after he had a meeting with this Angotti. He was stabbed with a long, thin blade, like a stiletto."

"He probably deserved it, then."

Frank couldn't argue with that. "The dead man was a friend of Felix Decker."

"Mrs. Brandt's father?"

Frank didn't like the way Donatelli's face lit up when he said Sarah's name. The boy adored her. "That's right, and he was just as rich as Decker, too, so a lot of people want to find out who killed him."

"Why would a man like that be meeting with Mr. Angotti?"

"Devries owns a lot of tenements. Angotti's goons help get rid of tenants who don't pay their rent."

"Which means Mr. Angotti has a good reason to keep this Mr. Devries alive and healthy."

"Up until a month ago, Angotti never even met Devries. He just dealt with Devries's goons. But Devries had a job, something personal, he wanted Angotti to handle. I need to find out what it was."

Donatelli was already shaking his head. "You can't go to a man like this and accuse him of murder, Mr. Malloy."

Frank bristled, even though he knew Donatelli was right. "I'm not going to accuse him of anything. I just want to know why Devries wanted to see him."

"He's not stupid. He'll know what you're trying to do. If this rich fellow was murdered, the police would love to get an Italian for it."

"If he did it, he deserves it."

"I don't think he did."

Angry now, Frank forgot to whisper. "You don't know anything about it."

Donatelli glanced around to see if they were attracting any attention. Frank realized everyone in the café was watching them intently even though they couldn't have overheard much of the conversation.

Donatelli leaned over the table, practically whispering. "I know Salvatore Angotti isn't going to stick a knife into some rich man in this city no matter how much he might want to. Something like that would ruin him."

"One of his goons did, then."

"Nothing that could be traced back to him. I told you, he's not stupid. The police, we don't care what he does to his own people so long as he doesn't scare the legal citizens who vote, but if he raises his hand against somebody important . . ." Gino shook his head.

"Then he needs to help me find out who really killed this Devries fellow, because if I don't, sooner or later somebody is going to figure out how easy it would be to convince a jury he did it."

Plainly, Gino didn't like any of this. He sipped from his tiny cup, probably trying to decide if he could refuse to help. "That might work."

"What might work?"

"Telling Angotti you're trying to help him."

The very thought made Frank wince, but he said, "Would he believe it?"

"No, but it would get you in to see him. After that, it's up to you to find out what you need to know."

"Can you arrange it?"

Frank waited patiently while Gino thought this over. If necessary, Frank would remind him of the way he'd let Gino assist him on cases when no other Irish detective on the force would have worked with an Italian. But Frank didn't think that would be necessary. Italians never forgot a slight, but they never forgot a favor, either.

"You'll have to show him respect," Gino said.

"What does that mean?"

"It means you can't slap him around or insult him. They'll kill you if you do."

That was plain enough. Frank couldn't help wondering if this was even worth the trouble. "So you're saying I should treat him like I'd treat Felix Decker."

Gino's grin flashed again, and he nodded. "That's right. You're asking for his help, because his name came up, and if he can help you find the one who really killed this rich fellow, you can keep the police from poking around in his business."

"He should appreciate that."

"He won't appreciate anything you do for him, but he understands how the city works, and he'll know it's in his best interest to do a favor for you. He might need one in return some day."

The knowledge that he would be in debt to a man like Salvatore Angotti left a bitter taste in Frank's mouth, but he said, "How soon can you set up a meeting?"

5

FRANK MADE HIS WAY TO THE CITY MORGUE THROUGH THE
crush of late afternoon traffic that clogged streets and sidewalks alike. The winter chill had seeped into his very bones
by the time he reached his destination. So, glad to be someplace warm, he didn't even mind the smell of death that always
hung so heavily in the air. He found Doc Haynes in his office,
writing out autopsy reports.

Frank flopped wearily down into the single chair available
for visitors in the Spartan room. "Did you finish with
Devries yet?"

Haynes frowned and started shuffling through the
stacks of papers on his battered desk. He looked as if he
needed a long rest in the country someplace. Frank probably
did, too.

"Just like I thought," Haynes said, pulling the report from
the mess. "Stabbed with something long and thin. The blade

punctured a kidney, and he bled to death internally. It was a lucky punch, too."

"What do you mean?"

"I mean whoever did it managed to slip it in between two ribs. A fraction of an inch up or down and it would've just nicked the skin. Instead, it slipped right in."

"Any idea what he was stabbed with?"

"Something small."

"You said it was long."

"Maybe six inches at most, but narrow, much narrower than a regular knife."

"A stiletto, then?"

"Maybe."

Frank sighed. "What do you mean, *maybe*?"

"I mean, I've never seen a knife—not even a stiletto—make a hole that small."

Frank raised his eyebrows. "You think it really was a hat pin?"

"I think something more like an ice pick."

An ice pick? That opened up all sorts of possibilities. "But it could still be a stiletto?"

"A small one, I guess. I'd have to see it."

Frank was trying to imagine how Devries could've been stabbed with an ice pick. Every house had one, of course, but they weren't just lying around handy, in case you got mad and wanted to stick one into somebody. An ice pick would normally be in the kitchen, and Frank didn't think Devries spent much time in the kitchen. "Did you find anything else?"

"Yeah, and I'm surprised you didn't notice it yourself. No holes in his clothes."

"What does that mean?"

"It means he wasn't wearing those clothes when he got stabbed."

Frank blinked. Of course. He *should* have noticed that himself. He'd been too busy worrying about Felix Decker and his damn Knickerbocker Club. "So he was naked when he was stabbed."

"At least from the waist up. Or else he was wearing different clothes when he got stabbed."

Remembering what Devries had been doing that morning, he most certainly would have been in some stage of undress when he was with Norah English. He'd bathed at his home and changed his clothes, so he'd been naked around Roderick. Frank couldn't imagine how Roderick could've stabbed his employer without Devries noticing, but it was still a possibility. And then there was always the possibility that Devries had cozied up to Lizzie the maid in the kitchen and she'd stuck an ice pick in his back.

Frank almost smiled at the ridiculous image.

"I guess I've got to go back to the man's house and find out if he's got holes in any of his other clothes."

"I guess you do. He was in good health otherwise. Might've lived to a ripe old age if he hadn't died."

Frank pushed himself wearily to his feet. "You could say that about anybody."

SARAH AND MAEVE WERE CLEANING WHEN THEY HEARD the doorbell the next morning.

"This time I hope it's a delivery," Sarah said, pulling off the kerchief she'd been wearing to protect her hair from dust. "I do have to earn a living, you know."

Maeve grinned. "Especially now that you have a family to support. I'll get it."

Sarah removed her apron and made a few repairs to her hair before following the girl out to the front room, where she found Maeve making Garnet Devries welcome.

"Mrs. Devries," Sarah said. "What a nice surprise."

"I'm sure you didn't expect to see me so soon, but my mother-in-law went to see her dressmaker this morning, so I took the opportunity to slip out myself."

"I'm glad you did. Have you met Maeve? She helps take care of my daughter, Catherine."

"Yes, and this must be Catherine," Garnet said, smiling at the child who had crept silently down the stairs to see their visitor.

Maeve took Garnet's cloak while everyone made the proper introductory greetings, and then Maeve and Catherine went back upstairs.

"Would you like some coffee? I'm afraid we'll have to sit in the kitchen."

"That would be lovely," Garnet said. "I haven't sat in a kitchen since I got married."

"You sound sorry about that."

"I'm sorry about a lot of things."

Good manners forbade Sarah from asking what she meant by that, but she had a feeling that if she gave Garnet Devries the opportunity, she would explain herself without being asked. Sarah led her to the kitchen, where she poured them both coffee from the pot left over from breakfast.

"Would you like some pie? Maeve and Catherine have become very good cooks since my neighbor took them in hand."

"No, thank you. I . . ." She pressed her fingers to her lips for a moment, a gesture Sarah had seen before. Suddenly, she understood why Garnet Devries had been so anxious to see her.

"Are you with child?"

Garnet's eyes widened. "Can you tell simply by looking at a woman?"

"Not exactly, but you put your fingers to your lips, as if the thought of the pie nauseated you."

"Not the pie in particular."

"No, just any food at all, I expect. It's called morning sickness. Many women suffer from it during the first few months. How far along are you?"

"I don't know. I wasn't even sure . . . I'm still not."

She hadn't touched her coffee, and Sarah noticed how pale she had grown now that the ruddiness from the cold had faded from her cheeks. Sarah saw no spark of joy in her lovely eyes at the thought of a new life, either. But perhaps she was just frightened. Childbirth could be terrifying.

Sarah began asking her the routine questions about her menstrual cycle and other changes she would have noticed in her body. Her answers confirmed Sarah's suspicions. "It's still very early, but I think you can expect a baby late this summer."

"You couldn't be mistaken?"

"I don't think so."

Garnet frowned. "If it's still early, then there's a chance I might miscarry, isn't there?"

"Have you ever miscarried before?"

"No."

"It's possible, of course, but it's much more likely you'll have a healthy baby." Sarah smiled to reassure her, but Garnet didn't look reassured. Instead she glanced around the room, as if noticing it for the first time.

"How nice that you have your own home. Do you support yourself completely?"

Sarah blinked. "Yes."

"How long did it take for you to learn to be a midwife?"

"I took training as a nurse, and then I worked with another midwife for a year or so. About three years total, I guess."

The news seemed to disappoint her. "That's a long time."

"Are you interested in becoming a midwife?"

"Not really. I just . . . I'm interested in how a woman can make her own way in the world."

Once again, Sarah considered what good manners required of her, but this time she chose to ignore them. "Why?"

Garnet seemed shocked. Probably no one had ever asked her such a rude question before. "I . . . I suppose you have a right to wonder."

"No, I don't, but I admit I'm curious. Most women would kill to be in your position." Seeing Garnet's wince, Sarah instantly regretted her choice of words. "I'm so sorry. That was thoughtless—"

"Oh, no, don't apologize. You're absolutely right. My husband is now one of the richest men in the city. I live in a beautiful home with servants to wait on me. I have every luxury available. I should want for nothing."

"And yet you're asking me how a woman can make her own way in the world."

Color bloomed in Garnet's cheeks, and she started to rise. "I shouldn't have come . . ."

"Oh, please, don't go! I'm sorry, I shouldn't have—"

"You did nothing wrong, Mrs. Brandt. I was just being foolish."

Sarah cast about for a way to make her stay. "I . . . Do you have any questions about the baby?"

Her lips stretched into a grin, a ghastly expression that spoke of pain and bitterness. "No, no questions. My mother-in-law will be thrilled. She so wants the Devries name to continue."

"You could send her away, you know," Sarah said, thinking she knew the source of Garnet's pain. "Your mother-in-law, I mean. You're the mistress of the house now. You could send her to live with one of her daughters, or surely the family has a house in Newport or someplace where she could go."

"My husband would have to agree to send her away." Plainly, Garnet didn't believe that would ever happen.

"Then you could go yourself. For your health. For the baby."

"For the baby. Of course." For a second, an emotion that might have been despair twisted her lovely face, and then it was gone. She smiled the way girls like them had been taught to smile their entire lives, politely and insincerely. "Thank you for seeing me, Mrs. Brandt."

"Please, come back anytime. I will always be happy to see you."

"That's good to know."

Sarah followed her back to the front room and helped her with her cloak. "I would be happy to attend you, if your family approves."

This time, Garnet's smile was merely sad. "I'm sure I will be attended by the best doctors in the city, although you understand, that would not be my choice."

"I do understand. But I can always be your friend."

Tears flooded Garnet's eyes. "You shouldn't make such rash promises, Mrs. Brandt."

Before Sarah could reply, she was gone, throwing open the front door and practically fleeing. Sarah wanted to call her back, but as Garnet reached the foot of the front steps, she nearly collided with Sarah's elderly neighbor, Mrs. Ellsworth, who carried a napkin-wrapped plate of goodies she must be bringing for the girls. Sarah rushed to save Mrs. Ellsworth and the plate from falling, and by the time she had, Garnet had disappeared around the corner.

"Who was that?" Mrs. Ellsworth asked, breathless.

"A new friend," Sarah said. "I'm sorry. She was a little upset."

"At you?" Mrs. Ellsworth asked as they climbed the front steps.

"Oh, no." At least Sarah didn't think so, although she had no idea what Garnet was really upset about. She tried to distract Mrs. Ellsworth. "What have you brought us?"

"Cookies. Just shortbread, I'm afraid, but they're Nelson's favorite. He won't eat many of them, though, so I brought you the rest."

"How is Nelson?"

"He's very happy. Did I tell you he's keeping company with a young lady?"

"At least a dozen times," Sarah said with a smile.

"I do wish my son would settle down and start a family. I would love to dandle some grandchildren on my knee while I'm still able."

Sarah took Mrs. Ellsworth's coat and called the girls to come down and greet her. A few minutes later, they were in the kitchen enjoying the cookies when Sarah's front bell rang again. This time, a very excited young man had come to tell Sarah his wife was in labor and she had to come right away.

"I knew it," Mrs. Ellsworth said as they helped Sarah pack her medical bag. "I saw four crows on the back fence this morning. You know what they say, one crow means sorrow, two crows mean joy, three crows a wedding, and four a birth."

"What do five crows mean?" Catherine asked.

"A mess in your yard," Maeve said.

FRANK STOPPED BY HEADQUARTERS TO SEE IF DONATELLI had left him a message about the meeting with Angotti. Finding nothing, he headed back to the Devrieses' house. This time he went to the back door, where the cook reluctantly admitted him when he said he needed to speak to Roderick again. She rang for the valet.

"You can wait right here where I can see you until he comes," she said, eyeing him warily as she continued to knead an enormous mound of dough.

"Afraid I'll run off with the silver?"

"Coppers don't seem to mind taking what they want, I've noticed, although they get right annoyed if anybody else does."

Frank decided not to comment. "I guess the staff is pretty upset about Mr. Devries dying like that."

She gave him a look, as if judging the sincerity of his sympathy. "It was a shock, no doubt about it."

"His son is very different, isn't he?"

"Mr. Paul is an angel," she sniffed, expertly flipping the dough. "Never has a cross word to say."

"Didn't he ever argue with his father? I never knew a son who didn't."

She glared at him. "I meant to the staff. He didn't say much to Mr. Devries neither, though. Nobody did. Wouldn't do any good. He did what he wanted, that one."

"Speaking ill of the dead?" Frank asked with a knowing grin.

"If there's nothing else you can say," she replied.

"I guess you know about the young lady who lives on Mercer Street."

"She ain't no lady."

"So you do know about her."

"We all do, and I can't say we minded. Kept him away from here, didn't it?"

"You approve of a man neglecting his family?"

She scooped up the dough and plopped it into a large crockery bowl. "I do if neglecting means leaving them in peace."

"Mrs. O'Brien, that's enough," Roderick said from the doorway.

She sniffed. "Mind your own business." She draped a towel over the bowl and carried it over to the stove where the dough could rise in the warmth.

"Mr. Malloy, we can use the butler's pantry," he said, and led Frank through the kitchen to the tidy room lined with cabinets. They sat at the small table in the center of the room. "Mrs. O'Brien has a loose tongue."

"I like a woman who speaks her mind."

Roderick frowned but said, "Why did you want to see me?"

"The medical examiner thinks Mr. Devries was stabbed with something long and thin, but the clothing he was wearing when he died didn't have any holes in it."

"Of course not. Do you think Mr. Devries would wear clothing with holes in it?"

Frank managed not to sigh. "Whatever stabbed him would've made a hole in whatever he was wearing. We don't know when he was stabbed, but if we found clothing with a hole in it, we could figure out when he was wearing it and know when it happened."

Roderick considered this information. "Then you would also be able to figure out who could have stabbed him."

Frank saw no reason to respond. He simply waited.

Roderick took his time with his reply. "I did not notice damage to any of Mr. Devries's clothes."

"The hole might've been very small. Maybe you over-looked it."

"That's . . . possible." Plainly, he didn't think so.

"Can you remember what clothing he was wearing when he came home from Miss English's house yesterday?"

"I believe I can."

"Good. Let's go take a look at them."

Roderick stiffened. "What do you mean?"

"I mean I want to go with you to look at them. And if we don't find any holes, I want to look at all his other clothes."

"I'm sure Mrs. Devries wouldn't approve."

Frank wasn't sure if she wouldn't approve of Frank looking at Devries's clothes or of him going upstairs in the house, but he didn't much care. "I won't tell her. Now are you going to take me or should I try to find my own way?"

The thought of Frank wandering around the house by himself was enough to persuade Roderick of the lesser of two evils. Without a word, he rose and left the room, Frank at his heels. They climbed two sets of stairs and silently strode down a long corridor to one of several doors and entered Chilton Devries's bedroom. The dark, masculine furnishings told Frank he did not share this room with his wife.

Frank could never understand why rich people kept separate bedrooms. He recalled sharing a bed with his wife as one of the best parts of being married. But rich people did manage to have children, so he supposed they got together sometimes. Frank could only be glad he wasn't invading a room shared by Mrs. Devries. She'd probably have his job for that. Or at least his head.

The room contained a large mahogany bed with elaborately carved head- and footboards. A fireplace dominated one wall, and two stuffed chairs had been placed in front of it. A table between them held a nut bowl and a tray with some glasses and a crystal decanter, the kind used to serve liquor, although this one was empty at the moment. The nut bowl was a fancy one with a holder in the center for the nutcracker and other implements. It was half full of walnuts.

Roderick closed the door behind them, then went to a door on the left side wall. This opened into a dressing room with built-in drawers and cabinets. In one corner was a basket that apparently contained dirty clothes. Roderick started picking through them, and pulled out a man's white dress shirt.

"I believe this is the one he was wearing when he arrived home that morning." He held it up, and he and Frank examined the back of it. Frank had hoped for a bloodstain, but he didn't even find a hole.

Roderick seemed even more disappointed. Frank could understand that. Roderick would probably be very happy to discover Miss English had stabbed his master.

"What else was he wearing?" Frank asked.

"If the shirt doesn't have a hole—"

"What else?"

Roderick sighed with long-suffering and found a set of balbriggans, an undershirt, and long johns. The undershirt was also undamaged, although Frank couldn't help noticing how much finer the fabric was than the set he was wearing. They examined all the rest of the clothing in the basket, but found nothing with a hole in it.

"All right, tell me everything Mr. Devries did that morning while he was here."

For a second Frank thought he might refuse, but he squared his shoulders as if preparing for a fight, and said, "I already told you."

"Tell me again."

Another sigh. "He took a bath."

"Did you help him undress?"

"I already told you, yes. And I saw no evidence that he was injured."

"Where did he take a bath?"

"In the bathroom."

Frank managed not to lose his temper. "Show me."

With obvious reluctance, Roderick took him back into the bedroom and to a door on the opposite side of the room. This led to a fully equipped bathroom, with a tub, a commode, and a sink. Which Devries obviously had all to himself. Being rich did have its advantages.

"After his bath, did he get dressed in here?"

"No, he put on his robe." Roderick indicated a garment hanging on the back of the door.

Frank snatched it down and examined it. No blood. No holes.

"Then what did he do?"

"He . . . He called for some breakfast to be sent up."

"What did he do while he waited?"

"Read the paper."

"You said he had a fight with his son."

"I never said any such thing."

Frank gave him the stare that usually frightened hardened criminals into cooperating. Roderick gulped audibly. "Mr. Paul came in while Mr. Devries was reading his paper. I do not know what they discussed. I left the room."

"Did you go downstairs?"

"No, I went into the dressing room."

"Then you know what they argued about."

"I most certainly do not. I do not eavesdrop."

"But you couldn't have helped overhearing, especially if they were shouting."

But Roderick wasn't going to betray his master, even if he was dead. "I did not hear anything."

Frank nodded in silent acknowledgment of Roderick's victory. "After Paul left, then what happened?"

"I came out to help Mr. Devries get dressed."

"He was still wearing his robe?"

Roderick hesitated. "I . . . No, he wasn't."

"What was he wearing?"

"Nothing."

"He was naked?"

"Yes, he . . . he was probably expecting me to dress him, so he'd removed his robe."

"Did he remove it while Paul was still there?"

"I don't know."

Frank thought this, at least was the truth. Roderick looked too worried about the implications to be lying.

Frank couldn't imagine prancing around naked in front of people, but since Roderick helped Devries dress and undress every day, he supposed Devries would've thought nothing of it. The question was, did he think nothing of being naked in front of his son, who might've stabbed him in the back when he took off his robe?

But what would the son have stabbed him with? Frank didn't see an ice pick or even a hat pin lying around.

"So Devries was just walking around the room, naked?"

"He was eating a walnut."

"What?"

"A walnut." Roderick indicated the bowl on the table near the fireplace. "Mr. Devries is . . . was very fond of walnuts."

Frank was fairly certain Devries hadn't been stabbed with a walnut. Or a nutcracker either. "Then what happened?"

"Someone knocked on the door. I thought it was the girl bringing up the breakfast tray, so I opened the door, but it was Mrs. Devries."

"And she came in?"

Roderick flinched a little at the memory. "Yes."

Frank could imagine her reaction to finding her naked

husband standing there eating a walnut. "Did you leave the room again?"

"Very quickly."

"And did you hear—"

"Before I left, I heard her say Paul had told her about their argument, but I didn't listen to any more. If you want to know what they discussed, you will have to ask Mrs. Devries."

Frank couldn't imagine doing any such thing, but maybe Sarah could do it. Did women talk about things like that? He had no idea, but he would find out. From Sarah.

"Did Mr. Devries put his robe back on when his wife came in?"

"No. At least not that I know of. He was still naked when she left and I returned to the room."

"Maybe he thought if he was naked, she'd leave."

Roderick had to make an effort not to smile. "Or at least not stay as long."

"Then what happened?"

"I brought him his underwear, and he started to dress, but the girl finally delivered the breakfast tray, and he stopped to eat."

"Was he still naked when the girl delivered the tray?"

"Not completely, no."

"Did the girl see him?"

Roderick stiffened again.

"Did the girl often see him naked?" Frank guessed.

"Mr. Devries was not a modest man."

"Did he make use of the maids?" Frank understood this was not an uncommon practice in wealthy households.

"Oh, no, not . . . not at all. He just liked to shock them, I think."

The maids and his wife and his son. Very interesting. "He ate his breakfast. Then what?"

"He finished dressing. Then he left the house."

"To meet with Mr. Angotti."

Roderick had no reply to that.

"And he never mentioned being injured or having pain or anything like that?"

"I don't recall anything out of the ordinary. Mr. Devries was not a man to complain. He felt it was a sign of weakness."

"Too bad. It might've saved his life. I don't suppose Paul Devries is at home."

"Yes, but he has a visitor."

"Does he now? Who is visiting him?"

"I'm sure that's none of your business."

"Maybe I'll just go see for myself. I think I remember where the parlor is."

Roderick flushed with the effort of holding his temper. "Mr. Hugh Zeller arrived to offer his condolences."

"And who is Mr. Zeller?"

"Mr. Paul's oldest friend."

"Then he's like a member of the family. I'm sure he won't mind if I ask Mr. Paul a few questions."

"You can't—" Roderick protested, but Frank was already in the hallway. He found the main staircase with no trouble at all and was halfway down them when Roderick caught up.

"At least let me announce you!"

Frank knew this was not a task someone in Roderick's position would ever stoop to, so he agreed, wondering why Roderick was so protective of Paul Devries.

The parlor door was closed, and Roderick knocked rather loudly and waited for a summons before entering. "Mr. Malloy from the police is here. He'd like to speak with you, Mr. Devries."

Frank didn't wait for a reply. He had to give Roderick a slight shove, but he managed to squeeze through the door before Devries could refuse to see him.

While Roderick stammered an apology for Frank's rudeness, the two young men standing in the middle of the room gaped at him. Hugh Zeller was a strapping fellow with chiseled features and a lot of money to spend on clothes.

"Excuse the intrusion," Frank said when Roderick at last fell silent. "I need to ask you a few questions before I go."

Paul glanced at Zeller, as if asking permission or perhaps seeking advice. Zeller simply shrugged.

"I suppose it would be all right," Paul said. "Just a few, you said?"

"That's right." Frank looked at Roderick expectantly.

Plainly, he didn't want to leave, but he said, "If you need me, Mr. Devries, I'll be right outside."

This made Zeller grin, and when Roderick had closed the door behind himself, he said, "I guess Old Roderick is afraid you're going to give Paul here the third degree."

"What's the third degree?" Paul asked.

"Where they beat a confession out of you," Zeller said.

Paul saw no humor in that. "Do you really beat people?"

"Only if they don't answer my questions," Frank said, making Zeller grin again.

Paul actually blanched, but Zeller said, "He's just teasing you." To Frank, he said, "I tell him all the time he's too serious." Zeller clapped a hand on Paul's shoulder and said, "Let's sit down so Mr. Malloy can do what he needs to do and get on with it."

The two men sat side by side on a sofa, and Frank chose a nearby chair.

Paul wrung his hands. "I don't know what I can tell you, Mr. Malloy. I don't have any idea what happened to my father."

"I'm just trying to figure out everything that happened that day, and you can help me by telling me what you saw. Roderick said you went to see your father that morning in his room."

Paul glanced at Zeller, who nodded encouragement. "Yes, I . . . I was only there a few minutes."

"What did you talk about?"

He stiffened. "I don't see what that has to do with anything."

"Roderick said you argued."

Paul flushed. "We often argued."

Zeller placed a hand on Paul's shoulder. "Was it about me?"

"No!" Paul shook off the hand and glared at Frank. "It had nothing to do with his death."

"How can you be sure?" Frank asked.

"He can't hurt you anymore," Zeller said. "Why would you want to protect him?"

"I don't want to protect *him*!" Paul closed his eyes as he struggled with some emotion. When he opened them, they were cold. "He'd been very cruel to Garnet. I . . . I told him to stop." He turned to Zeller, as if explaining to him was what mattered. "She didn't deserve it. She didn't even want to marry me."

"I know, Old Man, I know," Zeller said.

Paul turned back to Frank. "She's a sweet girl. She deserves to be happy, but he was never going to allow it."

"What wasn't he going to allow her to do?"

"To divorce me."

6

"THAT'S NOT VERY FLATTERING, OLD MAN," ZELLER SAID. "I wonder you'd admit such a thing to a stranger."

Paul didn't even acknowledge him. He was watching Frank, who didn't quite know what to make of this. "Your wife wanted to divorce you?"

"She's not like us. She didn't come from here, and she hated all the rules and restrictions. She hated living here with my parents."

"That part I can understand," Zeller said.

"Why didn't you just get a house of your own?" Frank asked.

"Because I don't have any money of my own, and Father would never have allowed it. He wanted to keep me under his thumb."

Now this was getting interesting. "So as long as your father was alive, you had to depend on him for everything."

"Exactly," Paul said.

Zeller sighed dramatically. "Old Man, I think you just admitted you had a reason to want your father dead."

"Oh, no," Frank lied. "I think most young men feel like that about their fathers. Tell me, Mr. Devries, how was your father dressed when you went to his room the day he died?"

Paul shifted uneasily. "Dressed?"

"Yes, what was he wearing?"

Paul glanced at Zeller again. His friend was smiling, as if this whole thing amused him tremendously. "He had on a robe."

"Was he wearing it the entire time you were with him?"

The color rose in Paul's face. "What does that matter?"

"I thought you might have noticed a wound on your father's back. Did he remove his robe while you were there?"

"Yes." He spit the word out as if it tasted vile.

Zeller muttered something that might have been an oath.

"He liked to show off," Paul said, angry now. "He thought himself a fine specimen of a man, and he knew I could never compare, so he'd do it to make me feel inferior."

"And did you?" Frank asked.

"Did I what?"

"Feel inferior?"

"Mostly I just felt furious. What kind of a thing is that to do? Who displays himself like that?"

Frank didn't know the answer, so he said, "And did you notice anything unusual?"

"I didn't look at him. I never do. I wouldn't have noticed if he'd cut off one of his arms."

Frank wanted to ask if he'd stabbed his father, but he'd wait on that. "And did he agree to stop being cruel to your wife?"

"Of course not. He just laughed at me. He knows . . . knew I couldn't do anything about it. And poor Garnet, she couldn't do anything about it either."

"And now you're both free," Frank said.

Zeller leaned close to Paul and pretended to whisper. "He's thinking you killed the old bugger."

"Well, I didn't. I almost wish I had. At least then Garnet would respect me."

"Now you've got all your father's money," Frank said. "Or at least I assume you're his heir. I know rich families sometimes don't like to divide up the family fortune, so they only leave the money to one of the sons, like Vanderbilt did, but you're the only son."

"I haven't thought about it," Paul said.

"You should," Frank said. "Women usually respect men with money."

"He's right, Old Man," Zeller said. "You can buy her that house now. That'll cheer her up."

Paul didn't look too sure of that. "Not having Father around anymore will cheer her up."

Frank thought Paul would have to dispose of his mother, too, if he really wanted his wife to be happy, but he didn't say so. "What did you do when you left your father's room?"

"I . . . uh, I went to my mother's room," he replied as if he needed a second to catch up with the change of subject.

"What did you talk about?"

"I told her how angry I was at Father."

"Did she offer any advice?"

Paul sighed. "She didn't know how to handle him either."

"But she went to see him just the same."

"Oh, yes, she stormed off and gave him what for, but it didn't do any good. It never does. He knows . . . knew he could do whatever he wanted to us and there was nothing we could do about it."

"That's true," Zeller said. "He's even threatened to put his wife in an insane asylum if she caused him too much trouble."

Frank wished he could be shocked by the revelation, but other men had done that very thing. The law gave them absolute power over wives and children, and many a man had gotten away with murder just because the victim shared his house and his name.

"Did he threaten your wife, too?"

"My wife didn't kill him, either, Mr. Malloy. You're wasting your time here. You should be talking to that woman he kept."

Ah, so Paul knew about the mistress, too. "Don't worry, I will." Frank managed not to sigh. He didn't think he'd learned much in this interview, but at least he'd managed to fill some time. Maybe when he got back to Police Headquarters, he'd have a message from Donatelli.

"YOU'VE GOTTA HOLD YOUR TEMPER, MR. MALLOY," Donatelli told Frank for at least the fourth time. "No matter what he says, you just let it pass."

"If you tell me that one more time, I'm not gonna let it pass," Frank said. He instantly felt bad for alarming Donatelli, who was obviously terrified of this Angotti character. "Don't worry, I know how to act."

"I think if you treat him like you do Mr. Decker, you'll do fine."

Frank didn't think Decker had ever burned down somebody's store or had them killed because they didn't show him enough respect, but he understood the connection. Felix

Decker's techniques might be more refined, but he could ruin a man just as effectively as Angotti.

"What is this place you're taking me?" Frank asked. They'd been walking through Little Italy for a couple blocks now, and they stopped to let a gaggle of ragged children race by, running from a street vendor whose wares they had pilfered.

Donatelli had to shout over their screams. "It's a club. Normally you have to be a member to get in, unless you're a guest of Mr. Angotti."

This was too much like the Knickerbocker Club—only members were welcome, and no Irish need apply.

The similarities ended there, however. This club met in a nondescript building on a narrow side street with no sign alerting passersby to what went on inside. A burly fellow stood outside, ready to keep out unwelcome visitors. He eyed Frank and Gino suspiciously.

"This is Detective Sergeant Malloy. Mr. Angotti is expecting him," Donatelli said.

The fellow grunted and rapped on the door. Another unfriendly-looking fellow opened it a crack. The two men exchanged some words in Italian, and the door swung wide. Donatelli let Frank go in first. Frank suspected it wasn't out of courtesy.

Little sunlight penetrated into the main room. Dark curtains covered the windows, shielding the occupants from observation by anyone passing by on the street outside. Gaslights illuminated tables where men played cards or other games of chance. He felt as much as saw the players peering at him through the haze of cigarette smoke. All conversation ceased. Frank felt their hostility like a force as he followed his guide through the room to another door on the far side.

"Wait here." The man knocked, then went inside.

Frank couldn't help thinking how easy it would be to stick a knife in him and dump his body in the river. Would Donatelli defend him or would he side with his own people? Was he a cop first or an Italian? Frank didn't know. He didn't even know if *he* was a cop first or an Irishman.

The door opened and his guide beckoned them inside.

This smaller room was furnished like a parlor, with sofas and chairs and side tables arranged around a fireplace. A gaming table stood off to one side, almost as an afterthought. The light in here was better, and the cigarette smoke not so thick. Several somber men stood around, their attention focused on Frank and Donatelli. Frank soon realized his host was the well-dressed man seated on one of the sofas.

"Gino," he said, reaching out a languid hand.

Donatelli stepped forward and took the hand, nodding respectfully. "Thank you for seeing us, Don Angotti."

"How is your mother?"

"She's very well. She said to tell you she is baking you a *cassata* to thank you for your help."

"I should tell you that isn't necessary, but I like your mother's *cassata* too much to do that."

They both chuckled.

"You have brought someone to see me," Angotti said.

Angotti's accent was slight but unmistakable. Frank suddenly realized they were speaking English for his benefit.

"Yes, Don Angotti. This is Detective Sergeant Malloy, the man I told you about."

Frank stepped forward and waited for Angotti to size him up. Angotti wasn't a big man, but his dark eyes were shrewd and cunning. He didn't have to use his muscles to get what he wanted. The suit he wore probably cost more than Frank made in a month, and Felix Decker probably didn't own a finer one. His shirt was pristine.

"Gino speaks highly of you, Detective Sergeant Malloy."

"Officer Donatelli is one of our finest men."

Angotti's lip curled. "It is a pity to waste him on the police department."

Frank refused to be baited. He merely nodded.

Donatelli cleared his throat. "Mr. Malloy would like to ask you some questions."

"And I will decide if I answer them or not."

"Of course," Frank said. "You know we are investigating the death of Chilton Devries."

"So Gino tells me."

"He had an appointment with you the day he died."

"Did he?"

"He thought so. The question is, did you see him that day?"

Angotti's gaze was sharp as broken glass. "And if I did?"

"Mr. Angotti, Chilton Devries died because somebody stabbed him in the back."

"Gino told me he died at his club. Have you questioned the men he saw there?"

"He died there, but he was stabbed someplace else. He was stabbed with something long and thin . . . like an ice pick."

"Or a stiletto, Gino tells me."

"Or a stiletto. He probably didn't know how badly he was injured, and he didn't bleed much on the outside. But he did bleed to death, and he died at his club, but he'd been stabbed earlier in the day."

"And you think I stabbed him?" He seemed only mildly concerned.

"No, but Mr. Devries was a wealthy man with lots of powerful friends. His family is telling them that he came to see you that day, and then he died. I believe his family and his friends would be happy to blame you for killing him."

"Because I am a foreigner."

"Because you're not one of them."

"And why are you telling me this?"

"Because I want to find out who did kill him, and I need your help."

Angotti frowned. "I do not understand you, Mr. Malloy. Why do you not want to blame me when everyone else does?"

"I told you, I want to find out who really did it."

"And you do not think I did?"

"No, I think you're too smart to kill someone like Chilton Devries, even if you wanted to, and I can't figure out any reason why you would."

"That is because you did not know Mr. Devries very well. If you did, you could figure out many reasons."

"Are you saying you had a reason to kill him?"

"Not personally, but I know things about him that make me glad he is dead."

"Could you tell me what those things are?"

"Why should I?"

"So I can find out who really killed him and make sure nobody bothers you about it."

"Why would you do this for me?"

"I'm not doing it for you. I'm doing it because I want to find out the truth."

Angotti chuckled again. "No man cares so much for the truth, Mr. Malloy. Why are you really doing it?"

"Because one of Devries's powerful friends asked me to, and he does care for the truth."

"Would this friend not be happy to find out a foreigner killed Mr. Devries?"

"He would be very happy, but only if it was true."

"I would like to meet this friend. He sounds like a man worth knowing."

Frank let a moment go by, in case Angotti had something else to say. "So, did you see Devries yesterday?"

"He came here, yes."

"I know he'd seen you before. Can you tell me what he wanted?"

Angotti studied Frank with his sharp gaze. "He wanted me to kill someone."

Frank blinked, and Gino Donatelli gasped.

"Who? Why?"

Angotti smiled, amused by their reaction. "I would be very foolish to tell you who I killed, would I not?"

He would, indeed, even though Frank knew he wouldn't have done the work himself.

Before Frank could figure out how to answer him, Angotti said, "Yes, I would be foolish to tell you if I had killed someone, but I did not, Mr. Malloy. Would you like to know why?"

"Yes, I would." Frank was glad to hear his voice didn't sound as flustered as he felt.

"Mr. Devries came to see me. He thought I was a man who would do anything for money. He did not have respect for me. He told me a story about a woman. He told me she was evil and had done terrible things. He wanted me to have her killed."

"But you didn't."

"No. I did not believe Mr. Devries. I thought the story he told me about this woman was a lie, but I did not say this to him. Instead I went to see this woman. She told me a very different story, and I believed her."

"So she's still alive."

"She was when I last saw her."

"When was that?"

"A few days ago. Then Mr. Devries came to see me yesterday. He was going to pay me for killing this woman, but I
told him I did not kill her. I told him he was a liar."

Frank couldn't help grinning at the image of Angotti calling Devries a liar. "I guess he was mad."

"Yes, but he could do nothing about it." Angotti gestured
to indicate the men standing around the room.

"And a few hours later, he was dead." Then Frank had an
unsettling thought. "Could he have gone to see this woman
himself?"

Angotti's eyes widened. "You think he may have killed her
himself?"

"And maybe she was the one who stabbed him. Do you
remember what time he left here?"

Angotti looked over at his men, who had a brief discussion
in Italian. "Around noon."

Frank wasn't sure exactly when Devries had arrived at his
club, but if he'd had the time . . . "Can you tell me where to
find this woman?"

Angotti gestured to one of his men who gave Frank an
address not too far from where Norah English lived.

"What is this woman's name?" Frank asked.

"Mrs. Richmond. I am sure you will enjoy her story as
much as I did."

FRANK DIDN'T REALLY EXPECT FELIX DECKER TO BE AT
home yet. In fact, he was hoping he wasn't. He really wanted
to talk to Mrs. Decker. She apparently wanted to speak to him,
too, because she only kept him waiting a few minutes in the

small receiving room before the maid escorted him up to the parlor. Not the front parlor, either, but the one the family used for every day. Mrs. Decker no longer considered him company.

"Mr. Malloy, how delightful to see you," she said, giving him her hand when the maid had shown him in. "I'm sorry my husband isn't home yet, but I expect him within the hour if you'd like to wait."

"Thank you, I would."

She smiled conspiratorially. "Good. I ordered coffee, unless you'd like something stronger."

"Coffee is fine."

"Please, have a seat and tell me what you've been up to. I went to Sarah's house earlier today, but she's out on a delivery."

She sat with him on one of the comfortable sofas, her lovely face alight with interest. Frank couldn't help noticing how much she and Sarah looked alike, except for the spark of spirit that made Sarah different from all the other rich women he'd met. He thought maybe living a lifetime in luxury killed that spirit, and Sarah had escaped just in time. Then again, maybe she was the only one who had it, and that's why she had escaped in the first place.

"I've been learning some things about Mr. Devries that aren't very nice."

"Oh, dear. But I guess that isn't surprising. Nice people seldom get murdered, do they?"

Frank couldn't help grinning. "No, they don't. I haven't had a chance to find out how your visit with Mrs. Devries went."

"I'm afraid we didn't learn very much that will be of use to you."

"Did you learn anything at all?"

Mrs. Decker frowned. "Let me see. We learned that Garnet and Paul have been married for two years but have no children.

This is a source of disappointment for Mrs. Devries, who wants to see the family name continue. Oh, and Garnet expressed a desire to get to know Sarah better. She was very interested in Sarah's work."

"Her work as a midwife?"

"Yes, she may hope Sarah can help her have a child, although Sarah insists she can't."

"Did she tell Garnet Devries that?"

"No. We didn't actually discuss the subject, you understand. This is all conjecture, the part about her wanting Sarah's help, I mean. Sarah disagrees."

"What does she think Garnet wants?"

"She doesn't know, but Maeve told me Garnet visited her earlier today, just before Sarah went out to the delivery, so perhaps we'll find out when she returns. Oh, and we learned Garnet's family is from the south, Virginia I believe she said. Her father moved the family here because of his business and tried to join the Knickerbocker Club, which is how he met Chilton. I gather Chilton met the rest of the family and decided Garnet would be a suitable wife for Paul."

"Does that happen a lot?"

"What? Trying to join the Knickerbocker?"

"No, parents choosing a mate for their child. I thought only kings and queens did that."

Mrs. Decker smiled. "I never thought of it that way, although . . . Well, you probably remember poor Consuelo Vanderbilt's marriage to an English duke last year. That was certainly an arranged marriage. Consuelo was only eighteen and most likely had no desire to marry a man a foot shorter than she was who lived all the way across the ocean from her friends and family, but Alva—Alva is her mother, you know—

insisted she was doing it so Consuelo would have an opportunity to live a much more interesting life."

"How would her life be more interesting?"

Mrs. Decker shrugged delicately. "I'm not sure, having never actually met a duchess, you understand, but according to Alva, upper-class women in Europe have many more interests than American women. They are even active in politics. Maybe . . ."

"Maybe what?"

"This will sound silly, but maybe I should have married Sarah off to a duke."

Frank could see her point. If Sarah had found her prospects as the wife of a rich man the least bit interesting, she probably wouldn't have married a poor doctor and become a midwife. "And she wouldn't be an embarrassment to you now."

"Oh, Mr. Malloy, you mustn't think I'm ashamed of her," she said, the color rising in her fair cheeks. "I'm very proud of her, in fact. I just . . . I worry about her, you know, traveling around the city at all hours. She does without so many things, too."

"I don't think she minds."

"Of course she doesn't, but . . . You must think me very shallow."

"No, not at all." Once he had. Now he knew her better.

"I didn't really mean that, about marrying her to a duke. But sometimes I think how different things might have been if she could have been content with her lot in life. But you didn't come here to listen to my regrets. To answer your question, no, we don't typically arrange marriages, at least not in America, but parents do take a hand in these matters."

"How?"

"By making sure our children socialize with only the right people. By pointing out a certain young man's good qualities. By letting the child know how happy such a union would make us. Parents can be very influential."

"So you think that's what happened with Paul and Garnet Devries?"

She had to consider this. "I suppose at first I just assumed that when Chilton met Garnet, he thought Paul would like her, too, so he brought them together. Then the two young people fell in love on their own, as attractive young people often do."

"Do you still think that?"

"Now that you've asked me about it, no, I don't. The way Garnet told it, I got the idea she and Paul—or at least *she*—didn't have much say in the matter. She certainly doesn't seem very happy, either, although that might not be Paul's fault. I haven't seen them together, so I can't judge."

"I have, and he's sure not doing much to help."

Before she could reply, the coffee arrived. Mrs. Decker served them both, and then said, "I know you've been investigating, too. What have you discovered?"

Which reminded Frank of why he'd come here in the first place. "Do you know a woman named Mrs. Richmond?"

"Richmond?" She frowned, then rose and went to a desk on the far side of the room. She returned with a small book bound in rose-colored leather. As she flipped through it, he saw it contained names and addresses. "No, I'm afraid I don't. I didn't think the name sounded familiar, but I wanted to be sure. Who is this Mrs. Richmond?"

Frank told her about Devries having an appointment with Salvatore Angotti on the day he died and what Angotti had told him about Devries wanting to have Mrs. Richmond murdered.

"Oh, my," she said for at least the third time during his narrative. "Do you think this Italian gentleman could be lying? Maybe he stabbed Chilton himself and is just trying to divert your attention."

"Anything's possible, but a man like Angotti always looks after his own best interest first. Killing a man like Devries would not be in his own best interest, especially because Devries was no threat to him."

"Yes, I see. What would Mr. Angotti get out of killing Chilton except a lot of trouble?"

Frank nodded, glad to see Mrs. Decker was as insightful as her daughter.

"Would you like me to go see this Mrs. Richmond?"

"*No!*" Frank saw the flash of disappointment in her eyes and instantly felt guilty for his vehement response. "I mean, that won't be necessary. I just wanted to find out everything I could about her before going to see her. If she's a society lady like you, I'd have to be more careful about how I approach her."

Mrs. Decker sighed. "I should so love to help you with something, Mr. Malloy. Couldn't you at least pretend you need it?"

For a second, Frank didn't know what to say, and then he saw the twinkle in her eyes and burst out laughing. They were still laughing when Felix Decker walked in.

Frank sobered instantly, jumping to his feet and feeling oddly guilty, as if he'd been caught doing something unseemly with another man's wife.

Decker had hesitated in the doorway, and he looked more disturbed now than he had when he'd been telling Frank about finding a dead man in his club.

Mrs. Decker gave him a dazzling smile. "Hello, my dear. I've been telling Mr. Malloy about our visit to Lucretia while we waited for you to arrive."

"I had no idea your visit had been so hilarious," Decker said with some asperity. "Mr. Malloy, you could have come to my office."

"But he wouldn't have been able to see *me* at your office," Mrs. Decker said. "And he needed to hear my report, didn't you, Mr. Malloy?"

Frank wasn't sure what the proper response to that should be, but he said, "I also needed to consult with Mrs. Decker about another matter."

"Yes," she said. "He was hoping I knew the lady Chilton Devries wanted to have murdered so I could make an introduction."

The usually unflappable Decker looked positively apoplectic. "Really, Mr. Malloy—"

"Oh, Felix, the expression on your face," his wife said, enjoying it immensely. "You can't really think for a moment that Mr. Malloy would do any such thing, but I couldn't resist teasing you."

Decker gave Frank an accusing glare.

"I did ask Mrs. Decker if she knew Mrs. Richmond, but I would never—"

"Richmond? Did you say Richmond?" Decker asked.

"Yes. Do *you* know her?"

"No, not a *Mrs.* Richmond, but . . . Did you say Chilton wanted to have this woman *murdered?*"

Frank was beginning to feel sorry for the man.

"Come and sit down, dear," his wife said. "We'd better start at the beginning."

"I think that would be an excellent idea," Decker said. "By the way, Mr. Malloy, you haven't inquired, but I thought you'd like to know that we have asked everyone who was at the club the day Chilton died, and he didn't speak with anyone except to exchange a greeting."

Frank nodded his acknowledgment as they all took their seats. He'd held out little hope the club members would have any helpful information anyway.

Mrs. Decker graciously allowed Frank to tell Decker the story while she served her husband a cup of coffee, for which he seemed grateful, even though it was probably cold by now.

"You didn't tell me you'd seen Angotti at his *club*," Mrs. Decker said when he'd finished. "How funny to think a man like that has a club. Is it very much like the Knickerbocker?"

"Not in any way," Frank said, deciding not to mention his observation that the Irish would not be welcome in either establishment.

She started to ask another question, but her husband stopped her with an impatient gesture. "Mr. Malloy, how can you possibly believe this Angotti was telling the truth?"

"I can't, but I'm going to see Mrs. Richmond tomorrow and find out."

Decker glanced at his wife.

"No, I won't leave you two alone," she said. "And you might as well let me stay. It will save you the trouble of telling me everything later."

Decker sighed, and Frank had to bite his lip to keep from grinning. "Mr. Malloy, I can't believe Chilton Devries would ever associate with a man like Angotti, much less that he would try to arrange for a woman—any woman—to be murdered."

Frank could have predicted that Decker wouldn't have the stomach for this kind of business. "Do you want me to stop investigating?"

"Heavens no," Mrs. Decker said, earning a glare from her husband.

"This is not your decision, Elizabeth."

"Forgive me," she said with mock sincerity. "I forgot myself for a moment. But you can't allow Mr. Malloy to quit now."

"I most certainly can."

"Mrs. Decker," Frank said in an attempt to rescue Decker from his wife's wrath, "considering what I've found out about Mr. Devries so far, I think we can guess that the rest of it will be even worse. I might find out things that will disgrace his family and still not be able to figure out who killed him. A lot of innocent people might suffer."

"Apparently, a lot of innocent people have already suffered," she said. "What about this Mrs. Richmond? What if Chilton hired someone else to kill her? Shouldn't she at least be warned? Felix, I can't believe you'd stand by and—"

"Elizabeth, enough!" Decker said. "Of course I won't stand by and allow this woman to come to harm. Mr. Malloy will go see her tomorrow no matter what else we decide to do."

"And do you agree that Mr. Malloy should stop his investigation to protect the family?" she asked.

Decker turned to Frank. "I think I'd like to find out what this Mrs. Richmond has to say before I make my decision."

"If she's still alive," Frank said.

Mrs. Decker gasped.

"What do you mean?" Decker asked.

"I mean if Devries wanted her dead and Angotti wouldn't do it, he might've done it himself."

"I don't believe it!" Decker said.

"Why not?" his wife asked. "Because you wouldn't do it yourself? I don't think you would've tried to hire someone to do it either, but Chilton apparently did."

"We only have that Italian's word for it."

"Honestly, Felix, just because the man was a member of your club doesn't mean he was a saint."

"And if he killed Mrs. Richmond, or tried to, and she put up a fight, that could explain how he got stabbed," Frank said.

"Oh, my goodness, you're right," Mrs. Decker said.

Decker frowned, but he said, "It would also explain why he didn't tell anyone he'd been injured."

Mrs. Decker smiled at her husband with apparent approval. "Of course. How *could* he have explained it?" To Frank, she said, "Shouldn't you go right over to see this Mrs. Richmond instead of waiting until tomorrow?"

"I don't think there's any hurry. If she's dead, I can't help her, and if not, I don't want to alarm her by calling on her after dark.

"But if Chilton hired someone else to kill her—"

"He didn't find out Angotti wouldn't do it until a few hours before he died, so I doubt he had time to arrange anything else. Finding someone to commit murder isn't that easy, even in New York."

"But you'll let us know immediately what you find out, won't you?" she asked.

"Elizabeth, Mr. Malloy will report to me in good time."

She didn't even acknowledge him. "You will, won't you?"

"Of course." Before Decker could object, he added, "Now tell me, was the English duke really a foot shorter than Miss Vanderbilt?"

"Oh, dear, did I say that?" she asked, her face lighting with delight. "Not a whole foot, surely, but at least half a foot. She's quite tall, you see, and he is . . . a bit runty."

"Elizabeth, really," her husband said.

"Well, he is, even if he is a duke. He was rather penniless, too, so he came out on the better side of the bargain. They had to honeymoon for a year while he used her dowry to refurbish his castle because it wasn't fit for human habitation."

Frank couldn't wait to tell Sarah her mother thought she should have married her off to a duke. "Mr. Decker, I'll report back to you as soon as I know anything important. Mrs. Decker, thank you for your hospitality."

The Deckers murmured all the appropriate responses as Frank took his leave. Just as the maid showed him out, he heard Decker say to his wife, "Now tell me what Mr. Malloy said to you that was so funny."

7

Sarah was just finishing the enormous breakfast Maeve and Catherine had prepared for her after she arrived home from the delivery that morning when the doorbell rang. They all groaned, thinking she was being summoned to another birth, but the girls' laughter when they answered the front door told Sarah their visitor was a friend. The rumble of a male voice prompted her to smooth her hair, but she had no time for any additional primping before the girls escorted Malloy into the kitchen.

Well, he'd seen her looking far worse than this. "Malloy," she said, returning his smile of greeting.

"Good morning, Mrs. Brandt. I was hoping to catch you at home."

Maeve poured him some coffee and gave him a few minutes to exchange some nonsense with Catherine before taking the child upstairs so he and Sarah could speak privately.

"I suppose you're wondering what Mother and I found out from Mrs. Devries," she said when the girls were gone.

"Oh, no. Your mother already told me all about it."

Sarah's jaw dropped open, and she closed it with a snap. "When did my mother tell you all about it?"

"Yesterday, when I went to see her. You weren't home," he added.

"Maeve didn't tell me you'd stopped by."

"I didn't."

Sarah managed not to gape at him again. "You mean you just went to my mother's house without even checking with me first?"

"I needed to see your father, so I figured if I got there early enough, he wouldn't be home yet, and I could talk to her in private."

"She must have loved that."

"She didn't say, but she did seem happy to see me."

Sarah could just imagine. "What did she tell you?"

"She told me the marriage between Paul and Garnet Devries was arranged, sort of like the one with Consuelo Vanderbilt and the duke."

"She didn't tell you any such thing."

"I'm sure she did. You can ask her yourself. In fact, she also told me . . . Well, another time. Anyway, she said they aren't happily married—Paul and Garnet, although I think Consuelo and the duke couldn't be very happy either—and they don't have any children, which proves it."

"They were happy at least once, because Garnet is now with child."

Sarah had the satisfaction of seeing Malloy choke on his coffee. "Your mother didn't tell me that."

"She doesn't know. Garnet came by to visit me yesterday."

"Oh, right. Your mother stopped by to see you yesterday after you left for the delivery, and Maeve told her Garnet had been here. So that's why she was so interested in your work. Your mother did tell me that, at least."

"Yes, Garnet asked me a lot of questions about being a midwife, and she asked some more when she was here yesterday. I had the oddest feeling she was really just interested in how she might earn her own living, though."

"Ah."

"What do you mean, *ah*?"

"Paul mentioned that Garnet wanted to divorce him."

"Oh!"

Malloy frowned. "What do you mean, *oh*?"

"I mean that would explain why Garnet wasn't very happy about having a baby. If she is really considering a divorce, a baby would complicate matters. When did you talk to Paul?"

"I met him when I went back to the house yesterday to look at Devries's clothes."

Sarah blinked. "I get the feeling you have a lot of things to tell me."

"Let me start with what I've found out since I saw you last, and then you can do the same."

"Sounds like a good plan, but don't dawdle. I was up all night, and I might drift off at any moment."

"I'll do my best to keep you awake. I guess I should start by telling you about my visit with the mistress."

Sarah no longer felt a bit sleepy. "I'd completely forgotten about her. What's she like?"

"Not like I expected. She's young and . . ."

"And what?"

"I feel silly saying *innocent*, considering what she is, but she

seems like a fresh-faced country girl who just got lost on her
way to the market."

"How sad. What's going to become of her now?"

"I don't know, but she's got a maid who'll look after her, I
think."

"A maid?"

"Well, she was got up as a maid, and she answered the door
and fetched Miss English like a maid would, but when Miss
English got hysterical, this woman slapped her right in the
face."

"The maid *slapped* her?"

"Yeah. Have you ever seen anything like that before?"

"I've heard about a very ill-mannered houseguest slapping
a maid once, but never the other way around. She'd be turned
out without a reference and would never get work in another
house in the city."

"Which is why I thought maybe she wasn't really a maid."

"Or maybe she was the girl's nursemaid or something and
just stayed with her when she fell on hard times or . . . I don't
know. Did you ask my mother what she thought about it?"

"Of course not. Do you think I was going to talk about
Devries's mistress with your mother?"

Sarah had to smile at the image. "No, but I assure you, she
would have loved it."

"Which is exactly why I didn't do it. So this girl and her
maid are living in this house, but I'm sure Paul Devries will
turn them out as soon as he thinks about it, if he hasn't done
it already. That's why the girl got hysterical, by the way. She
didn't seem too upset that Devries was dead until she realized
what it meant to her. That's when she started carrying on."

"How interesting that no one seems particularly upset the
man is dead."

"Not really. A lot of people who end up murdered aren't well liked."

"I don't suppose she happened to mention that she'd stabbed him in the back before he left her that morning."

"No, but she did admit they had an argument."

"What about?"

"The maid said Miss English wanted to go out to the theater or something, and Devries wouldn't allow it. But that's just what the maid said. They could've been fighting about anything."

"Do you think the girl might have done it? Even by accident?"

"I don't know. Maybe by accident, but I didn't ask her outright. She would've just denied it, and I would've lost my chance to surprise her with it. I think the maid could've done it, but the thing is . . ." Malloy shifted, obviously uncomfortable.

Sarah straightened in her chair. "What?"

"I'm starting to think Devries was naked when he got stabbed."

"Why do you think that?"

"The medical examiner noticed there are no holes in the clothes he was wearing when we found him dead at the club, so he wasn't wearing them when he got stabbed."

"He could have been wearing different clothes or . . ." Sarah tried to imagine some possible scenarios. "You said he spent the night with his mistress. He would have taken off his clothes then, to sleep if nothing else. He might've been wearing a nightshirt, and . . . Would he have taken the nightshirt home with him?"

"I've never kept a mistress myself, but I doubt a man would carry a bag of nightclothes and a change of underwear when he went back and forth between her place and his house."

"No, you're right, he'd keep clothes there. But what about the clothes he wore home from her place? They might have been different from the clothes he wore later in the day."

"His valet couldn't find anything at the house that had holes in it."

"If he was undressed when he got stabbed, it must have happened at the mistress's house, then."

"Not necessarily. He also happened to be naked when he had an argument with his son and then later with his wife."

Sarah watched Malloy's face slowly growing red. No matter how many times they discussed things like this, Malloy still got embarrassed. Her medical training had hardened her to such things, and she sometimes wondered if Malloy thought her unfeminine because of it. "I'm guessing you didn't discuss any of this with my mother either." From the expression on his face, he didn't think that was funny. "So, I can understand why a man might be undressed when with his wife, but how did it happen with his son as well?"

"Apparently, Devries and his wife don't spend much time together anymore, dressed or not, so it was unusual for the wife, too. According to the valet, Devries came home and took a bath, as he usually did when returning from visiting Miss English."

Sarah bit her tongue to keep from making a remark that might embarrass Malloy further and simply nodded.

"He was in his room, waiting for his breakfast tray to be brought up, when Paul came in."

"Mr. Devries was waiting in his room without any clothes on?"

"No, he wore a robe, but at some time during his argument with Paul, he removed it. Paul said he did it to make him feel inferior."

"How would removing his robe make Paul feel inferior?"

"That's not something I'm going to explain to you, but it doesn't matter anyway. I think Devries had another purpose in mind."

"What?"

"Nothing I'm prepared to tell you about, and don't bother pouting because it won't work."

"I'm not pouting!"

"So Devries was naked when Paul left the room."

Sarah sighed. "What did they argue about?"

"Paul said Devries had been cruel to Garnet, and he was telling him to stop."

"That doesn't sound right."

"Why not?"

"You told me Garnet wanted to divorce Paul, and we know they weren't particularly happy together. Why would he care if his father was mean to her?"

Malloy leaned back in his chair. "That's a good question. Maybe because of the baby."

"I don't think he knows about the baby. His mother certainly doesn't. She actually told us Garnet is barren, so *she* couldn't know, and I'm guessing if Paul knew, he would have told her instantly."

"Then I'll have to find out why he was so anxious to defend his wife."

"Find out what the father was doing to her, too. Maybe he made Garnet mad enough to stab him."

Malloy grinned at that image. "I'd rather put my money on Mrs. Devries."

"Oh, yes, how did she happen to visit her husband, since you said they don't spend much time together?"

"Paul went straight to her to complain about his father, and she went to see Devries herself. According to the valet, Devries was not a modest man, and he made no move to cover himself when she came in."

"Oh, dear, I can just imagine her reaction."

"Yeah, well, she probably didn't stay long, but she was there, so I have to consider her."

"She didn't like him much, either, and she probably knows about the mistress, so she'd be mad about that, too." Sarah shook her head. "I don't suppose anyone else was in the room with them."

"The valet claims he withdrew and didn't see or hear a thing."

"He might not have seen, but I'll bet he heard plenty."

"I'm sure he did, but he's not going to talk, at least not yet."

Sarah considered what Malloy had told her. "So both the wife and the son could have done it."

"Yes, except for one thing."

"What's that?"

"I don't have any idea what they could've stabbed him with."

"I thought it was a stiletto."

"What would either of them be doing with a stiletto? Besides, Doc Haynes says it was thinner than that. Something like an ice pick."

"An ice pick? Where would they have gotten an ice pick?"

"Just what I was wondering." Malloy glanced around the kitchen and pointed to the top of her icebox. "There's yours, right where it's handy if you want to chip off some ice for something."

"Or if I wanted to stab someone with it."

"But it would only be handy for that if you wanted to stab somebody in the kitchen."

"Oh, I see what you mean."

"And while you spend a lot of time in your kitchen, I doubt Paul or his mother ever go there."

"And if one of them had decided to murder Mr. Devries with an ice pick, they would have had to go down to the kitchen and get it without anybody noticing or wondering about it and carry it upstairs and . . ." She shook her head. "It just doesn't make any sense."

"I know." Malloy sighed.

"What about the Italian man Mr. Devries was going to see?"

"Oh, yes, Mr. Angotti. He was interesting."

"You met him?"

"Gino Donatelli made the introduction."

Sarah smiled. "How is Gino doing?"

For some reason, Malloy frowned. "He's still with the department, at least so far, but I don't know how much longer that will last."

"Are things very different now that Theodore is gone?" Police Commissioner Theodore Roosevelt had instituted many reforms in the department, but he'd left a few months earlier for a job in Washington, D.C.

"Everything is different, but with all the Italians in the city, it's still good to have some cops on the force who know the language and the neighborhood."

"Are things different for you?"

He didn't answer right away, and when he did, his voice held no emotion. "Having Felix Decker ask for me by name will keep me in good graces for a while. Now, you were asking about Angotti."

"Yes, did you find out why Devries went to see him?"

"Devries wanted Angotti to kill a woman for him."

"Good heavens! You can't be serious!"

"I'm perfectly serious. Devries wanted this woman, a Mrs. Richmond, murdered, and he tried to hire Angotti to do it."

"Why on earth did he want someone murdered?"

"I don't know yet. I have to go see this Mrs. Richmond to find out."

"Then Angotti didn't kill her?"

"He claimed he didn't. He said when he heard her story, he decided she didn't deserve to be killed and told Devries his decision on the day he died."

"Do you suppose there's a chance Devries went to see Mrs. Richmond and took his clothes off for some reason?"

"I did think he might've tried to kill her himself and got stabbed in the process, but I won't know until I see Mrs. Richmond."

"She isn't likely to admit to something like that, especially if she knows he's dead now."

"Let's hope she doesn't. It hasn't been in the papers yet."

"Do you have any idea why Devries wanted her dead?"

"None. Angotti wasn't going to help me any more than he had to."

"I'm sorry I can't help you more."

"I'm not. You're already more involved in this than you should be."

"Maybe I could call on Garnet again, just to see how she's doing."

"Somebody in that house might be a killer."

"They wouldn't have any idea I was helping with the investigation, though. I'm just a concerned friend."

"Sarah . . ."

"All right, all right. But if Garnet calls on me again, I'm not going to turn her away."

Malloy didn't roll his eyes, but she suspected he wanted to.

"What are you going to do today?" she asked.

"Go see Mrs. Richmond, and if she doesn't confess to stabbing Devries, then I'll go see Miss English again and ask if any of Devries's clothes have holes in them."

"That should be interesting. And if neither woman confesses, what will you do next?"

"Go see your father, tell him Mrs. Richmond's story, and find out if he wants me to quit."

"*Quit?* Why would he want you to quit?"

"So I don't embarrass the family."

Sarah couldn't believe it. "Yes, I'm sure it would be terribly embarrassing to find out Mrs. Devries killed her husband."

Malloy grinned. "I don't think he's afraid of that. He's afraid I'll find out even worse things about the Devrieses than I already have and his family will have to live with the shame of it, whether I find the real killer or not."

"I suppose I should be proud of my father for being so considerate."

"You may not like Mrs. Devries, but what about Garnet? Did she do anything to deserve a scandal? Or Paul?"

"I suppose you're right."

"Stop pouting."

"I'm not—" Sarah caught herself when she saw his grin. "Malloy, I think you're enjoying this case."

His grin faded. "Truthfully, I'm not. I don't like anything about it."

"Do you normally like murder cases?"

"Not *like*, but . . . I don't know how to explain it. The whole thing makes me uneasy, like I'm going to find out something I shouldn't find out. Something *nobody* should find out. When your father said he was thinking about putting an end to it, I was actually relieved."

"You were just relieved that you wouldn't have to work with my father anymore."

To her surprise, he shook his head. "I would've thought that was true, too, before I worked with him, but he's . . ."

"He's what?" Sarah found herself intensely interested in his opinion of her father.

"Reasonable."

Sarah's jaw dropped again, and she didn't even bother to close it. "I would never describe my father as reasonable. You know very well how *un*reasonable he can be."

"Yes, I do, but in this . . . Well, maybe he's changed. Tragedy can change a man."

It could change a woman, too. The tragedy of her sister's death had changed Sarah from a careless girl to the woman she was today. Could it have changed her father, albeit more slowly? She would like to think so. "Maybe I should discuss the case with him."

He grinned. "Be sure to include your mother. It will save him the trouble of having to tell her everything you talked about later."

FRANK WASN'T SURE HOW EARLY WAS TOO EARLY TO CALL on Mrs. Richmond, but he couldn't imagine it mattered. He wouldn't be welcome at any time, so he went straight to the address Angotti had given him when he left Sarah's house. The once-respectable neighborhood was slowly going to seed as immigrants moved whole families into one or two rooms of what had formerly been a single-family home. The address Frank sought was a large house badly in need of paint. A sign in the front window said ROOMS TO RENT. Mrs. Richmond had fallen on hard times if she had to take in boarders.

A harried woman of middle years answered his knock—the bell no longer worked. Although she wore an apron, she was clearly the lady of the house and not a maid. She looked him up and down. "I only rent to ladies."

"Mrs. Richmond?" he asked.

She planted her fists on her ample hips. "No, I'm not Mrs. Richmond, and what would you be wanting with her?"

Frank decided not to embarrass Mrs. Richmond if he didn't have to, so he didn't mention he was with the police. "I have a business matter to discuss with her. Is she at home?"

"Where else do you think she would be?"

"Would you tell her she has a visitor?"

"What do I look like, her social secretary? I don't allow any men in the house except in the front parlor. I run a respectable place, so no funny business." Before Frank could manage a reply, she started walking away, muttering under her breath. She walked like someone whose feet hurt. When she was halfway down the hall, she called back over her shoulder, "Well, come on in and close the door. You're letting in the cold."

Frank did as instructed, closing the door carefully. The hallway was indeed just as cold as outside. Faded wallpaper curled at the edges, and the floor could have used a good scrubbing. Frank had misjudged. Mrs. Richmond wasn't taking in boarders. She *was* a boarder. Many respectable women who had fallen on hard times lived in places like this, along with shopgirls and teachers and others whose wages didn't allow them the luxury of having their own place. He was glad he hadn't brought Mrs. Decker along.

He found what must be the front parlor, a shabby room

full of worn-out furniture. He didn't want to risk any of it, so
he was still standing with his coat on when he heard footsteps
in the hall. This room was cold, too. There was no fire in the
grate.

"I don't know who he is," the woman who had answered
the door said, making no effort to keep her voice down. "He
ain't that Italian, if that's what you're wondering. This one's
Irish and a copper if I don't miss my guess. I run a respectable
place here, Mrs. Richmond, and I told you when you come
here that I don't allow male visitors, especially Italians and
coppers."

Another voice replied but too softly for Frank to make out
the words. Then a woman appeared in the parlor doorway. She
was probably in her forties and had been a beauty in her youth.
Her dress was far from new but of good quality, and she had
wrapped a cashmere shawl tightly around her shoulders, probably to protect against the chill. He noticed a small hole in
the wool near her shoulder. Still, he could tell instantly who
and what she was, or rather what she had once been. She held
herself erect and met his gaze squarely, the way rich people
did when they wanted to put you in your place.

"Who are you?" Her well-modulated voice held the ring of
authority.

"Detective Sergeant Frank Malloy of the New York City
Police."

Her eyes widened but she did a good job of pretending she
wasn't afraid. "What do you want?"

"Are you Mrs. Richmond?"

"Terry Richmond, yes."

"I need to ask you some questions about Chilton Devries."

Color flooded her face, but more from anger than fear, Frank
judged. "Did he send you here to harass me?"

Good. She didn't know he was dead. "No, he didn't. Salvatore Angotti told me where to find you."

Her composure cracked just a bit. "I don't understand."

"Maybe we could sit down and talk for a few minutes. This won't take long."

She didn't look like she believed him, but she said, "Yes, of course. Please excuse me. I've forgotten my manners."

He waited until she'd chosen a chair—the one farthest from the still-open parlor door, Frank noticed. They would have to keep the door open for propriety, and the landlady might well be lurking. Frank knew the type. She'd feel it was her duty to know what went on in her house. He snagged a wooden chair from the corner and set it close to Mrs. Richmond's so they could keep their voices low. She raised her eyebrows at this but didn't protest. She probably didn't want the landlady eavesdropping either.

"How long have you lived here?" he asked.

"A few weeks." He noticed she sat on the edge of the seat, her back straight and not touching the chair, the way Mrs. Decker sat.

"I'm guessing you never had to live in a boardinghouse before."

Her expression hardened. "I thought you wanted to ask me about Mr. Devries."

"We'll get to him. Angotti told me he came to see you. He told me Devries wanted him to kill you."

She trembled, or maybe she shivered, but she didn't speak.

"Why did Devries want you dead?"

"Why don't you ask him that?"

"I'm asking you."

"Why do you care?"

"Mrs. Richmond, I'm trying to be nice here, but I can just

as easily send for a Black Maria and have you taken down to Police Headquarters and locked up instead."

"You can't lock me up! I haven't done anything wrong."

"I can do anything I want because I'm with the police. Now are you going to answer my questions or not?"

The look she gave him could've drawn blood, but she said, "What do you want to know?"

"Why did Devries want you dead?"

"I don't know. That's the truth, Mr. Malloy," she added when he frowned. "I had no idea he was interested in me at all until Mr. Angotti called on me last week."

"What did Angotti tell you?"

"I . . . He's such a strange man. He's so polite and so well dressed, but he's terrifying."

"I guess he was if he told you he was supposed to murder you."

"He didn't tell me that, not at first. At first he just said Mr. Devries had sent him."

"How do you know Devries?"

"I . . . My husband knew him."

"How?"

"They were business associates."

"But not anymore?"

"My husband is dead."

Frank glanced meaningfully around the boardinghouse parlor. "He didn't leave you very well off."

"My husband was a fool."

So much for the grieving widow. "I guess he didn't manage his money very well."

"Devries cheated him."

"How did he do that?"

"I don't understand business, Mr. Malloy, and my husband

wasn't eager to explain to me exactly how he'd been tricked into giving Devries all of our money, but it had something to do with a new railroad. My husband was quite flattered when Devries suggested he invest in the project. That's what he called it, a *project*. We would make millions, Keith told me. I didn't want him to do it, but he said there was nothing to worry about because rich men were investing, and they must know it was safe."

"But the railroad didn't succeed?"

"I don't know what happened. Something to do with stock and prices dropping. It was very confusing, and I don't think Keith really understood either. All I know is that we lost everything."

"What about your husband's own business? I'm guessing he earned his living somehow before this happened."

"He lost that, too. He'd borrowed against it, I think. He didn't even have the courage to tell me any of this himself. I had to find out after he . . . died."

"How did he die?"

"He killed himself."

Frank winced inwardly. "And then you found out you'd lost everything."

"I didn't lose it. Keith did." He could see her anger had burned itself down to a white-hot core of resentment.

"But you're the one who had to suffer. Did you ask Devries for help?"

"Not at first. I didn't understand how bad it was at first. Then I started getting letters from creditors, and I soon realized. I sold our house and everything in it. I even sold my jewelry and some of my clothes. Mr. Devries was very helpful. He found buyers for me, although I'm sure he managed to cheat me somehow on that, too."

Frank suspected she was right. "And you ended up here?"

"No, I left New York and went home, to my parents' house. My father is dead, and my mother was glad to have me with her."

"What brought you back here?"

"My daughter needed me."

"Your daughter?"

Frank remembered how Mrs. Decker's face lit up whenever she talked about Sarah, but Mrs. Richmond's face did not light up. Her eyes were bleak and her voice flat when she said, "Yes. You see, Mr. Devries had told me he was able to salvage some monies from my husband's investments, and he arranged for me to have a small annuity. Without it I would have had nothing. You understand what that would have meant?"

He did. Women in that situation were fished out of the East River or found starved to death in their rented rooms. A young woman might survive by selling herself, but not a woman of Mrs. Richmond's age. "That was generous of Mr. Devries. Sounds like he was trying to make it up to you for cheating your husband."

"You must not know Mr. Devries very well. He never does anything out of the goodness of his heart, and he certainly never lets feelings of guilt influence him. This was a business transaction, pure and simple. He wanted something of mine and was willing to pay for it."

"What did he want?"

"My daughter."

Suddenly, everything fell into place. Norah English, the innocent young girl with the phony name. Frank nodded. "I've met her."

"She was willing," Mrs. Richmond told him, her composure slipping at last. "You must believe that. I didn't force her. I would never have forced her to do anything against her will. I couldn't take care of her myself anymore, and no one else would marry her, not with no dowry and a father who'd killed himself. Keith had ruined my life and her prospects completely. She would never have gotten a better offer, and she knew that as well as I."

Frank had heard stories like this before. "So you turned her over to Devries and left town."

"She begged me to go, and I really had no choice. This is how I have to live here in the city, and she couldn't bear the thought of it, or so she said. But she also . . ." Mrs. Richmond pulled a handkerchief out of her pocket and pressed it to her lips.

"She what?" he asked.

"I think she also didn't want me to see how miserable she really was."

That made sense. What girl would? "What brought you back?"

"Her letters. She didn't tell me, not outright, but I knew something was wrong. I came for a visit, and when I found out . . ." She pressed the handkerchief to her lips again.

"What did Norah tell you?" he asked as gently as he could.

She looked up in surprise. "Who?"

"Norah, your daughter."

"My daughter's name is Garnet."

8

Frank needed a few seconds to recover. *"Garnet?"*

"Who is this Norah?" she asked, as confused as Frank.

"Uh, nobody. I . . . Your daughter is married to Paul Devries?"

"Yes. You said you'd met her."

"I have. Do you know why your daughter was unhappy?"

"I can't imagine that's any of your business, Mr. Malloy."

Frank sighed. She kept forgetting she didn't have money anymore, and he really hated having to remind her. "If it had something to do with why Devries wanted you killed, then it's my business."

"I already told you, I have no idea why."

"Then let's figure it out."

"What good would that do?"

Frank studied her for a long moment and realized that she really wasn't as unmoved as she was trying to convince him she was. He could see it now in the tightness of her jaw and the way she clutched the handkerchief in her lap. Underneath her manners and her hauteur, she was afraid. He could deal with that.

"Mrs. Richmond," he said softly, "a strange man came to see you the other day and told you that your son-in-law's father had hired him to murder you. I don't think for one minute that you don't know why or at least suspect," he added when she would have protested. "We can also guess that it has something to do with your daughter, and if you're in danger, she probably is, too."

The blood drained from her face. "No, I don't believe it!"

"That doesn't mean it isn't true. Even if you don't care about yourself, you should care about your daughter."

Frank could see that a lifetime of training in how a lady should conduct herself was the only thing preventing her from collapsing into hysteria. Tears flooded her eyes, and she dashed them angrily away. "He wouldn't hurt Garnet, would he?"

"Why would he hurt you?"

"I told you—"

"And *I* told *you*, let's figure it out. When did you first start thinking something was wrong with your daughter?"

She drew a deep breath. "I don't . . . I can't remember exactly, but maybe four months ago. Her letters . . . She'd never seemed particularly happy in her marriage, but suddenly, she wrote asking if she could come to live with me at her grandmother's house. I thought she meant a visit, and I told her she would always be welcome, but she asked if her grandmother would welcome her if she wanted to stay."

"What did you tell her?"

"I didn't know what to tell her. I couldn't ask my mother a question like that, could I? She'd want to know what was wrong with Garnet and . . . Well, I must confess, I don't think my mother would approve of a woman leaving her husband like that. It just isn't done."

"So what did you tell her?"

"I asked her what was wrong, and I told her I would be glad to give her the benefit of my wisdom to help her solve whatever problem she might be having with her husband."

"But she didn't tell you what was wrong."

"She only said that nothing I could say would help."

Frank sat back in his chair. "That sounds like a serious problem."

"I was frightened, Mr. Malloy. My daughter was talking about leaving her husband, and I could tell from the tone of her letters that she was in despair. I couldn't invite her to come to me, so I came to her."

"And what did she tell you when you got here?"

"Not much more than I've already told you. I've only seen her three times since I've been here. I couldn't invite myself to stay at the Devrieses' house, so I stayed in a hotel at first. I called on Garnet, but Mrs. Devries was very cold. She made it clear I was not welcome. I couldn't believe it, but I suppose she was only expressing her husband's wishes. Mr. Devries had no desire to be reminded of how badly he had treated my husband, I'm sure."

Frank wasn't so sure. He didn't think Devries had much of a conscience, so why would seeing Mrs. Richmond bother him? "Paul Devries said he and his father argued because Devries was being cruel to Garnet. Maybe she wanted to get away from *him*, not Paul."

"I know Garnet despised him, but that started long before she married Paul. She blamed him for her father's death."

"Did Garnet say anything to you about Devries? Give you

any idea what he might have done recently that was especially cruel?"

"No, she . . . In fact, at first I thought she might want to escape from *Mrs.* Devries. The woman is intolerable, and she dotes on Paul. No woman would ever be good enough for him, especially not Garnet."

Frank had no trouble at all believing that. "Lots of women hate their mothers-in-law. That doesn't make them want a divorce. Didn't Garnet tell you anything at all about why she wanted to leave Paul?"

Mrs. Richmond hesitated, then shook her head. "No, she didn't tell me anything."

But Frank had seen the hesitation. "You have an idea, though, don't you? Is it something about Paul?"

"No, I don't . . . I told you, she never told me."

"But she hinted. She said something that made you suspect." Frank took a chance. "Something about why they don't have any children."

She sprang to her feet, her face flaming. "How dare you?" she cried. "Get out of here! Get out of here right now before I call . . ."

"Who?" Frank taunted. "The police?"

"Mrs. Higgins."

"The landlady?" he scoffed. "She's more likely to put *you* out. You're trouble, Mrs. Richmond. First an Italian thug calls on you, and then a police detective. She runs a respectable house. She doesn't need you spoiling her good reputation."

Mrs. Richmond glared at him as if she'd like to scratch his eyes out, trembling with fury and frustration. He felt sorry for her, but he couldn't let that stop him from finding out the truth. "I'm not going anywhere until you tell me what I need to know, so why don't you sit down, Mrs. Richmond?"

He could see the effort it cost to pull herself together, and he admired her strength. She sat down as reluctantly as if the seat were covered with broken glass. At least the fear had vanished from her eyes. All he saw there now was anger.

He knew she wasn't going to answer any more questions, so he decided to tell her what he'd guessed so far and let her respond. "You don't think Paul was much of a husband to Garnet. Maybe she told you he spent all his time with his good friend Zeller and ignored her."

Mrs. Richmond's eyes widened, telling him he was at least close to the truth.

"You tried to get Garnet to tell you why she wanted to leave Paul, but she wouldn't. You said you'd seen her three times since you've been in town. Did she visit you here?"

He had to wait a full minute before she finally said, "Yes."

"She came here to see you, but she wouldn't tell you what was wrong. Did she want you to go home or did she want you to stay?"

"Go home," she said through gritted teeth.

"Did you ask her to go with you?"

No answer.

"Did you talk about it, at least?"

Her cheeks flamed again. "I have no home of my own to offer her." The pain behind the words tore at him, but he couldn't stop now.

"And what did you think when she told you about the baby?"

She jerked as if he'd slapped her. "What baby?"

"The baby she's going to have."

She uttered a strangled cry and fainted dead away.

Frank swore as he jumped to catch her before she hit the floor. He lowered her as gently as he could to the worn carpet and hollered for the landlady. The woman came stomping into the room, probably intending to give Frank a piece of her mind, but she stopped short when she saw Mrs. Richmond.

"Good heavens, what've you done to her?"

"She fainted."

"How do I know that? Maybe you did something to her!"

"You can ask her when she wakes up."

She sighed with long-suffering. "I'll get my salts."

Frank tried to remember what you were supposed to do when someone fainted. All he could think of was loosening their clothes and chaffing their wrists. He decided just to wait for the smelling salts. Mrs. Higgins returned with a vial. She pulled the cork and waved it under Mrs. Richmond's nose.

Soon Mrs. Richmond was conscious and back sitting in her chair, but she was still furious at Frank, and now Mrs. Higgins was, too.

"I don't know who you think you are, but you got no right coming in here and upsetting people like this," the landlady said.

Frank figured Mrs. Richmond wasn't going to tell him anything else, at least not today, but first he had to find out if she could have killed Devries. "You said an Italian visited Mrs. Richmond," he said to Mrs. Higgins. "Did she have any other visitors? Any other men, I mean."

"What business is it of yours?"

"It's police business, and if you'd like to avoid spending a night locked up in a cell, you'll answer me."

"It's all right," Mrs. Richmond said wearily. "Who do you think visited me?"

"Did Devries himself call on you?"

Her eyes widened. "No!"

He looked at the landlady for confirmation. "It would've been last Tuesday."

"Tuesday? No, and not any other day, either. The only one I know who called before you was the Italian."

At least he wouldn't have to ask Mrs. Richmond if Devries had undressed in her presence. He'd probably need more than smelling salts to revive her after that. "Devries is dead."

Mrs. Richmond blinked. "What?"

"Devries?" Mrs. Higgins said. "That's your daughter's name, ain't it? You mean her daughter's husband is dead?"

"No, his father."

Mrs. Richmond couldn't seem to comprehend. "Dead? But how . . . ?"

"Somebody stabbed him."

All the blood drained from her face, and he was very much afraid she was going to faint again. "I . . . I need to go to my daughter."

"Of course you do," Mrs. Higgins said and turned to Frank. "You've done enough damage here. You'd better go."

He couldn't argue with that.

FRANK DIDN'T KNOW WHAT WAS WRONG WITH HIM. HE didn't usually jump to conclusions, but after hearing Mrs. Richmond's story about how Devries had cheated her husband, he'd assumed Devries had taken her daughter as his mistress. Maybe because he'd recently heard a story just like that. But Devries hadn't taken her for himself. Instead, he'd married her off to his son. He really wanted to talk to Sarah about this, but he couldn't possibly wake her up to talk about this now. He'd have to wait until this evening.

Meanwhile, he needed to see Miss Norah English.

Lizzie the maid opened the door. "You're like a bad penny, ain't you?"

"I'm glad to see you're still here." Frank didn't wait for an invitation to come in, and Lizzie's frantic attempt to shut the door in his face failed.

Sputtering indignantly, she slammed the door behind him, surrendering to the inevitable. "What do you want?"

"I want to see Miss English, if she's still here."

"Where else would she be?"

"I was afraid somebody would've sent her packing by now."

"Why would you be afraid of that?"

"Because then I would've had to waste a lot of time hunting her down."

"Lizzie? Who's there?" Miss English called from upstairs.

"It's that copper what was here the other day. Don't you worry none. I'll just—"

"Miss English, I need to speak with you again," Frank called, silencing Lizzie with the glare that usually put a stop to interference.

"Don't you go scaring her," Lizzie whispered, not nearly as frightened as she should have been. "She never hurt nobody in this world, and you got no right to upset her."

Frank would have told her he had every right, but Miss English appeared on the landing above them. Today she seemed even more innocent than she had two days ago. Her brown eyes wide and frightened, she stared down at him, her fingers fiddling nervously with the ruffles on her dress.

Frank tried a reassuring smile. At least he hoped it was reassuring. "I just have a few more questions for you, Miss English."

She wrung her plump hands. "What should I do, Lizzie?"

Lizzie gave him a murderous look, but she said, "I guess you better talk to him. I doubt he'll leave until you do."

Miss English descended the stairs, still watching him warily, as if afraid he might do something terrible to her. He found himself feeling sorry for her, too, and instantly caught himself. He'd never felt sympathy for murder suspects before. What was wrong with him?

"You can go in the parlor," Lizzie said when Miss English glanced around uncertainly.

"It's cold in there," Miss English said.

"He won't be long," Lizzie said, giving Frank a meaningful glance that he ignored.

He followed Miss English into the parlor and found the room was indeed cold. "Maybe you should get Miss English a shawl," he said to the maid.

Lizzie stationed herself in the open doorway and crossed her arms. "She'll be fine."

Frank sighed. "Has anybody been to see you, Miss English?"

"You said Mr. Devries is dead," she said.

"He means anybody else," Lizzie said.

"But he's the only one who ever came. He never let me see anybody else except Lizzie."

"Maybe we could sit down," Frank said, glancing at Lizzie in case she wanted to protest, but she nodded.

Miss English sat down on the threadbare sofa, and Frank took the nearest chair.

"I want to ask you about the morning that Mr. Devries died. The last time you saw him."

She waited, still staring at him with her innocent brown eyes.

"Did he sleep with you that night?" Lizzie made an outraged noise, so he quickly added, "I mean, did he sleep in the same bed?"

"Yes. We only have the one bed. Well, and Lizzie's bed, of course."

"What did Mr. Devries wear to bed?"

"What in God's name does that matter?" Lizzie asked.

Frank sighed again. "It matters. Now if you'd rather I took Miss English down to Police Headquarters to answer these questions, I'd be happy to do that."

"I don't want to go to Police Headquarters," Miss English said.

Lizzie frowned ferociously, but she said, "He ain't taking you anywhere. Just tell him what he wants to know."

Miss English looked back at Frank. "What did you ask me?"

"What did Mr. Devries wear to bed?"

"A nightshirt."

"I'll need to see it. In fact, I'll need for you to pack up all of his clothes. I'll take them back to his house."

"How do I know you won't just keep them for yourself?" Lizzie asked.

"You don't, but I need to look at his clothes, and if you won't pack them up for me, I'll ask somebody from Mr. Devries office to come here and do it, and when they realize you're living here for free, they'll probably throw you both out into the street."

"I knew that's what would happen," Miss English said. "I told you, Lizzie."

"I'll give him the clothes. Nobody's going to throw us out, not yet anyways."

Frank didn't acknowledge her surrender. He kept his gaze on Miss English. "Did you get up at the same time as Mr. Devries that last morning he was here?"

"No, not that morning. I usually do because he always wants to—" Her eyes widened as she realized what she'd almost confessed. Her smooth, round cheeks flushed becomingly, and she glanced at Lizzie in dismay.

"But he didn't want you that morning?" Frank asked.

"Don't you have no manners at all?" Lizzie asked.

"Not when I'm investigating a murder. So he usually wanted you in the mornings, but not that day. Is that why you argued?"

"Why would they argue about that?" Lizzie asked.

"I'm asking *her*."

Miss English blinked her big, brown eyes. "I didn't argue with him, not ever."

"How could she?" Lizzie said. "If he got mad at her, he could put her out."

"But you did complain about not being able to go out, didn't you?"

"I asked him if I could go to a play or something, and he got mad. He said I shouldn't cause him any bother. He said . . ." Her voice broke and she looked down to where her hands were twisting in her lap.

"What did he say?" Frank asked as gently as he could.

She drew an uneven breath. "He said there were lots of girls who would take my place in a minute."

"Did that make you angry?"

She looked up in surprise. "Oh, no, not angry. It just made me scared. He's right, you know. There *are* lots of girls who would take my place."

"But that was a mean thing to say. Didn't it make you mad, too?"

"It made *me* mad, I can tell you," Lizzie said. "Old goat."

"Did *you* have an argument with Devries?" he asked her.

"Me? I'm not likely to argue with the likes of him, am I? If there's lots of girls to take her place, there's thousands to take mine."

Frank turned back to Miss English. "You said he didn't want you that morning. Was that something new?"

Lizzie muttered her disapproval, and Miss English turned red again. "I . . . Not . . . Sometimes . . ."

"Did he seem to be losing interest in you?" he tried somewhat desperately.

"Yes." She sighed, relieved he had finally asked a question she could decently answer.

"How long since you first noticed he wasn't as . . . attentive?"

"A few months, I think."

"He still came here regular," Lizzie said. "I think he just liked being away from his wife, if you want the truth."

"But he wasn't as interested in Miss English as before."

"He said I was boring."

"Boring," Lizzie sniffed. "Can you imagine?"

Actually, he could. "Do you think he had another mistress?"

The women exchanged a puzzled glance. Lizzie said, "Why would he keep two women? If he was tired of Miss English, why not just put her out and put the one he liked better in here?"

A good question, Frank thought. Devries wasn't known for his kindness, so that couldn't be the reason. Maybe he just hadn't gotten the new woman to agree yet, if there even was a new woman. And if there was, how would he find out? At least Devries hadn't had time to visit her the day he died. Or had he?

Frank felt a headache coming on. He stood. "Thank you for answering my questions, Miss English."

"What's going to happen to us now?" she asked.

"I don't know."

"Are you going to tell them about us?" Lizzie asked. "The people at Devries's office, I mean?"

"No, that's none of my business. You can stay here forever as far as I'm concerned."

"But we don't have any money," Miss English protested.

Frank couldn't help her there. "Can you pack up Mr. Devries's clothes for me?" he asked Lizzie.

She grumbled a bit, but she stomped off.

Frank realized this was his chance to question Miss English alone, but he couldn't think of anything of importance that he hadn't already asked her about. "How did you meet Mr. Devries?"

"My uncle."

"Your *uncle* introduced you?"

She shrugged. "He was my guardian after my father died. He had to support us, and he didn't like it. He said we cost too much money. One day he told me he'd found somebody who would take me off his hands. I thought I was going to get married." She gave him a sad little smile.

"Who is *us*?"

"Me and Lizzie."

"Has she always worked for you?"

"Oh, no, she's . . ." She quickly covered her mouth.

"She's what? Not your maid, I guess. Don't worry, I won't tell anybody."

"My stepmother. My father married her after my mother died, so he'd have somebody to take care of me, but then he died, too."

Although he'd never given it much thought before, Frank realized he hated the fact that women like Mrs. Richmond and Garnet and Norah English were at the mercy of men like Chilton Devries. A decent woman left penniless and alone had few options in life, and those that didn't require the kindness of some man were immoral or illegal. He'd once looked down on women who worked for their living, like Sarah Brandt, but now he understood how difficult and amazing it was for a woman to make her own way in the world. No wonder Garnet Devries had been interested in how Sarah had accomplished it.

"Do you think your uncle would take you back?"

"Not now. I'm a fallen woman."

Frank doubted the uncle would see that as hypocritical. "I'll bet if you write him a letter telling him Devries is dead and he's got to take you in again, he'll find you another protector, at least."

"Oh, my, I never thought of that! You're very clever."

Frank didn't feel clever. He felt ashamed of all the men who had abused this poor girl and who would continue to. She'd said they didn't have any money, and she would need some to tide her over. He glanced around, trying to spot anything of value that she could sell, and something shiny on one of the tables caught his eye. A fancy silver bowl with a handle, half full of walnuts. The nutcracker and other implements lay nestled in the nuts. Chilton Devries had been fond of walnuts, he remembered.

"If that's real silver, you could pawn it."

Miss English stared at him in shock. "I couldn't do that! Mr. Devries would never . . . Oh!"

"Right. He won't know. And nobody else will know what was here, either. You should probably gather up everything you could pawn and sell it right away. You don't know how much longer you'll be here, and if somebody evicts you, it'll be too late."

"What're you telling the girl?" Lizzie asked from the doorway.

"He said we should sell the nut bowl, and there's another one upstairs. He said we should do it right away, before they put us out. Oh, and Mr. Devries's shaving set. That's silver, too."

"Hush," Lizzie said, frowning at Frank.

"Don't worry, I don't care what you do."

"Here," she said, thrusting a bulging pillowcase at him. "That's all his clothes. You can be on your way now."

Frank wanted to look through the clothes, but he could wait. He took his leave, and as Lizzie was closing the door behind him, he heard Miss English say, "He said we should ask Uncle Ned to find me another protector."

Frank shook his head.

FRANK STOPPED OFF AT POLICE HEADQUARTERS AND WENT through the bag of clothing. He found the nightshirt and several changes of linen, but nothing had a hole in it. If Norah English had stabbed Devries, she'd done it while he was naked. The trouble was, he didn't think she had. She was just too simple to lie well, and a girl too honest to hock someone else's silver would never be able to hide a murder.

He'd put it off as long as he could. He needed to report what he'd learned to Felix Decker. As much as he would have enjoyed chatting with Mrs. Decker, he figured he shouldn't risk the old man's wrath by going to his house again.

He reached the office by midafternoon, half frozen and cursing the wintry wind that whipped mercilessly down the city's streets. Decker's secretary—an old-fashioned, middle-aged gentleman; no girl secretaries for Felix Decker—recognized him and only kept him waiting a few minutes before ushering him into the inner office.

Decker didn't rise, but Frank noticed he'd put aside the papers he'd been working on to give Frank his full attention.

"Mr. Malloy, I'd given you up."

"I had to go see Miss English, too."

"The mistress? Was that Italian supposed to kill her, too?"

"Not that I know of, but I figured if I found a nightshirt with a bloody hole in it at her house, we could all rest a little easier."

"But you didn't."

"No, I didn't."

"And what about this Mrs. Richmond? Is she still alive?"

"Oh, yes. She's also Garnet Devries's mother."

"Good God!"

"I thought you must know that."

"No, not . . ." Decker shifted uneasily.

"But you knew the name Richmond when I said it yesterday."

Frank watched Decker's inner struggle. Normally, Decker probably wouldn't share much information with anyone, not even his closest friends. An intensely private man, he had also assigned Frank a difficult task, and withholding information would only hinder him in accomplishing that task. "I knew a man named Richmond."

"Devries cheated him in a business deal."

"No, he didn't. At least he didn't actually cheat him. He merely offered him the opportunity to invest. He gave me the same opportunity."

"And did you take it?"

"Yes, but I wasn't impressed with the possibilities, so I only put in fifty thousand."

Frank didn't think he'd ever heard the word *only* used in conjunction with fifty thousand dollars. "And you lost your money?"

"Along with everyone else who invested. The difference was that I could afford to lose. Richmond couldn't."

"Then why did he do it?"

"Why does anyone do something stupid? He wanted to make money, I suppose, but more likely, he wanted to be seen as an equal to men like Devries."

"And you."

Decker shrugged. "Richmond came to the club when he heard the deal had gone sour. He made an ugly scene and had to be escorted out. I saw his obituary two days later."

"He killed himself, leaving his wife and daughter with nothing."

Decker considered this information. "What does this have to do with Chilton's death?"

"I don't know yet. I'm still trying to figure out why he wanted Mrs. Richmond dead."

"Then you think the Italian was telling the truth?"

"Mrs. Richmond said he came to see her. He told her Devries had hired him to have her killed."

"He must be a charming man."

"She was pretty scared, but Angotti just wanted to know *why* Devries wanted her dead. I got the feeling from Angotti that he wasn't above having one of his men kill a woman if she deserved it, but he wanted to be sure, so he asked her. She didn't know why Devries wanted her dead, but she told him her story, and Angotti decided not to kill her."

"A compassionate gangster."

"Thank God for that. The important thing is why did Devries want her dead in the first place? I think it has something to do with her daughter."

"Garnet? What makes you think that?"

"Because that was her only connection to Devries. And the

more I think about it, the more I think Devries ruined Richmond on purpose."

"That's ridiculous! Do you think he talked his friends into investing in a scheme he knew would fail?"

"Why not? You said yourself you didn't have much confidence in the scheme. And none of his other friends got ruined. They're like you. They can afford to take a risk and lose now and then, but not Richmond. And why go to Richmond in the first place? The man wasn't rich. He couldn't even get into your club."

Decker tapped a finger on his desk for several moments. "I did wonder about that afterwards, but perhaps Chilton didn't know his true situation. Remember they met when Richmond applied to join the Knickerbocker. One would assume he had the means for such a venture, even if he didn't have any social standing in the city yet. And don't forget, Chilton seemed very confident. He managed to convince several of us to take a chance. Maybe he thought he'd do Richmond a good turn by letting him in."

"Have you ever known Devries to do somebody a good turn for no reason?"

Decker had no answer.

"I'll tell you what I think. I think he ruined Richmond on purpose so he could get Garnet."

"What do you mean?"

"I mean he wanted a wife for his son."

"Chilton didn't have to scheme to bring that about. Paul Devries could marry anyone he wanted."

"Could he?"

"What do you mean?"

"Have you met Paul's friend, Hugh Zeller?"

"What are you talking about?"

"You know what I'm talking about. Paul and Hugh Zeller

are very close friends. They're such close friends that Paul would probably not be interested in women."

Decker simply stared back at Frank across his desk, his expression stony.

"I think Devries wanted his son comfortably and safely married, but he couldn't take the chance of marrying him off to a girl who might be disappointed in Paul and reveal his secret."

"A girl whose family would be outraged," Decker said. "A family with power and influence who would make sure Devries and his family were socially ostracized for tricking a young woman like that."

"Then he met Garnet Richmond, and he decided she would be the perfect wife for Paul, if he could make her desperate enough that she would take him and stay with him under any circumstances."

"Good God," Decker said, this time in a horrified whisper. "But he'd already gotten what he wanted. Why did he want to kill Mrs. Richmond?"

"I'm not sure yet, but Paul told me Garnet wanted a divorce. Mrs. Richmond came to New York to see her daughter, and maybe Devries thought she would help Garnet leave."

Decker shook his head as if trying to clear it. "But does this have anything at all to do with why somebody stabbed Chilton?"

"I don't know yet. The question is, do you want me to keep on trying to find out?"

9

WHEN SARAH WOKE UP, SHE WAS DELIGHTED TO FIND HER mother had stopped by for a visit. Mrs. Decker had been only too happy to join Catherine and Maeve upstairs for some make-believe involving the dollhouse while she waited for Sarah to finish her nap.

Maeve and Catherine had fixed her a sandwich to tide her over until supper, then the girls went back upstairs so Sarah and her mother could speak privately. They shared the details of their respective visits with Malloy while Sarah ate her sandwich at the kitchen table.

"Do you think Father will allow him to continue the investigation?" Sarah asked.

"I have no idea, although I will certainly encourage him to, if I can. I simply can't get over Garnet being with child, though. Why wouldn't she have told Paul and Lucretia? I gathered that her failure to produce a son to carry on the family name was a major source of Lucretia's disappointment in her."

"Maybe she didn't want to say anything until she was certain. Claiming to be with child when you're not can cause even more resentment."

"Perhaps, but still . . . You said she wasn't happy about the baby."

"No, and that's puzzling. Of course, if she wanted to end her marriage, a child would complicate matters tremendously."

"Yes, it would. Although she would be a fool to divorce Paul; if she wanted her freedom badly enough, she might be willing to tolerate the disgrace and being left with nothing."

Sarah tried to remember anything she might know about a society divorce. Alva and William Vanderbilt, Consuelo's parents, were divorced, but Alva had somehow managed to remarry another millionaire almost immediately, so their situation was hardly comparable to Garnet and Paul Devries. Besides the Vanderbilts, she couldn't think of any other examples. "Garnet could go back to her family, I suppose, if they would take her in, but Mrs. Devries would never allow her to take her child."

"Heavens, no, and the law would support that. Paul would get the child, and Garnet would never see it again. That would explain her unhappiness about the baby, at least."

"The choice between staying in an unhappy marriage or never seeing your child again is awful."

"Women stay in unhappy marriages for far less noble reasons all the time," her mother said. "And how unhappy can she be? Lucretia is a harridan, to be sure, but I can't believe Paul is a problem. Surely, he doesn't beat her or starve her or keep her locked away in the cellar. The worst I can imagine is that he neglects her, and many women would consider that a benefit."

Her mother was right, of course. Chilton and Lucretia Devries apparently had just such an arrangement. She and her mother had reached no conclusions a few minutes later when the doorbell brought Catherine and Maeve clamoring downstairs to greet the visitor.

"Just as I hoped," her mother said when they recognized Frank Malloy's deep voice. "I knew he wouldn't dare come to our house again, but I felt sure he'd be here sooner or later."

Sarah bit back a smile. Her mother was obviously enjoying the novelty of having a murder to investigate. Or perhaps she had simply grown fond of Frank Malloy.

In a few more moments, Malloy appeared in the doorway, carrying a delighted Catherine. Sarah felt her smile growing at the sight. She had grown very fond of Frank Malloy herself.

"Mrs. Decker, I was hoping you'd be here," he said with a grin.

"Great minds think alike, Mr. Malloy," she replied.

"What does that mean?" Catherine asked.

"I'll explain it to you later," Maeve said. "Now tell Mr. Malloy good-bye. The grown-ups need to talk for a while."

"Then can I come back?"

"Of course," Malloy said. "Now give me a kiss before you go."

Catherine giggled and pecked him on the cheek. Children, Sarah reflected, are excellent judges of character.

When the girls were gone, Malloy took a seat at the kitchen table. Without asking, Sarah poured him a cup of coffee.

"Have you been busy today, Mr. Malloy?" her mother asked.

"Yes, I have. I visited Mrs. Richmond and Miss English."

"Miss English is Mr. Devries's mistress, Mother."

"I don't suppose you would need me to see her as well," her mother said. "I've never actually met anyone's mistress before."

"No, I would not," Malloy said quite firmly.

"Pity. Oh, well, at least you can tell us what you've learned from these two ladies. Oh, dear, does one call a mistress a lady? I don't believe this was covered in my deportment classes at Miss Lydia's Finishing School."

"Behave yourself, Mother. Poor Mr. Malloy doesn't know you're teasing him."

"I think he probably does, but I should allow him to tell his story. That *was* covered in deportment classes. One always defers to the gentleman in conversation."

"Which means you have to suffer through a lot of dull conversations, I'd guess," Malloy said.

"But never when I am in your company, Mr. Malloy."

Malloy raised his eyebrows, but he said, "I am happy to report that Mrs. Richmond is alive and well."

"That's good news," Sarah said.

"What is her first name? I keep thinking I must know her."

"Terry, she said."

"What an odd name. I suppose it's short for Theresa or something. It still doesn't ring a bell, although the Richmond part does."

"I don't think you'd know her, except that she's Garnet Devries's mother."

Sarah and her mother gaped at him. "Her *mother*?" Sarah said.

"Yes. Remember when I told you that Angotti went to see her, and when he heard her story, he decided she didn't deserve to be murdered? That's what he told Devries the day he died, at least."

"I can't believe Chilton would want to harm his son's mother-in-law. That doesn't make any sense," her mother said.

"It makes more sense when you find out how Garnet came to marry Paul Devries."

"Was it an arranged marriage as you suspected?"

Sarah looked at her mother in surprise. "Was that how you got on the subject of Consuelo Vanderbilt?"

"Don't interrupt, dear."

Sarah could see that Malloy tried very hard not to smile, but he failed. "It *was* an arranged marriage, but the circumstances were a little different than we thought. It turns out Devries got Garnet's father to invest all his money in a business deal, and he lost everything. Her father killed himself, and left Garnet and her mother penniless."

"We've heard stories like that before," Sarah said.

"This one is a little different, though, because Devries offered Mrs. Richmond a settlement if Garnet would marry Paul."

"How odd," her mother said.

"And not at all how things are done," Sarah said. "If money changes hands, it's usually the other way around. The bride pays a dowry to the groom's family."

"But why would Chilton have to pay someone to marry his son? None of this makes any sense."

Both women looked to Malloy for an explanation, but he just stared back at them, looking extremely uncomfortable. Casting about for a reason for his unease, Sarah said, "Does Paul have some unspeakable disease?"

Malloy studied his coffee cup for a long moment. "Maybe you already know this, but some men prefer the company of other men."

"Of course they do," her mother said. "That's why they have all those clubs where no women are allowed."

But Sarah knew that wasn't what he meant. "Do you mean romantically?"

He continued to study his cup. "That's one way to put it."

"And you think Paul . . . ?"

"He has a friend named Hugh Zeller. Do you know him?"

"I know his family," her mother said, frowning. "What do you mean *romantically*?"

Malloy gave Sarah a desperate look. She rescued him. "Mother, some men are attracted to other men in the same way most men are attracted to women."

"You mean . . . *romantically*?"

Sarah nodded.

"But that's ridiculous! It's . . . It's not even possible!"

Sarah would save explanations for sometime when Malloy wasn't present. "Nevertheless, it's true."

Sarah's mother needed only a few moments to come to terms with such an amazing fact. "So you think Paul is one of these men?"

"I suspect it, yes," Malloy said.

"But if he prefers men, why would he get married at all?"

"To conceal it, Mother. Men like that usually find themselves the subject of ridicule and worse. Paul would probably be ostracized from society if people suspected."

"Oh, my, now that you say it . . . Is that why Harold Lake went off to Europe and never came home?"

"Yes, it is."

"Oh, my. I always wondered, but no one would ever tell me a reason. How awful for him."

"And Paul would suffer, too," Sarah said.

"So it would also explain why Devries chose to marry his son off to a girl whose family had no power or influence," Malloy said.

"And who wouldn't complain or cause a scandal when she found out her groom preferred the best man," Sarah said.

"But Garnet is with child. You told me so yourself," her mother said.

Malloy cleared his throat. "Just because Paul prefers the companionship of men doesn't mean he wouldn't fulfill his marital duties, too. I understand his mother is anxious for a grandson to carry on the family name, so he probably felt a . . . a duty."

"Mother and I have been trying to figure out why Garnet would have wanted a divorce. This would explain it."

"But we still don't know why Chilton wanted to kill Garnet's mother," her mother said.

"I have a theory about that, too," Malloy said.

Sarah and her mother both looked at him expectantly.

"Mrs. Richmond said that Garnet had written to her asking if she could come to live with her. Mrs. Richmond had moved back to Virginia and was staying with her own mother. She said she knew Garnet was unhappy, but she wouldn't tell her why, so Mrs. Richmond came to the city a few weeks ago to find out what was wrong. Garnet still wouldn't tell her, but Devries might've been afraid Mrs. Richmond knew about Paul and would cause trouble and maybe even help Garnet get away."

"That's not much of a reason to murder someone," her mother said.

"There really aren't many *good* reasons to murder someone," Malloy said. "Most times it's some stupid thing nobody else cares about. Protecting his family's good name was probably important to Devries, though, so it might've been enough for him."

"I should like to meet this Italian gentleman who refused

to kill Mrs. Richmond," her mother said. "How interesting that he seems to have more honor than Chilton Devries."

Malloy rolled his eyes, but her mother didn't notice.

"I don't suppose you learned anything useful from Miss English," Sarah said.

"Just that Devries wasn't stabbed through any of the clothing he kept there either."

"But wouldn't a man sometimes be undressed when in the presence of his mistress?" her mother asked. "I mean, that is the nature of their relationship, isn't it?"

Malloy managed to maintain his composure, although his face grew extremely red. "Miss English isn't the sort of girl who could stick a knife into a man."

"Nonsense. Every girl could stick a knife into a man with the right provocation."

"But Miss English also isn't the sort of girl who could lie about it afterwards. I wish I thought she did it, but she's just not that clever."

"What about the maid?" Sarah asked. "You said she might be capable."

"She's not really the maid. She's Miss English's stepmother."

"How interesting," her mother said. "I had no idea that one could bring along family members when one became a man's mistress."

This time Sarah rolled her eyes. "I'm sure there's a lot you don't know about mistresses, Mother."

"Quite the contrary, my dear. Mistresses are often the topic of conversation among my friends. I know a great deal about them, although this Miss English sounds a bit out of the ordinary. Most of them, I'm told, are wicked and scheming women whose primary interest is using their charms to amass jewels and money from rich, besotted men before their beauty begins to fade."

"Maybe Miss English will learn to be wicked and scheming as time goes on, but for now she's just a silly girl whose protector is dead and who doesn't know where her next meal is coming from."

"Good heavens! You make her sound pathetic."

"She is."

"Sarah, isn't there someone who could help her?" her mother asked. "One of those charities you're always getting involved with?"

"She would be welcome at Hope's Daughters, but I can't imagine she'd be willing to go there," Sarah said, naming the mission where she volunteered.

"We could visit her and suggest it," her mother said.

Sarah and Malloy both stared in admiration at the way she had so neatly contrived a way for her to visit the girl. "Mother, Father would murder *me* if I allowed you to call on Chilton Devries's mistress."

"Only if he found out," her mother said slyly.

Malloy cleared his throat again, drawing their attention. "I do have a visit you *can* make. I need for you to call on Mrs. Devries again, Mrs. Decker."

"Whatever for?"

"To distract her, because I really need Sarah to visit Garnet Devries. Mrs. Richmond doesn't know what drove Garnet to consider divorcing Paul, but maybe Sarah can find out now that we've figured out Paul's secret."

"How can I distract her? Lucretia will never allow Sarah to be alone with Garnet."

"She won't know about it. I've been thinking about this,

and I think it will work, but you're the ones who know all the rules about rich women visiting each other, so tell me if you think so, too. Mrs. Decker, you call on Mrs. Devries alone. While the two of you are busy in the parlor, Sarah arrives and asks to see Garnet. I'm going to guess Garnet will be happy for a visitor, and Sarah can insist she doesn't want to bother Mrs. Devries or something. Is that possible?"

Her mother frowned, but Sarah thought of a way she could get in. "What if I was bringing her something?"

"What could you be bringing her?" her mother asked.

"I don't know. It doesn't even have to be anything real. I could carry a basket filled with towels and covered with a napkin. I don't have to say what I've brought her, just that it's important for me to give it to her myself, and the maid won't dare question me."

"Could you ask to see Garnet privately?" Malloy asked.

"Of course I could. I could say it was personal. The only problem would be if Garnet refuses to see me."

"And we won't know that until you try," her mother said. "We need to hurry, too. I saw Chilton's obituary in the newspaper today. The funeral is set for Monday, and I'm sure Lucretia will leave the city immediately afterwards."

"Where will she go?" Malloy asked.

"Probably to Europe. Someplace warm where she doesn't have to observe the strict rules of full mourning the way she would here where people know her. Nothing is duller than New York when you're in mourning."

"Would she take Paul and Garnet with her?"

"I don't know, but I will certainly ask her tomorrow," her mother said with a smile.

"Before we go any further with this plan," Sarah said, "we need to know if you've reported all this to my father."

"Yes, I saw him just before I got here."

"Oh, my," her mother said. "I just remembered that he was going to decide whether you should continue your investigation or not."

"Yes, he was."

"Did you tell him your suspicions about Paul Devries?" Sarah asked.

"Yes."

She winced. Her father detested scandal. She couldn't imagine him allowing such a thing to become public knowledge, and if Malloy continued to investigate, it probably would.

"Mother, I believe we will need to keep our visit to the Devrieses a secret from Father."

"Oh, no," Malloy said in surprise. "The whole thing was his idea."

SARAH SHOULD HAVE BEEN USED TO WAITING. SHE MADE her living waiting for babies to be born, and they were notorious for taking their time about it. Still, the fifteen minutes she and her mother had decided she should wait in her mother's carriage before trying to get in to see Garnet Devries seemed to stretch interminably. They had determined her mother might need a little extra time in case Lucretia Devries kept *her* waiting. Finally, the watch pinned to her bodice showed she could safely begin her attempt to see Garnet.

The maid who answered the door seemed harried and dismayed to find a second visitor on the doorstep in so short a time. "We're in mourning, miss," she said, glancing meaningfully at the enormous black wreath hanging on the door.

"This isn't a social call," Sarah said. "Mrs. Paul Devries called on me at my office the other day, and I promised to bring her a remedy." She nodded at the basked she carried over one arm. "If you would just tell her I'm here."

"A remedy?" Plainly, she wanted to know what it was a remedy for, but her training forbade her from inquiring. "Couldn't you just leave it for her?"

"Oh, no, I must give her instructions, and they are quite detailed. Really, I'm sure she'll be happy to see me. And if not, I'll be on my way." Sarah smiled, trying to look nonthreatening.

The maid didn't smile back. "Please wait here."

Another eternity stretched as Sarah stood in the foyer studying the very ugly wallpaper and hoping no one would alert Mrs. Devries that someone else had arrived. To her relief, the maid seemed much happier when she returned.

"Mrs. Paul Devries will see you. She said you should go to her bedroom."

"That will be fine."

The girl led her up two flights of stairs to the third story of the house. Several doors opened off the hallway. The girl took her to one of them and knocked, then opened it for Sarah.

The room was a surprise. Furnished with intricately carved mahogany furniture, it was decorated in shades of dark red. Burgundy silk covered the walls and hung in heavy folds at the windows. The coverlet on the canopy bed was striped in cream and crimson. Not what Sarah would have considered restful colors, but the décor set off Garnet Devries's dark beauty and complemented her name.

Garnet stood in the middle of the room, her hands clutched anxiously in front of her. "It really is you," she said when the maid was gone.

"Of course. How are you feeling?"

She looked pale and drawn, and she still wore a dressing gown. "The girl said you brought me a remedy." She glanced at the basket.

"I'm afraid that was a lie I used to convince her to let me see you."

Her shoulders sagged with what might have been disappointment, although Sarah couldn't imagine why she'd be disappointed. "Oh. I thought . . . Well, no matter. I'm still pleased to see you, although you didn't have to lie. I would have welcomed a visit from anyone."

"I wanted to talk to you privately, and I thought if I simply called on you, your mother-in-law would insist on intruding."

"I'm sure she would have, but I believe she already has a visitor."

"Yes, my mother."

Garnet blinked and then smiled her appreciation. "How very clever of you, Mrs. Brandt. I find I like you more and more with each meeting. Please, sit down."

Garnet's spacious bedroom had a small sitting area near the fireplace. One overstuffed chair with an ottoman dominated the area, and several slipper chairs stood nearby. A hastily discarded blanket indicated Garnet had been curled up in the chair when Sarah's visit had disturbed her. She took her seat again and propped her feet on the ottoman. Sarah took one of the slipper chairs and set her basket on another.

"What's in there?" Garnet asked, indicating the basket.

"Just a folded towel. How *are* you feeling? You look a bit . . . tired."

"How tactful of you. I look haggard and ill. Mother Devries has told me so more than once."

"But surely she understands that in your condition—"

"She knows nothing about my condition."

Sarah raised her eyebrows with a silent question, but Garnet did not answer it. "You won't be able to hide it forever," Sarah said finally.

"No, I won't."

Sarah had no idea what to say next. She stared at Garnet, trying to read the emotions behind her calm façade, but Garnet had learned to hide them too well. Where should she start? How much should she confess to already knowing about her? What question would Malloy ask to get the conversation started? Something shocking, she was sure. She settled for, "Have you told Paul about the baby?"

She stiffened. "No. He wouldn't have been able to keep it secret from his mother, and I don't want her to know."

"Why not?"

Garnet seemed almost amused by the question. "Really, Mrs. Brandt, I don't think I've ever encountered anyone quite like you."

Sarah winced in dismay. She was making a botch of this. "Oh, dear, I suppose I've forgotten everything my mother ever taught me about good manners, haven't I?"

"I'm not sure if it's good manners or not, but certainly no one in society would have ever asked such an honest question."

"I don't suppose they would, and I shouldn't have either. Your decisions are none of my business."

"But I can't fault you for being curious, I suppose. Most women in my position would be thrilled to find themselves with child, wouldn't they?"

"Most of them, yes, but not if they were so unhappy they were contemplating divorce."

Her eyes widened. "Who told you that?"

"Then it's true?"

"I'm sure every married woman has contemplated divorce at one time or another."

"I doubt many of their husbands are aware of it, though."

"Ah, Paul told you. No, wait, he wouldn't have told *you*. He would have told that policeman your father brought here. Did *he* tell you? Is that how you found out?"

Sarah could also choose not to answer questions. "I also know about Paul."

This time, Sarah saw real emotion flicker across her face. For just an instant, Garnet was afraid, but she hid it quickly. "What do you know about Paul?"

"I know about his friend Mr. Zeller. I know they're more than friends."

The color rose in her face. "I don't know what you're talking about."

"That's the wrong answer, Mrs. Devries. You should have said, *Of course they're more than friends. They've known each other for years. They're more like brothers.* Or something like that, if you want to pretend ignorance."

"I'll try to remember that next time someone pries into my husband's private life."

"I'm sorry. I've angered you."

"I don't think you're sorry at all. I think you intentionally angered me."

"I wasn't sure talking about Paul would make you angry. I had to find out."

"Why?"

"Because I want to find out the truth."

"The truth is that Mr. Devries is dead and no one really cares, so why should you?"

Sarah was starting to wonder herself. "My father cares. He wants to know what happened."

"And what good will that do?"

"You'll have to ask him, I'm afraid. He feels he has a duty to an old friend, I believe."

"Chilton Devries was no one's friend."

"I'm not surprised you think so, after what he did to your father."

This did shock her. "What do you know about my father?"

"I know Mr. Devries convinced him to invest in a business venture that failed."

"I thought you said you were interested in the truth. That isn't the truth."

"What is the truth?"

"He cheated my father and ruined him. He did it on purpose, too."

"What makes you think so?"

"I don't think it; I know it. Oh, he pretended to be sorry when my father killed himself. I don't think he expected that. He just wanted my father to be humbled and compliant so when he suggested I marry Paul, he wouldn't be able to refuse."

"*You* could have refused."

Garnet actually laughed at that, an ugly, bitter sound that held no hint of happiness at all. "Oh, yes, I could have refused, and my mother and I could have moved into a tenement and eked out a living making paper flowers or rolling cigars for sweatshops, the way immigrant women do, until we starved to death."

"Didn't you have anyone you could turn to?"

"My grandmother, but she's what we call *the genteel poor*. She owns a large house and a lot of land, but she can't farm it herself. She rents out the fields to tenant farmers and lives on the pittance they pay her if the crops don't fail. She can hardly keep herself, so no, there's no one. When Devries offered my mother a settlement, we couldn't turn it down."

"That was kind of him."

"So we thought at first, or that maybe he felt guilty, but I didn't know him very well then. He was simply buying Paul a wife, and he got off cheap. When he suggested I marry Paul, I was actually relieved. I liked Paul, you see. He can be charming, and I thought . . . Well, I didn't know anything then. My mother would be taken care of, and I would have a husband and a home. I thought we would both be safe."

The despair in her voice cut Sarah like a knife. "I'm so sorry."

"Are you? Then perhaps you'll really bring me a remedy."

Sarah frowned. "What?"

"A remedy. For this thing." She touched her abdomen. "Don't midwives know secret medicines that can solve a problem like this?"

Sarah shook her head. "I don't . . . I can't help you."

"Can't or won't?"

"Garnet, what you're asking is . . . I know you're angry and upset right now, but this baby is part of you, too. You can learn to love it . . ."

Fury flashed in her eyes. "Love it? How can I love something spawned by a monster?"

Sarah instinctively reached out and touched Garnet's arm. "I know how shocked you must have been when you found out about Paul and his friend, but he's not a monster. If you find it too difficult to live with him, I'm sure he'll provide a house for you someplace else now that his father is dead and he has control of everything. I know several couples who live apart except for certain social engagements where they must be seen together. An arrangement like that could suit you very well. You might even bring your mother to live with you."

"And Paul's mother would want the child," she said, her voice oddly hollow.

"Don't be too hasty. You may want it yourself when you see it."

She smiled then, but it was little more than a grimace. "You are a good person, Mrs. Brandt."

"I don't think I'm particularly good. I'm just trying to be a friend to you."

"Thank you for that. No one has been kind to me in a very long time."

Sarah's heart ached at the pain behind her words. "Did your mother come to see you yesterday?"

"Oh, yes, and now I know how she found out about the child. You told her, didn't you?"

"No, I haven't met your mother. I told Mr. Malloy."

"Ah, and he's also the one who told her Devries was dead, I suppose. She doesn't think I should leave Paul either."

"You should certainly consider it very carefully before making a decision. Has anyone explained to you what will happen if you do leave him?"

"I haven't really inquired. Divorce isn't a subject one raises in casual conversation."

"Then allow me to. If you had come into the marriage with any property or a dowry—"

"Which I did not."

"But if you had, it became your husband's when you married. If you divorce, he would keep it all, every penny. He would be under no obligation to give you anything except the clothes on your back. He could put you out without so much as a change of linen."

"I couldn't even keep my clothes?"

"Not if he didn't allow it. And needless to say, he would no longer support you in any way. And your children are also his property. I know you think you don't want this baby, but you may feel differently when it's real and you can see it. If he chooses, you would never be allowed to see your child again. You're a lovely young woman, and if you had been widowed, you might be able to remarry, but few respectable men would be interested in a divorced woman except as a mistress. You'd also find none of your current friends would receive you any longer."

"You make the tenement life sound almost attractive, Mrs. Brandt."

"The tenement life might still be in your future. You need to know what you'll be facing."

"And yet you've managed without a husband."

"I was fortunate to have a trade. I'd learned to be a midwife before I met my husband."

"And he left you a respectable widow. I don't think Paul will be so obliging."

Sarah couldn't conceal her astonishment.

"Oh, I've shocked you. I'm sorry. I didn't mean it, you know. Poor Paul."

How odd. She sounded almost as if she felt sorry for him, when moments ago she'd called him a monster.

Garnet sat up a little straighter. "Well, in any case, things have changed now that the old man is dead."

"Yes, they have."

"Do you . . . ? Does Mr. Malloy have any idea who . . . how it happened?"

"I'm afraid not. Except we know someone stabbed him, of course."

"Stabbed him with a knife, you mean?"

"They aren't certain what it was."

"I see. What else has Mr. Malloy found out?"

"Oh, yes, he also suspects Mr. Devries was undressed when he was stabbed."

Her eyes widened. "Undressed? How can he possibly know that?"

"Because he hasn't found holes in any of Mr. Devries's clothing."

"Holes?"

"Yes, if someone stabbed him through his clothing, there would be a hole."

"Oh, of course."

Sarah thought Malloy would probably ask her something directly, if he were here. "Do you think . . . ?"

She stiffened slightly. "Do I think what?"

"Do you think Paul could have stabbed his father? I understand his father was undressed when they argued that morning."

She seemed to grow even paler. "I . . . I don't know."

"Or Mrs. Devries? She saw him that morning as well."

Garnet had gone very still. "Anything is possible, I suppose. They certainly hated each other."

"Do you know what Paul and his father argued about that morning?"

Sarah saw the emotion flicker across her face again. Anger. Or something very close to it. But she said, "I have no idea."

Sarah knew they had argued about Garnet, and she could tell Garnet knew it, too. But why would she lie about it? "Paul said his father was being cruel to you."

"I suppose Paul said he was defending me."

"Do you doubt that?"

She shrugged one shoulder. "What does it matter? The old man did what he wanted, and nothing Paul said would change that. Now, Mrs. Brandt, I'm afraid I'm not feeling well. I'm going to have to ask you to leave."

10

SARAH FELT A LITTLE SILLY STEALING DOWN THE STAIRS with her towel-filled basket after Garnet had so unceremoniously sent her packing, but she hadn't wanted to wait for a maid to escort her out. Garnet truly did look unwell, and Sarah didn't have the heart to upset her any more today. She had reached the bottom of the first flight of stairs when a maid emerged from a door that must lead to the servants' stairway and hurried to the parlor.

Sarah froze, hoping to escape notice. The maid didn't even glance in her direction, but her luck didn't hold. When the girl opened the parlor door, her mother and Mrs. Devries were standing just inside, obviously waiting for a servant to show her mother out. Both of the older women saw Sarah at once.

"Mrs. Brandt, whatever are you doing out there all by yourself?" Mrs. Devries asked, her displeasure obvious.

Sarah saw no reason to lie, although she also didn't see any reason to tell the entire truth, either. "Hello, Mrs. Devries, Mother. I stopped by to see Garnet."

"Whatever for?" Mrs. Devries's eyes narrowed as she took in Sarah from head to foot, focusing finally on the basket.

"When I was here before, I got the impression she would welcome some advice."

"What kind of advice could you possibly give her?"

"Do you really need to ask, Lucretia?" her mother said. "You made it very clear how disappointed you are that Paul and Garnet have no children. Sarah is a midwife."

The maid's wide-eyed gaze kept darting back and forth as each woman spoke, and Mrs. Devries finally noticed her rapt attention. "Run along, Mary Catherine. Mrs. Decker isn't leaving just yet. Mrs. Brandt, please, come inside and tell me what advice you've given my daughter-in-law."

Sarah had no intention of doing any such thing, but she accepted Mrs. Devries's invitation and joined the two older women in the parlor. Sarah couldn't help noticing Mrs. Devries wore a new gown of black bombazine with jet buttons. Her dressmaker had done well in providing her with stylish mourning clothes.

When they were seated, Mrs. Devries looked at Sarah expectantly. Sarah returned her stare with what she hoped was a maddeningly blank expression. Apparently, it was.

"Really, Mrs. Brandt, I'm waiting."

Sarah smiled politely. "What exactly are you waiting for?"

"For you to tell me what you and Garnet talked about."

"Oh, my, so many things . . . Let's see, she told me her mother had been to visit her. Her mother lives in Virginia, I believe," she told her own mother.

"Mrs. Brandt, what did you tell Garnet about having a baby?" Mrs. Devries asked.

"Oh, I told her not to give up hope. Sometimes it takes years, but she's still young, so she has plenty of time."

Mrs. Devries frowned, her eyes fairly glittering with rage, but her mother had to cover a smile.

"We also spoke about Mr. Devries's death. She wanted to know if I'd heard anything about the investigation."

"Why would *you* hear anything?" Mrs. Devries asked.

"Because of my father, I suppose. He's the one who asked the police to investigate in the first place."

"A lot of nonsense, if you ask me," Mrs. Devries said. "How can someone die from a pinprick?"

"I gather it was more than a pinprick," her mother said. "Didn't Mr. Malloy say something about an ice pick?"

This time, Sarah had to cover a smile when she saw Mrs. Devries's expression. "How on earth did you hear such a thing, Elizabeth?"

"From Mr. Malloy, of course. Didn't I just say so?"

Sarah noticed Mrs. Devries was turning an unbecoming shade of purple. "From the policeman himself? I can't believe Felix allows you to associate with someone like that!"

"Mr. Malloy is a family friend," her mother said.

"A *policeman* is a family friend?"

Sarah felt the heat rising in her own face at the sting of Mrs. Devries's contempt. How dare she judge Frank Malloy? But, of course, most everyone in the city would judge him exactly the same way. The police were, in many ways, no better than the criminals they chased. How was anyone to know that Frank Malloy was any different from the beat cop who collected protection money from the brothels or the police chief who collected bribes from politicians?

"Mr. Malloy has assisted my father on several important

matters," Sarah said. "Father specifically asked him to find out what happened to your husband."

"And you see how much good it did," Mrs. Devries said. "Five days have gone by, and we don't know any more than we did before."

"We know he was stabbed when he was naked," Sarah said, taking perverse pleasure in Mrs. Devries's shock.

"How can you possibly know that?"

"You'll have to discuss that with Mr. Malloy, I'm sure," her mother hastily replied, giving Sarah an exasperated glance.

"But he must have told you why he thinks so," Mrs. Devries said. "What a horrible thing to say, and if it's true . . ." She looked from Sarah to her mother and back again. "If it's true, then Roderick must have done it."

"Who's Roderick?" her mother asked.

"His valet. That's it. He's the one who dressed Chilly every day. He's the only one who ever saw him *un*dressed." Mrs. Devries sat back in her chair and folded her hands with a satisfied nod.

"Are you quite sure?" Sarah's mother asked with a confused frown that didn't fool Sarah for an instant. "I understand he wasn't yet dressed when he had a rather heated discussion with Paul that morning."

Mrs. Devries started turning purple again. "Who told you such a thing? Your policeman, I suppose."

"Yes, but I don't know who might have told him," Sarah lied. She knew Mrs. Devries had also visited her husband when he was undressed, but she waited to see if the woman would admit it.

"No one would have told him such a thing!" she said instead.

"I'm sure he wouldn't have made it up," Sarah said.

"Paul himself probably told him," Sarah's mother said, apparently trying to be helpful.

Mrs. Devries glared at her. "Nonsense! It was Roderick! He's always been a sly one. I've never trusted him myself, and now look, he's spreading all kinds of lies about our family."

"Why would he do that?" her mother asked.

"Why do people like him do anything? They hate us, that's why. They're jealous of anyone who's better than they are."

Sarah doubted the Devries family was truly better than their servants in any way, but she didn't think Mrs. Devries would appreciate hearing her explain why she thought so.

Sarah's mother was shaking her head. "I would sleep with one eye open if I thought my servants hated me."

"Oh, Elizabeth, you know I'm right. I told you, I think Roderick is the one who stabbed Chilly, and the more I think about it, the more convinced I am. And here I've kept him on even though he no longer has a thing to do with Chilly gone. I should have turned him out the instant I heard Chilly was dead. That's what I get for being so softhearted."

Sarah was sure no one had ever accused Mrs. Devries of being softhearted, and she certainly had no reason to accuse the poor valet of murdering her husband. "I can't imagine Mr. Devries would have allowed his valet to stab him and not have raised an alarm."

"Sarah's right," her mother said. "That makes no sense."

"It makes perfect sense to me," Mrs. Devries said. "That was Chilly. He allowed the servants too much freedom. He left it to me to enforce whatever trace of discipline we managed to maintain here. I doubt he would have raised an alarm if one of the servants tried to cut his throat!"

Sarah and her mother exchanged a horrified glance, but Mrs. Devries didn't appear to notice. She *had* noticed Sarah's basket again. Sarah had set it on the floor at her feet, hoping it wouldn't attract attention, but Mrs. Devries frowned at it.

"What on earth do you have in that basket?"

"Nothing." Before Mrs. Devries could pursue the matter, Sarah rose and snatched up the basket in question. "I'm afraid I must be going, Mrs. Devries. I have another appointment. Mother, I don't suppose you could give me a lift?"

Sarah's mother rose as well. "I'd be delighted, my dear. I was just leaving myself when we saw you on the stairs. Lucretia, thank you again for your hospitality."

Left with no choice, Mrs. Devries got up and rang for the maid again. "I suppose I'll see you at the funeral, Elizabeth."

"Of course."

"I'm dreading it so. I only hope I can hold up. I'm nearly prostrate with grief, you know. You can't imagine how shocking it was, losing Chilly in such a way."

"I'm sure it was difficult for Paul, too," her mother said, reminding Sarah what Malloy had told them about the way Paul and his mother had reacted to the news of Chilton Devries's death.

Mrs. Devries looked at her sharply, as if trying to judge her sincerity. "Of course it was, but Paul will be fine. Men don't feel things the way women do, do they?"

"I don't know about that," Sarah's mother said, but just then the maid knocked and opened the door. The ladies made their farewells to Mrs. Devries and managed to escape without having to answer any more awkward questions.

When they were back in the carriage, Sarah asked, "Were you able to learn anything interesting from Mrs. Devries?"

"Heavens no, not until you came in. She just kept complaining about the funeral arrangements and how tedious it all was. Can you believe she accused the poor valet of stabbing Chilton?"

"I'm feeling guilty about that, and Malloy will probably be furious."

"Why would he be furious?"

"Because I revealed that we suspect Devries was naked when he was stabbed."

Her mother frowned. "Why would that matter?"

"Because it narrows down the circumstances and the times when he could have been stabbed, which means Malloy knows it probably happened at his home or when he was with Miss English."

"If Lucretia even knows about Miss English."

"Do you think she does?"

"I'm sure she'd never admit it to me if she did, but I don't know how she could have failed to notice how many nights he spent away from home."

Her mother was probably right. But Miss English was the least of her worries. "What Malloy will chasten me about is that if the killer is someone at the Devrieses' house, I revealed that we know it was someone who was with Devries when he was undressed."

"I see, and because the number of people who did is small, the killer will know we suspect him."

"Or her."

"Oh, yes," her mother agreed. "We mustn't eliminate Lucretia as a possible killer. I can too easily imagine her plunging an ice pick into Chilton."

"Mother!"

"Oh, come now, Sarah. Can't you?"

Sarah had to admit she could, but she said, "I'm just afraid she's going to dismiss the valet now that I've reminded her of him."

"Oh, I'm sure she will. You heard what she said. I'd wager he knows more about Chilton's death than he admitted to Mr. Malloy, too."

"If anyone knows anything, he's the one. We should let Malloy know she's thinking about letting him go. He might be difficult to find if she did, and I'm sure Malloy doesn't want to waste time tracking him down later."

The carriage stopped, then swayed as the driver hopped down from his perch and opened the door. "We're here, Mrs. Decker."

Sarah and her mother stepped out onto the sidewalk in front of one of the dozens of tearooms that had sprung up around the city. They provided safe, respectable places for ladies to gather to gossip with their friends, which wasn't so very different from what they were planning to use it for themselves today.

Inside they found Frank Malloy trying to be inconspicuous behind a newspaper and failing miserably. As the only male on the premises, he would have been an object of curiosity to the other patrons, but because he also happened to be so obviously not the sort of gentleman the ladies here encountered, he had become fascinating. The room was abuzz with conversation and sly glances in his direction, but when the other ladies realized Sarah and her mother were heading for him, the room fell eerily silent.

Spotting them, Malloy lowered his newspaper and folded it with exaggerated care as they approached his table at the far back of the room. He laid it down and stood to greet them.

All the other women in the room began whispering behind their hands again, and Malloy rolled his eyes.

"I hope you haven't been waiting long," Sarah said, trying very hard not to grin at his obvious discomfort.

"At least a day and a half." He nodded at Mrs. Decker, who grinned in unabashed delight at his predicament. He pulled out chairs for them. They were delicate and gilt. Sarah wondered that any of them could hold his weight.

A young girl hurried over and took their order for tea and scones. Malloy requested a refill on his coffee.

When she was gone, Sarah said, "I did something stupid."

He raised his eyebrows and leaned back as far as he dared in the fragile chair. "Is that right?"

"I let it slip to Mrs. Devries that we know her husband was undressed when he was stabbed."

"And how did *that* subject happen to come up?"

Sarah winced a bit at the memory. "Mrs. Devries was annoying me."

He smiled slightly. "How did she do that?"

"If you must know," her mother said, "she was criticizing your ability to solve the case, and Sarah came to your defense."

"I'm touched."

He didn't look it. "She said you hadn't made any progress, so without thinking, I informed her that you certainly had and you knew Devries was undressed when he was stabbed, and I know it was foolish because if the killer is in that house, he'll know—"

"Or *she'll* know," her mother said.

"Mother wants Mrs. Devries to be the killer," Sarah explained.

"So do I," Malloy confided to Mrs. Decker, making her grin.

Sarah sighed. "At any rate, now she knows that you know Devries was naked."

"That isn't exactly true," Malloy said.

"What do you mean?" Sarah asked.

"It means we haven't found any of his clothes with a matching hole, but maybe the killer got rid of them. Or maybe he wasn't wearing any. So we don't really know for sure."

"Oh, my," Mrs. Decker said. "No wonder you enjoy this so much, Sarah. It's quite challenging to figure it all out, isn't it?"

"I don't *enjoy* this," Sarah said.

Her mother glared at her with disapproval, the way she used to do when Sarah was small and told a lie.

"At any rate, I told her," Sarah continued doggedly. "I know I shouldn't have."

He shrugged, as if it was of no consequence. "Did you find out anything useful from Garnet?"

Sarah described her conversation with the young woman.

"She's a very strange girl," her mother said.

"I'm sure I'd be acting strangely in her situation, too. She must feel she has no one to whom she can turn."

"Surely, her mother will be a comfort to her."

"I'm sure she'll try, but she can't offer much more than that."

"I wish I could feel more sympathy for her, but a woman who doesn't want her own child . . . It's unnatural."

"I've been trying to see things from her perspective, but the more I think about it, the more confused I become. She knows about Paul's, uh, *preference* for other men and is apparently appalled by it, so much so that she can't bear the thought of having his child. Yet when she speaks of him, she seems actually fond of him."

"As I said, she's a strange girl."

Sarah realized Malloy had made no comment about Garnet. "What are you thinking?"

"Something unthinkable. Did you find out anything interesting from Mrs. Devries?"

"Oh, my, yes. Sarah, tell him about the valet."

"Mrs. Devries said she thinks the valet stabbed Devries."

"Why would she think that?"

"Oh, I don't believe she really does," Sarah's mother said. "I think she has decided that solution would cause her the least inconvenience."

"She also said she should have dismissed him as soon as Devries died, since he doesn't have anything to do now, but Mother and I think he probably knows more than he's told you so far, so if you're going to question him again, you should do it before she puts him out."

"I didn't think about her dismissing him," Malloy said. "Wouldn't Paul need a valet?"

"He probably has his own."

The girl arrived with their order, and they spent a few minutes pouring tea and buttering scones.

"What will you do now, Mr. Malloy?" Sarah's mother asked.

"Go back to the Devrieses' house, I suppose. I'll need to put the fear of God into Roderick and find out what he hasn't told me so far. And then—"

"If you need someone to question Miss English again, Sarah and I would be happy to do so." Sarah's mother smiled innocently.

Malloy looked aghast, and Sarah almost choked on her tea.

"You've done more than enough already, Mrs. Decker," Malloy said after taking a moment, probably to choose the right words.

"Nonsense. I've hardly done anything at all."

"You've done more than your husband would approve of," he said.

"I'm sure he wouldn't be shocked to discover that, Mr. Malloy. I've often done more than he approves of."

"Yes," Sarah said, "but this time he will blame Malloy, not you."

That silenced her, but if she were concerned about getting Malloy in trouble with her husband, her expression did not reflect it.

"I suppose I should wait until after supper to call on the valet," Malloy said, checking his pocket watch.

"You'll attract less attention from the Devries family that way, I think," Sarah said. "They won't be going out this evening since they're in mourning, but they won't be making many demands on the servants at that hour, even if they're at home, so they won't even have to know you're there."

With that settled, Malloy finished his coffee and took his leave, thanking them for their assistance.

"I'm so sorry to have subjected you to the scrutiny of so many ladies," Sarah's mother said with another of her innocent smiles. "Perhaps next time we should arrange to meet you in a saloon."

"I'll be sure to suggest that to your husband, Mrs. Decker," he replied.

BY THE TIME FRANK RETURNED TO THE DEVRIESES' HOUSE, the winter darkness had settled over the city in earnest. The gaslights cast puddles of gold in the gloom, making little impact on it and doing nothing to alleviate the numbing cold. He hunkered in his overcoat, hands shoved deep into his pockets, as he waited for someone to answer his knock at the kitchen door.

The scullery maid opened it, peering out suspiciously, then taking a step back when she recognized him. "It's that policeman again," she reported to someone over her shoulder.

Frank could have easily pushed his way inside, the way he had at Miss English's house, but here he waited, showing respect for the servants until forced to do otherwise.

"What's he want now?" a woman asked. He recognized the cook's voice.

"I'd like to see Roderick again, if he's available."

"If he's available," the cook mocked. "He's always available now that Old Devries is dead."

The girl smirked and stepped aside to admit him. He wiped his feet ostentatiously before entering, showing consideration for those who'd have to clean up after him if he didn't.

"Tess, go fetch Roderick," Mrs. O'Brien said. She was sitting at the kitchen table, her feet up on another chair and a plate with the remnants of her own dinner in front of her. "Have you eaten, Mr. Malloy?"

"Yes, thank you, although I'm sure it wasn't as good as I'd have gotten here."

"You're right about that," she said. "Sit yourself down. Roderick won't be in no hurry to see you, I'm sure. Tell me, do you think he's the one what did for Old Devries?"

Frank pulled out a chair and sat. "I doubt it. I'm thinking the old man would've raised an alarm if his valet stuck him with something."

"You're right there. He'd have called the coppers if Roderick had nicked him shaving."

They both laughed at that.

"Who do *you* think might've done it?" he asked.

She sobered instantly. "I wouldn't like to guess."

"I understand. You don't want to get anybody in trouble."

"No, I don't want to see no one punished for it. Whoever stuck the old man done us all a service."

Before Frank could manage a reply, the sound of running feet on the back stairs distracted them.

The scullery maid burst out of the stairway, breathless. "Roderick's taken sick. We'd best send for a doctor!"

"He couldn't be that sick," the cook said, swinging her feet to the floor. "He was just fine at supper."

"He's taken real bad, I tell you!"

"Let me see him," Frank said.

At a nod from the cook, the girl started up the stairs again, with Frank at her heels. The servants' rooms were on the top floor, and Frank was panting by the time they reached it. The warmth of the other floors had only seeped up here and could barely cut the winter chill. The girl stopped outside an opened door and gestured helplessly. Frank could hear the man moaning before he even reached the door.

Roderick lay on his bed, fully clothed and curled in a ball, writhing in pain. The chamber pot held a malodorous stew of vomit and excrement.

"How long since he ate supper?" he asked the girl.

"I don't know!" she cried.

"Think! It's important."

"I . . . an hour maybe. No more than that."

"Did he come straight upstairs after that?"

"I . . . I think so."

Frank glanced around the Spartan room. Besides the plain iron bedstead, there was a wooden chair, a washstand with an enamel bowl and pitcher, and a small table. On the table sat a crystal decanter nearly full of amber liquid and an empty glass tumbler. Frank picked up the decanter and sniffed. Whiskey.

"Where'd this come from?" he asked.

"It was Mr. Devries's," the girl said. "He must've pinched it."

"No!" Roderick cried between groans.

"Where'd you get it then?"

"Gave it . . ."

"When?" Frank asked.

"Tonight," he gasped as another spasm shook him.

"What in heaven's name?" Mrs. O'Brien cried, having just arrived.

"Get a doctor here, right away," Frank said. "Tell them he might've been poisoned."

"Poisoned! I won't say no such thing!"

"Do you want him to die?"

The girl cried out. Other doors in the hallway were opening as the rest of the servants came to see what the commotion was.

"Somebody send for a doctor," Frank said. "Tell him Roderick will need his stomach pumped."

"I'll go," a young man said and hurried off.

"I never heard of such a thing," Mrs. O'Brien muttered.

"Get rid of this and bring in a clean one," Frank said, gesturing to the chamber pot. "And tell everybody to get back to their rooms."

The scullery maid reluctantly took charge of the chamber pot, and the cook started ushering the rest of the staff downstairs as they muttered and murmured their many questions.

When they were gone, Frank stood over the writhing man. "Who gave you the whiskey?"

Roderick looked up, his face twisted in agony. His lips moved, trying to form words, but no sound came out.

Frank leaned closer. "Tell me, man. Who gave it to you?"

Roderick's eyes glittered with rage, but as Frank waited, silently willing him to speak the name of his killer, the glitter faded and flickered out. The eyes rolled back. Roderick was dead.

FRANK USED THE DEVRIESES' TELEPHONE TO CALL THE medical examiner and Felix Decker. Decker arrived first. By then, Frank had enlisted the cooperation of all the servants to keep the death a secret from the Devrieses for the time being, and the maid showed Decker into the receiving room where Frank was waiting for him, without announcing his arrival to the family.

"How in God's name did something like this happen?" Decker demanded as soon as the door closed behind him.

"This afternoon, Mrs. Brandt let it slip to Mrs. Devries that I knew her husband was naked when he was stabbed."

"How would that result in a servant getting poisoned?"

"The three people who were with Devries when he was undressed were the valet, Paul, and Mrs. Devries. She would know that, too, which means either Paul or his mother stabbed him, and they must have been afraid Roderick knew it."

Decker scowled. Frank could see how little he liked this. "But didn't you also think the mistress might have done it?"

"I did, but if she was the killer, why would anyone need to get rid of Roderick?"

Decker muttered a very ungentlemanly curse. "But are you absolutely sure he was poisoned? Could it have been unintentional?"

"You mean something he ate? Not likely. All the other servants ate the same food he did for supper, and none of them are sick."

"Then how . . . ?"

"I found a decanter of whiskey in his room, and he'd apparently been drinking out of it. He could barely speak when I found him, but he managed to say someone had given it to him."

"No servant would have done that."

"No."

Decker sighed. "How did Paul and Lucretia behave when you told them?"

"I haven't told them yet. In fact, they don't even know I'm here or that Roderick is dead."

"You were waiting for me, I assume."

Frank hated himself for having to say it. "I need to know how you want this handled."

The muscles in Decker's jaw flexed. "You must have a low opinion of me, Mr. Malloy."

"What do you mean?"

"I mean because you felt you needed to ask that question. Yes, I wanted Chilton's death handled discreetly, but only because it might have been unintentional. This servant's death, however, is no accident. Someone killed the poor man with calculated cunning to cover their own guilt. I can't allow something like that to pass."

The knot of tension in Frank's belly loosened. He nodded. "I'm waiting for the medical examiner, and I'll need to tell the family. You don't have to stay for that."

Decker studied Frank for a long moment. "I won't have you think me a coward, either, Mr. Malloy. We'll tell them together."

The medical examiner arrived a few minutes later, and the noise of the man and his orderlies clomping up the stairs alerted the family that something was wrong, leaving Frank no choice but to go to them at once. He gave Doc Haynes his instructions, then followed Decker and the maid into the back parlor, where Mrs. Devries and her son had been spending a quiet evening.

"Felix, what on earth is going on?" she asked. "And what is that policeman doing here at this hour?"

"I'm afraid I have some more unpleasant news, Lucretia," Decker said.

"About my father's death?" Paul asked. He stood behind his mother's chair, as if they had determined to present a united front against the intruders.

"No, about someone else's death," Decker said.

"Someone else?" Paul said. "Don't tell me there's been another unfortunate accident."

"I'm not so sure it was an accident, but your father's valet is dead."

Paul seemed genuinely shocked. "Roderick? But that's impossible. I saw him just after supper, and he was perfectly fine."

"Be quiet, Paul," his mother said. "Don't say another word. What happened to him?"

"We aren't sure yet," Frank said, according to the plan he and Decker had made. "I came here tonight to ask him some more questions and found him very ill with gastric fever. We sent for the doctor, but Roderick died before he arrived."

"I knew it," Mrs. Devries said.

Frank and Decker gaped at her.

"What did you know?" Decker asked.

"Roderick. I knew he was the one who stabbed Chilly. I told Elizabeth exactly that this afternoon when she came to see me."

Her son looked down at her as if he thought she was insane. "Why would Roderick have stabbed Father?"

"Your father was a difficult man, my dear. You must know

that. I confess, I can't blame the poor fellow for wanting to put an end to his misery."

"You can't really believe that," Paul said.

"Paul, didn't I ask you not to say another word?" She looked at Decker again. "I'm afraid Paul was often blind to his father's faults, but we know, don't we?"

"Mother!"

She silenced him with a gesture. "He was poisoned, wasn't he?"

"That is what Mr. Malloy suspects," Decker said. "How did you know?"

"What else could it be? He must have been unable to bear the guilt for what he'd done to Chilly, and he took his own life. I'm surprised your Mr. Malloy hasn't figured that out himself."

11

Frank could hardly believe it. Did she really think anyone would accept such a ridiculous story?

"Mother, that hardly seems—"

"Enough, Paul. No one is interested in your opinion. Felix, I'm afraid I'm going to have to instruct the staff to stop admitting you. Every time you come, something awful has happened." She smiled as if to show she was joking, but Decker did not return it.

"So it seems. Mr. Malloy will need to question the staff before he leaves tonight."

"Is that really necessary? I won't have them upset. The house has been in an uproar for a week already."

"They will probably feel better if they think the police are going to sort it all out."

"Is that what you do, Mr. Malloy? Sort things out?" she asked.

"I try."

"I can't imagine what good it will do, but I don't suppose that will stop you, will it?"

She could have stopped him, but Frank chose not to inform her of that. "If Roderick killed himself, maybe he said something to one of the other servants or maybe one of them noticed something."

He didn't think she could argue with that, and apparently, she agreed. "I doubt a man intent on killing himself would confide in someone else, but I suppose anything is possible. Lord, such a fuss. I don't know how I can bear it. Paul, will you help me upstairs to my room?"

"Of course, Mother. I'll ring for someone to see you out, Mr. Decker."

"Don't bother. I know the way. Don't worry about a thing, Lucretia. Mr. Malloy will take care of everything."

The look she gave Frank didn't seem very appreciative.

"WHAT DO YOU THINK?" FRANK ASKED DOC HAYNES.

The two men stepped aside as the orderlies carried Roderick's body out of his room on a stretcher. "From what you describe, it does sound like poison, probably arsenic. I'll have them test the whiskey, of course."

"It *would* be arsenic."

"I know. Common as dishwater. Every house in the city has a box of rat poison in a cupboard somewhere. Do you know where he got the whiskey?"

"The scullery maid thought he'd stolen it, but he managed to say somebody gave it to him. He died before he could tell me who, though."

"Worst luck."

"How soon will you know?"

"Tomorrow is Sunday. Come see me Monday afternoon."

Frank swore. Monday was Devries's funeral. He was start-ing to feel like *he* might not be able to bear it either.

As he had before, Frank spoke with each of the servants one by one, hoping Roderick might have bragged to one of them about the gift someone had given him. This time the young man who had offered to summon the doctor took charge of organizing the interviews. As it turned out, young Winston was Paul's valet.

None of the other servants knew anything about the mys-terious decanter of whiskey, although one or two of them wouldn't have been surprised to learn Roderick had stolen it from Devries's room. He did like a nip now and then, although Devries didn't allow his servants to drink in the house. Frank had given up hope of learning anything important long before young Winston sat down with him in the receiving room, the last one to be questioned.

He lacked Roderick's air of confidence, but Frank figured time would take care of that. Paul was the master of the house now, and his valet would soon start to feel the importance of his position.

"When did you last see Roderick?" Frank asked, the same question he had asked all the others before him.

"At supper." The same answer the others had given.

"Did he seem ill or complain about not feeling well?"

"No, in fact . . ."

Frank's weariness evaporated. "In fact what?"

Plainly, Winston had been taught not to speak ill of the dead, so he hesitated diplomatically before saying, "He seemed rather jolly."

"Jolly?" No one else had mentioned this.

"Well, cheerful at least."

"Do you know why?"

Winston shifted uneasily in his chair. "He said . . . He said Mr. Paul had asked to see him."

"Why would that make him happy?"

"I don't know. See, we've all been talking, ever since Mr. Devries died. The servants, I mean. We've been wondering how long they'd keep Roderick, what with Mr. Devries being dead and not needing a valet anymore. We thought maybe they'd keep him until after the funeral, in case they needed him to choose his clothes or something, but Roderick thought different."

"What did he think?"

"I'm not sure, but he didn't think Mr. Paul was going to let him go."

"What did he say to you?"

Winston shifted again. "He said . . . Well, not in so many words, but he thought Mr. Paul was going to take him on and let *me* go."

"*Exactly* what did he tell you?"

Winston sighed. "He said, *Winston, old sport, we'll be sorry to see you go.*"

"He said this *before* he met with Paul Devries?"

"Yes."

"And what did you say?"

"What *could* I say? I know Mr. Paul has been very happy with my service, but I didn't know. Maybe Mr. Paul thought he should keep Roderick because he'd served his father or something. I was nervous, I can tell you."

"What did he say afterwards?"

"Nothing. I mean, I didn't see him again. I waited down in the kitchen for a while. I thought he would come and tell me I was out—he would've liked lording it over me—but he didn't. He just went right up to his room. That made me think Mr. Paul told him some bad news. Next thing I knew, I heard you yelling for somebody to call a doctor."

"Did you see the decanter we found in Roderick's room?"

"Yes."

"Do you know where it came from?"

"Mr. Devries had one like it in his room. I've seen it there. He likes his walnuts and his whiskey."

"Would Roderick have taken the decanter on his own? Without permission?"

"I couldn't say for sure, but I'd have to say no. Mrs. Devries, she'd be real hard on anybody who stole something."

"But if Paul Devries had just told him they were letting him go, maybe he didn't care."

"Oh, he'd need a reference from the family if he wanted to get another job. He wouldn't dare do anything to make them mad, even if they'd just turned him out."

"Winston, do you know what Paul and his father argued about the day Mr. Devries died?"

To Frank's surprise, the color drained from Winston's face. "Uh, no, I don't. Mr. Devries, he was always finding fault with Mr. Paul. It could've been anything at all."

"Roderick said they argued because Mr. Devries had been cruel to Garnet Devries."

He blinked. "Did he? Well, then, that must be it."

"What did Mr. Devries do that was cruel?"

He had to think about this for a moment. "He was always saying hurtful things to people. Yes, that's probably what it was. He'd said something to her and hurt her feelings."

Winston was a terrible liar, Frank noted. "Did he hurt Mr. Paul's feelings, too?"

Winston's expression hardened. "He'd say terrible things to him."

"What kind of things?"

"Accuse him of not being a real man. Of being soft and weak."

"Did he ever talk about Mr. Paul's friend, Hugh Zeller?"

Winston blanched at that, silently confessing that he knew about Paul's secret. "He . . . he didn't approve of Mr. Paul's friendship with Mr. Zeller."

"How does Mr. Paul get along with his wife?"

"What do you mean?"

"I mean, do they argue a lot?"

"Oh, no! They're right fond of each other. That's why Mr. Paul was so mad about his father not treating her well."

Which confirmed one of Frank's suspicions. "Did Mr. Paul think his father took an improper interest in his wife?"

Winston's eyes grew wide. "I don't know what you mean."

"I think you know exactly what I mean."

"I couldn't say. I won't say nothing about Mrs. Paul. You'll have to ask somebody else."

Which confirmed Frank's other suspicion.

"Take me up to Mr. Devries's bedroom."

"Whatever for?"

"I need to see where the decanter came from."

Winston obviously didn't like this, but he'd been instructed to assist Frank in his investigation, so he led the way up the back stairs to the third floor, where the family's bedrooms were located. Before opening the door from the stairway into the hall, he turned to Frank.

"Try not to make any noise. You don't want to disturb Mrs. Devries."

He was right about that, Frank thought, following him

down to the proper room. Winston closed the door behind them and leaned his back against it, silently telling Frank he was going to observe his every move. Frank remembered seeing a decanter on the table in the sitting area in front of the fireplace, and sure enough, the tray on which it had sat was still there, along with the matching glasses, but the decanter itself was gone.

"That's where the old man kept his whiskey, isn't it?" he asked Winston, nodding to the table.

"I believe so, yes."

"The last time I was here, I saw the decanter sitting on the tray, but it was empty."

"That's impossible. Roderick always kept it full for Mr. Devries."

"It was definitely empty when I saw it."

Winston frowned. "When was this?"

"A day or two after Devries died, I think."

Winston nodded. "Roderick had probably drunk it by then."

"Was he in the habit of doing that?"

"Not when Mr. Devries was alive, I don't think, but with him gone . . . I mean, who would know? Nobody comes in here but him now."

"Where is Mrs. Devries bedroom?"

Winston nodded to his left.

Frank pointed to the door on that wall. "Do the rooms connect?"

Winston smirked. "Sure, but there hasn't been a connection in a long time, if you know what I mean."

Frank returned his grin. "I suppose it's locked on her side."

"That's right."

Frank looked around again, and this time he noticed

something he hadn't before. He walked back over to the table where the decanter had sat. If Roderick had sampled the whiskey, he hadn't touched the walnuts. The bowl still held as many as Frank remembered from his previous visit. The implements stood neatly in their holders, polished and gleaming. Frank plucked one of them from its place, a nut pick, to examine it more closely.

Something long and thin, like an ice pick, Haynes had said. Testing the point with his thumb, he easily punctured the skin and drew a drop of crimson blood.

"What are you doing?" Winston asked in alarm.

Frank ignored him. He was noticing something else. "One of the nut picks is missing."

"You've got it in your hand," Winston said, hurrying over.

"No, there's an empty hole where another one should be. Where is it?"

"How should I know? Ask . . . Oh, I was going to say, ask Roderick," he said in dismay.

"I'd like to," Frank muttered.

"It seems like a strange thing to steal. It wouldn't be worth much."

"It's probably just lost," Frank said.

Winston brightened. "That's it. Mr. Devries, he was always walking around, eating his walnuts and dropping the shells everywhere. The maids complained about it all the time. He probably carried it with him someplace and left it."

He had, Frank remembered Roderick saying, been eating walnuts the morning he died.

Sarah and the girls had just finished washing up their Sunday dinner dishes when the front doorbell rang.

Maeve and Catherine ran to answer it, and from the laughter, Sarah knew she wasn't being summoned to a birth. She found the girls happily hanging up Malloy's coat and helping his son, Brian, off with his.

When Brian saw Sarah, he ran over and threw his arms around her. She caught him up and returned his hug, smiling as widely as she could to let him know how happy she was to see him, since she knew he couldn't hear her words. His small hands started making the signs he had learned at the New York Institution for the Deaf and Dumb where he attended school. Plainly, he had learned a lot, and Sarah sighed when she realized she could make little sense of them.

"Do you know what he's saying?" she asked Malloy.

"He's happy. I know that sign, at least."

"I'm happy, too," Sarah said, hugging him again.

But Catherine was tugging on Brian's arm. When he looked at her, she pointed at the stairs, and when Sarah released him, the two children raced away, clattering up the stairs to visit the toys in Catherine's room.

"They don't need words *or* signs," Maeve said, following them upstairs. "They understand each other just fine."

"Thank you for bringing Brian," Sarah said to Malloy. "Catherine loves playing with him."

"It makes him pretty happy, too."

"Come into the kitchen and tell me what you found out from the valet."

To her surprise, his expression darkened, but he followed her obediently. She set out cups and poured them some coffee. She thought he'd start talking the minute he sat down, but he waited until she'd served them both and taken a seat at the table herself.

"What's wrong?" she asked.

"Roderick is dead."

"The valet? What happened?"

"Someone poisoned him."

Sarah needed a minute for the words to register and another for the awful truth to dawn on her. "Oh, no!" she cried, covering her mouth as tears sprang to her eyes. "It's all my fault!"

"No, it's not!" Malloy said, taking her hand in a grip just short of painful. "It's not your fault, Sarah. You didn't kill him. Someone else killed him, and that's who's to blame."

"But if I hadn't said anything about him—"

"The killer would've thought of him sooner or later."

"But maybe not until later and maybe he still would've been alive when you arrested the killer."

"Stop it! You can't know that. You can't know anything, and *you* didn't kill him. Somebody else did, and that's whose fault it is. I won't have you taking on somebody else's guilt."

He was right, of course, but Sarah knew she would never forgive herself for losing her temper with Mrs. Devries. "That means Mrs. Devries must be the one who stabbed him!"

"I know that's what we were all hoping, but from what I've been able to find out, Paul seems to be the one who gave him the poison."

"Paul? I can't even imagine that. How could he have done it?"

"I don't even know for sure what the poison was yet, but the medical examiner and I think it was arsenic."

"Rat poison."

"Probably. It's pretty easy to find."

"But how—"

"Somebody gave him a decanter of whiskey."

"Who would do a thing like that?"

"I don't know that either, at least not for sure, but here is what I do know. Roderick seemed to think Paul was going to fire his own valet and keep Roderick on."

"Why did he think that?"

"I'm guessing, you understand, but remember we thought Roderick knew more about what happened the morning Devries got stabbed than he was saying. Maybe he knew who had stabbed him, and he thought that knowledge would protect him."

Sarah sighed. "When it really put him in mortal danger."

"Right after supper last night, Paul met with Roderick. Afterwards, Roderick went straight to his room, and an hour or so later, I arrived to question him. We found him writhing in agony, and a few minutes later he was dead."

"Didn't you ask him what happened?"

"Of course I did, but he couldn't speak. I saw the decanter of whiskey in his room. It was real fancy, not the regular kind of bottle whiskey comes in, but the kind rich people put it in to sit around and look nice."

"He might have *borrowed* it. Servants do that, you know."

"One of the maids said he'd probably pinched it, but Roderick managed to say someone had given it to him. Of course I asked him who," he added when she would have interrupted, "but he was too far gone. He never said another word before he died."

"How awful!"

"I've been trying to figure out what happened before I question Paul Devries, and here's what I think: I think Roderick knew who killed Devries, so when Paul realized it, he put the rat poison in the whiskey. Then he called Roderick in and told him he was going to let him go. Roderick would've been pretty disappointed. Maybe he even threatened Paul, but maybe he was afraid to. Whatever happened between them,

Paul knew he'd be upset so he told Roderick to take the decanter of whiskey to his room to drown his sorrows. What do you think?"

"It sounds logical, but do you really believe Paul Devries is a cold-blooded killer?"

Malloy frowned. "That's the part that bothers me, too, but if he killed his father—even by accident—he might be feeling desperate. He might be willing to do whatever he could to protect himself."

Sarah considered the possibilities. "Or maybe to protect someone he loves."

"His mother?" Malloy asked skeptically.

"We don't like her, but she's his mother, after all, and she apparently adores him."

"Winston said he's fond of his wife, too."

"He did?"

"He could've been lying, but I don't think so. I'm pretty sure they don't hate each other, at least. Paul was angry at his father for treating Garnet badly, remember."

"But why would he have to protect Garnet unless she was the one who stabbed Devries?"

"Maybe she was."

Sarah nearly choked on her coffee. "But . . . If he was naked . . ." She shook her head, unable to believe it.

"Something's going on in that house. Your father said it himself. He didn't think I had a chance of finding out what it was, so he asked you to help. I didn't want to say anything in front of your mother yesterday, but I've started suspecting that Devries had taken an improper interest in his daughter-in-law."

"That's a horrible suspicion!"

"I know, which is why I didn't want to say anything before,

but I've been noticing how the servants protect her and nobody will tell me exactly what Paul and his father were arguing about the day he died except that it was about Garnet. And now we know Garnet is expecting a baby she doesn't want. You thought that was because she didn't want a child by her husband, but what if Devries had fathered it?"

Sarah shuddered. "That would certainly explain why she said it had been spawned by a monster."

"Yes, it would. And if Devries had tried to have his way with her that morning, and she'd stuck him with a nut pick—"

"A *what*?"

"A nut pick. Those things you use to pick out the nut meat when you're eating walnuts?"

"Was that what killed Devries?"

"It's the right size and shape, and he really liked walnuts and ate them all the time, and one of the picks is missing from the nut bowl in his bedroom."

"Oh, my."

"Yes, oh, my."

"What are you going to do?"

"I'm not sure. First of all, I have to wait for the medical examiner to do the autopsy and tell me for sure what killed the valet. I can't accuse Paul Devries of murder and then find out he ate a bad oyster or something."

"You certainly can't. How soon will you know?"

"Not until tomorrow afternoon."

"Mr. Devries's funeral is tomorrow."

"I know. Are you going?"

"I hadn't thought about it. Will you be there?"

"I'll go to the church, but I won't be welcome back at the house afterwards. I'd like to know what goes on there."

Sarah had performed this duty for him before. "My parents will be going. I'm sure they'd take me with them."

"Would you mind?"

"Actually, I'd like an opportunity to see Garnet again. She asked me for a . . . She called it a *remedy*, something to get rid of the baby. I won't do that, but there are plenty of people in the city who would. I'm afraid she might do something dangerous."

"If Devries did what I think he did, I couldn't blame her."

"No matter what he did, I don't want to see anyone else die."

"So you'll go to the funeral?"

"Of course."

They both looked up when someone knocked on the back door. Sarah hurried to admit her neighbor, Mrs. Ellsworth.

"Why, Mr. Malloy, what a surprise," she exclaimed, a little breathless from the cold.

Malloy smiled. "Is it?" He knew Mrs. Ellsworth usually kept careful track of the comings and goings on Bank Street.

"Well, of course. If I'd known you were here, I'd have brought *two* pies, so you could take one home." She handed the basket she was carrying to Sarah. "Although I should have known you'd have a visitor because I dropped a spoon on the table while I was making breakfast this morning. It was a large spoon, though, which usually means a family of visitors." She shook her head as if baffled by such a mistake.

"Mr. Malloy brought Brian with him," Sarah said.

Mrs. Ellsworth smiled approvingly. "Oh, well, that explains it! How is that darling little boy of yours?"

"He's very well. You can see for yourself if you stay for a while."

"Would you like some coffee?" Sarah asked.

"I'd love some," she said, pulling out a chair. "I don't suppose you're working on an interesting case or anything, are you, Mr. Malloy?"

"As a matter of fact, I'd like to ask your opinion of something, Mrs. Ellsworth," he said solemnly.

"I'm sure my opinion would be of no help to you at all, but I'm happy to give it."

"Do you think someone could be murdered with a nut pick?"

SARAH'S PARENTS WERE HAPPY TO COME BY FOR HER ON their way to the funeral the next morning, but Sarah didn't have any opportunity to tell her mother Malloy's theories about Paul and Garnet Devries because she didn't want to discuss it in front of her father. Malloy himself should make that report and only after he'd been able to confirm or refute his suspicions about Garnet and Mr. Devries.

The service itself was an ordeal. She could hardly sit still while she listened to several of Chilton Devries's friends speak of him as if he'd been a paragon of virtue. Typically, the son of the deceased would also give a eulogy, but Paul remained in his seat, staring straight ahead, his pale face expressionless. Beside him, his heavily veiled mother appeared frail and distraught, clinging to his arm as if it were a lifeline. Of course, no one could actually see her expression through the veil, so for all anyone knew, she was snickering with delight.

Paul's sisters and their families took up the rest of the front pew and most of the second one. The girls looked appropriately bereaved, although Sarah never saw either of them shed a tear. The person Sarah had most wanted to see wasn't present, however. Garnet Devries had not come to the church.

If Malloy's suspicions were right, Sarah could certainly understand why Garnet had refused to mourn the man's death.

As they filed out of the church, Sarah's heart went cold when she overheard another guest say Garnet was too ill to attend. She thought of Roderick, poisoned and dying and how Malloy had found him too late. She was being silly, she knew, but she couldn't help feeling a sense of urgency to get to the Devrieses' house as quickly as possible to make sure.

"Mother, I'm going to go check on Garnet," she whispered as they made their way down the crowded aisle.

"But we have to go to the cemetery," her mother whispered back.

"You do, but I don't."

"But we'll have the carriage. How will you get there?"

"I'll walk." Sarah craned her neck. "Malloy is in the back. I'm sure he'll go with me."

No one seemed to notice when Sarah slipped away and found Malloy in the shadows.

"What's the matter?" he asked when she reached him.

"I heard someone say Garnet was too ill to attend. I want to go straight to the Devrieses' house and make sure she's all right."

"Do you really think somebody would've killed her right before the funeral?" he asked with a trace of amusement.

"I have no idea, but if somebody tried, I'd like to find out as soon as possible."

He couldn't argue with that logic. They found a side door to the church and slipped out into an alley so they would avoid the crush of mourners waiting in front of the church for their carriages.

"I doubt we can find a cab," Malloy said as they stepped out into the wintery air.

"We can walk. It's not far."

They walked a while in silence, making their way through the midday shoppers and nannies pushing baby buggies. Malloy moderated his pace to match her shorter one. Finally, he said, "If Paul was protecting Garnet, he's not likely to have killed her himself, you know."

"I'm afraid logic isn't going to have any effect on me today. I've been trying to convince myself that she's simply ill because she's with child or even that she pretended to be ill so she wouldn't have to sit and listen to those insufferable men talk about what a wonderful person Devries was. None of it has made me any less uneasy."

"What did your father say when you told him what we talked about yesterday?"

"I didn't tell him anything. We have no proof, and he won't be eager to believe one of his friends had forced himself on his daughter-in-law. I'm not anxious to believe it myself."

"Do you think you could get Garnet to admit it to you?"

"Perhaps, if I can meet with her alone, but even then, she may not admit it. Few women would, and Garnet isn't the sort who bares her soul easily. She didn't even confide in her own mother, and she was quite angry with me the last time we met, you'll remember."

"Try, at least, because if you can't, I doubt your father would approve of using my methods on her, so we might never find out."

Sarah sighed as they turned the corner and could see the Devrieses' house down the block. "I just remembered that my father called you in on this case because he thought he might not want to see the killer punished at all. I wonder if he still feels that way."

"We talked about that on Saturday night, and he's changed his mind."

Sarah blinked. "Why?"

"Because he wants to see Roderick's killer punished."

"He does? Good heavens!"

"Why are you so surprised?"

Sarah had to think about this for a moment. "Because . . . I'm afraid I would have thought my father would consider Roderick's death of little consequence, certainly as compared to the death of one of his friends, and he wasn't even sure he wanted to see Devries's killer punished."

"I would've thought that, too. In fact, I think he was a little hurt when I said so."

"Really?" Sarah could hardly believe they were talking about her father. "He's changed."

"Maybe."

"You don't think so?"

They'd almost reached the Devrieses' front steps, and they slowed their pace.

Malloy looked down at her. "I don't think a man can change who he really is."

"But he's behaving so differently than . . . than I've ever known him to. That's what he and my sister used to argue about. He didn't think people like Roderick were important."

"Maybe he's just changing his idea of what's important."

"I'd like to think so, but can he really do it? What if it turns out Garnet stabbed Devries while she was trying to protect her honor? Could you bring charges against her?"

"Not for killing Devries, but if she killed Roderick to cover it up, then, yes, I could."

"But would my father?"

"Let's hope we don't have to find out."

Sarah sighed again. They'd stopped at the foot of the Devrieses' front steps. "What are you going to do now?"

"I'm going to see the medical examiner and find out what killed Roderick. I'd like to question Paul Devries, but I guess I've got to wait until tomorrow to do it."

"Oh, yes. You wouldn't dare question him about killing his father on the very day of the funeral." She looked up at the Devrieses' front door with its black wreath. "But this is the perfect time to question Garnet about her demons."

The maid who answered the door stared at Sarah in alarm. "Are you coming from the funeral already?"

"Oh, no," Sarah said, feeling guilty for causing her a fright. "They're just on their way to the cemetery. I came to see Mrs. Paul Devries. I heard she wasn't feeling well, and I wanted to see if there was something I could do for her. I'm Mrs. Brandt. I was here to see her the other day, you'll remember."

The girl sighed with obvious relief and admitted Sarah. "I'll tell her you're here."

"Is she very ill?" Sarah asked, her earlier concerns rushing back.

"Oh, no," the girl started to say, then caught herself. "I mean, I'm sure I don't know."

Sarah felt her own surge of relief. "Is she in bed?"

"Oh, no, ma'am. She's up and dressed for the wake. She just didn't feel like she could make the trip to the church and out to the burial."

"If you'll take me to her, I'll see what I can do for her."

The girl would know she should announce Sarah and see if her visit was welcomed before taking her upstairs, but Sarah knew how harried she and the other servants would be preparing for the funeral dinner. She might be able to take advantage of this.

"There's no need to announce me. I'm sure Mrs. Paul will be happy to see me." And if she wasn't, the poor girl would probably never know it. Sarah smiled as reassuringly as she knew how, and finally the maid relented.

"Follow me, please."

She took Sarah up to the third floor, to Garnet's bedroom. At her knock, Garnet bid her enter, and she said, "Mrs. Brandt is here to see you."

Sarah didn't wait to hear what Garnet might have replied. She slipped in behind the maid and said, "When I heard you were ill, I came at once."

Sarah wasn't sure who was more startled, Garnet at Sarah bursting in on her or Sarah at finding she wasn't alone.

12

GARNET ROSE TO HER FEET, AND SO DID THE OTHER LADY who had been sitting with her in front of the fire. Both wore the unrelieved black of full mourning. The contrast of the black with Garnet's pale face was startling. She really did look ill, and Sarah wondered if she dared ask if Garnet had found the *remedy* she had been seeking. Common wisdom said there were mysterious herbs or potions a woman could take to rid herself of an unwanted pregnancy, but Sarah knew such treatments were either completely ineffectual or potentially lethal to the mother as well as her child. She couldn't ask until she knew who this other woman was, however.

"I'm sorry. I didn't know you had a visitor," Sarah said.

"Would that really have stopped you?" Garnet asked.

"Garnet," the other woman chided in a tone Sarah recognized instantly as one her mother often used on her. That and her slight resemblance to Garnet told her the woman's identity.

"You must be Mrs. Richmond," Sarah said. "I'm very pleased to meet you."

"And, Mother, this is Mrs. Brandt," Garnet said, "about whom you have heard me complain. Mary Catherine, could you bring us some tea and cakes? I know you're being run ragged, but I'm afraid my guests might grow faint if they have to wait until the funeral dinner for something to restore them."

"Yes, ma'am."

When the girl was gone, Garnet turned to Sarah. "I envy you. How delightful it must be to simply go wherever you wish and do whatever you wish with no regard for the consequences."

Mrs. Richmond gasped, but Sarah smiled. "I assure you, it is far from delightful, and I often must deal with consequences. For example, I must now feel terrible for interrupting your visit with your mother."

"Don't do that," Garnet said. "We actually welcome your arrival. I'm afraid we were simply wallowing in our mutual misery when you burst in."

Garnet sat down, signaling her guests to do the same.

When they were settled, Sarah turned to Mrs. Richmond. She was a handsome woman, and her gown had been made for her by a skilled dressmaker, but not recently. She, too, was pale and looked as if she hadn't been sleeping well. She also didn't know quite what to make of Sarah.

"My daughter is exaggerating," Mrs. Richmond said with a polite smile. "I've just been keeping her company while we wait for the rest of the family to return from the funeral."

"I'm sure she appreciates that." Sarah turned back to Garnet. "Someone told me at the church that you were too ill to come, so I thought I should make sure you were all right. I was afraid you might have taken something that didn't agree with you."

"Like poor Roderick?"

"Good heavens, Garnet, what a thing to say!" her mother cried.

"Mrs. Brandt isn't easily shocked. Are you, Mrs. Brandt?"

"Not at all. And I was sincerely hoping you hadn't suffered the same fate."

"Your concern is gratifying, but I assure you, I am perfectly safe."

"If you're feeling unwell because of the child, I can suggest some things to do that will make you more comfortable."

"My mother is ahead of you there. The two of you share a touching concern for my well-being. Did I tell you Mrs. Brandt is a midwife, Mother? She is a widow who earns her own bread."

"Isn't that really why you envy me?" Sarah asked.

Garnet widened her eyes. "Am I so transparent?"

"Not at all. Any woman could understand your interest."

"Any woman who had been left penniless and helpless, you mean."

"You aren't penniless," Mrs. Richmond said almost desperately.

"No, I'm not," Garnet agreed. "At least so long as I stay here, in this house, at the mercy of everyone in it."

Mrs. Richmond reached out and laid a hand on her daughter's arm. "But he's gone now, my darling. He can't hurt you anymore."

"Can't he? And what about you? He left you penniless and helpless, too."

From what Sarah knew about Mrs. Richmond, this was

certainly true, but to her surprise, Mrs. Richmond stiffened and snatched away her comforting hand. "Penniless, perhaps, but not completely helpless." For a moment, Sarah and Garnet stared at her in surprise, and seeing their reaction, Mrs. Richmond instantly softened her expression with a smile. "In many ways, we are the stronger sex, are we not, Mrs. Brandt?"

"Anyone who has seen a woman in childbirth would agree," Sarah said.

"A woman will do what she must to protect those she loves," Mrs. Richmond said. "My daughter is still learning this lesson."

Mrs. Richmond and Garnet exchanged a look. Sarah would have given much to know its true meaning, but Garnet said, "And a bitter lesson it is, too."

A knock at the door announced the arrival of the maid with their tea. Mrs. Richmond took charge of serving it, and like the proper hostess she had once been, she directed the conversation to trivialities. By asking Sarah about herself and her family with the skill of one who has been taught from birth how to fill the hours with conversation without ever touching on anything of real importance, she managed to pass the time until the maid came to inform them that the rest of the family had returned.

"Mrs. Devries wants you to help her greet the guests," the girl told Garnet.

Garnet actually winced.

"Mrs. Paul couldn't possibly stand on her feet for so long," Sarah said. "Please tell Mrs. Devries that she will be available in the parlor for anyone who wishes to see her."

"The *rear* parlor," Garnet added with a perverse smile. Few of the guests would find her there.

This time the maid winced, probably dreading Mrs.

Devries's reaction to this refusal. When she was gone, Garnet turned to Sarah. "Will you stay with me?"

Malloy had wanted her to report to him what happened at the house, and she would see little if she stayed with Garnet, but she said, "Of course."

Garnet turned to her mother and took her arm. "We will be as brave as Mrs. Brandt thinks we are."

An expression that might have been despair flickered across Mrs. Richmond's face, and she gave her daughter a brief, fierce hug. Then, smoothing out her expression to cool unconcern, she walked out with Garnet into the hallway.

For the next few hours, Garnet held court in the family parlor. As Sarah had predicted, few of the guests found her there. To Sarah's surprise, one of them was a handsome young man who greeted her warmly.

"Garnet, my darling," he said, taking her hand in both of his. "How are you bearing up?"

"I'm so much better now that you're here," she said.

"Of course you are," he said, winning from her the first true smile Sarah had seen that day.

From where she sat unobtrusively in the corner, Sarah was busily rethinking her opinion of Garnet, nearly convinced this fellow was her lover, when Garnet said, "Mother, allow me to present Paul's oldest friend, Hugh Zeller."

Hugh and Mrs. Richmond made all the correct responses to the introduction, and he accepted Garnet's invitation to sit with her.

"Paul sends his most affectionate regards," Zeller said, "and asks you to forgive him for not attending you sooner, but he will find you the moment the witch is done with him."

"I know he will. She's keeping him away from me as a punishment for not going to the funeral."

"Of course she is, and for not standing at her side while people gush about what a wonderful man her husband was. I keep telling Paul to stand up to her, but the habits of a lifetime are difficult to break."

"We all do what we must to protect those we love," Garnet said with a meaningful glance at her mother.

"Now tell me, my darling, are you really ill?" he asked, studying her intently. "You are as ravishing as ever, but I'm afraid now it is more in the manner of the tragic heroine wasting away for love."

"Not for love, surely," she said.

He grew solemn. "Tell me the truth. Are you really ill?"

"Nothing that time won't cure."

She was exactly right, Sarah thought.

"You know we would move heaven and earth for you. All you need do is ask."

Garnet smiled at him fondly and patted his hand. "I'm sure I won't require anything so ambitious as all that. Paul might, however, if you don't get him away from his mother soon."

"Have you assigned me a quest, fair lady?"

"I most certainly have."

He took her hand and bowed over it, then rose. "I will bring him back with his shield or on it."

"What did he mean by that?" Mrs. Richmond asked when he was gone.

"I have no idea. He always says the most outrageous things."

Sarah's parents came in then, distracting her from her eavesdropping. She greeted them, then introduced them to Mrs. Richmond. They didn't bother to express their condolences to Garnet, for which she was undoubtedly grateful. Sarah's mother, who was also a master of meaningless conversation, managed to get Mrs. Richmond's history in a few short minutes.

While the two women were chatting, Sarah's father drew her aside. "I see Garnet is still alive."

"Don't tease, Father. If Roderick was killed because he knew who the killer was, other people might be in danger as well."

"I wasn't teasing. I'm as relieved as you are. I just can't believe Paul or Lucretia would commit murder."

"Maybe they don't consider it murder if it's just a servant."

She saw her barb hit home, but he said, "Many in their place would not, I'm afraid."

"I'm glad you aren't one of them."

Her compliment seemed to please him. "Where is Mr. Malloy?"

"He's meeting with the medical examiner to make sure Roderick really was poisoned."

"Then I assume he'll question Paul."

"Yes, but not until tomorrow."

"Will he be able to find out the truth?"

Sarah didn't know the answer to that question.

FRANK HAD TO WAIT FOR DOC HAYNES, WHO WAS IN THE middle of an autopsy when he arrived. Sitting in Haynes's cluttered office, Frank spent the time mulling over all that he had learned about Chilton Devries. Usually, when he investigated a murder, all he needed to do was figure out who would profit most from the person's death. In this case, however, he wasn't even sure the person who stabbed Devries had intended to kill him. The weapon—which might've been a nut pick, of all things—wasn't particularly large or dangerous enough to give the person wielding it confidence in its ability to do serious damage.

No, the incident that caused Devries's death had probably been a spontaneous act of anger or frustration meant only to cause him pain or divert him from causing it to someone else. If Felix Decker had left it alone, that person would have gone unpunished but rightly so, in all probability. And Roderick would still be alive. If Sarah felt guilt about that, Frank felt even more. He should have used his considerable skill to force Roderick to tell him everything he knew about Devries's encounters with his family when he'd first had the chance. Instead he'd chosen to bide his time and win Roderick's cooperation. That decision had cost Roderick his life.

When Doc Haynes finally returned to his office, he plopped wearily into his chair and peered at Frank with bloodshot eyes. "Killers have no imagination, Malloy."

"If they did, maybe they could figure out a better way to deal with their problems."

"You're probably right. The whiskey had been laced with arsenic, just like you thought. Rat poison, straight out of the box. It works pretty fast if you take enough of it, and there was plenty in the bottle. I'm surprised he didn't balk at the taste."

"He'd only had a glass or so, judging from how much was left."

"So maybe he did notice the taste, but he'd already drunk enough. Any idea who did the deed?"

"Yes, unfortunately. A bunch of swells."

Haynes muttered a curse. "Poor fellow. He was the butler or something, wasn't he?"

"Valet to Chilton Devries."

"Oh, the one I saw last week."

"Yeah, and I wanted to ask you something. Do you think a nut pick could've made the wound that killed Devries?"

"A nut pick?"

"Yes, that thing you use to pick out the inside of a walnut when you've cracked it open. It's about this long—"

"I know what it is. Would it be sharp enough?"

"It's got a point, and if somebody stabbed hard enough, I think it would probably break the skin."

Haynes considered the possibilities. "Could be. It's the right size and shape. What made you think of that?"

"Devries liked walnuts. He was always walking around, eating them and dropping the shells. And one of the nut picks is missing from a set he had in his bedroom."

"So you need to find out who has the missing nut pick."

Frank was very much afraid he already knew.

SARAH'S PARENTS HAD LONG SINCE WITHDRAWN. GARNET and her mother had easily dealt with the trickle of mourners who found them, accepting their condolences with such a blatant lack of appreciation that they soon fled.

At last Paul appeared, followed by Hugh Zeller. He hurried to Garnet's side. "How are you feeling?"

"I'm fine," she said with a small smile.

"This must be ghastly for you."

"No worse than it is for you, and Mother has been keeping me company."

Paul seemed to notice his mother-in-law for the first time. "I'm so glad you could be here for Garnet, Terry. Thank you for coming."

She seemed almost offended by his gratitude. "I would do anything for my daughter."

Paul gave her a crooked smile. "I know, but this must tax even your motherly devotion."

Some emotion flickered across her face, but she returned his smile with a sad one of her own. "Nothing could do that."

Paul turned back to Garnet. "Have you eaten anything?"

"No, she hasn't," Mrs. Richmond said.

"Let me take you to the dining room, then. You can see my mother and my sisters there for a few minutes, then go back to your room."

"I couldn't eat a bite," Garnet said.

"You won't have to. Just stand there looking appropriately somber and murmur your thanks if anyone speaks to you. I'll make sure you don't have to stay long."

Hugh Zeller stepped forward. "And I'll escort you, Mrs. Richmond. Two pariahs together," he added with a knowing smile.

His frankness seemed to disconcert her, but she rose and took his offered arm. They waited for Paul and Garnet to precede them, but as they moved to the door, Garnet stopped. "What about Mrs. Brandt? You've been so quiet, I almost forgot about you!"

"Don't worry about me," Sarah said. "I'll find my parents."

"Sarah?" Paul peered at her with a puzzled frown. "Sarah Decker?"

"I'm Sarah Brandt now, Paul. It's nice to see you."

"It's nice to see you, too, but what on earth are you doing here?"

"Paul!" Garnet said in dismay.

"Oh, I'm sorry. I didn't mean it like that," he said. "It's just that I haven't seen you in so long and . . . I'm surprised you're here today."

"Mrs. Brandt is my friend," Garnet said. "She came to support me."

This news surprised Paul even more, but he seemed pleased by it just the same. "Then I'm very grateful to you."

"I'm glad I could come," Sarah said.

"Hugh, would you escort Mrs. Brandt as well?" Paul asked.

"I would be delighted."

Paul quickly introduced the two.

As they moved out of the room and down the hallway toward the dining room, Sarah tried to hear what Paul and Garnet were saying to each other as they walked on ahead, but Zeller distracted her.

"Paul called you Sarah Decker. Are you any relation to Felix Decker?"

"He's my father."

"Ah, then perhaps you know why he's so anxious to blame someone for old Devries's demise."

Zeller's smile was charming and his tone light, but Sarah saw the sharp intelligence in his eyes. He was more than a little interested in her reply. "He and Mr. Devries were old friends."

"Then he must know whoever killed Devries did us all a favor."

Beside him, Mrs. Richmond stumbled, and he caught her.

"Are you all right?" he asked.

"Yes, I'm sorry," she said unsteadily. "I just . . . Perhaps I'll go back to the parlor and wait for Garnet there."

"Would you like me to go with you?" Sarah asked.

"No, no, I'll be fine. I just . . . I'm not looking forward to seeing Mrs. Devries, and I'd rather not cause a scene. For Garnet's sake, you understand."

"Of course," Zeller said. "Although her scenes can be amusing if one isn't involved in them."

Mrs. Richmond smiled weakly. "I'm sure. Please tell Garnet where I've gone." Before they could reply, she fled back down the hall.

"Do you think she'll be all right?" Zeller asked Sarah.

Sarah had no idea. "I'll be sure to check on her in a few minutes."

But when she did, Mrs. Richmond was gone.

SARAH HAD BEEN WAITING FOR MALLOY ALL EVENING. As she had half expected, he didn't arrive until after Catherine's bedtime, when he knew her house would be quiet and free from unexpected visitors. Even Maeve had gone to bed.

When she served him coffee, she noticed he wrapped both hands around the cup to absorb its warmth.

"I don't suppose you learned anything unexpected from the medical examiner," she said, sitting down with him at the table.

"No. Arsenic, just as we thought. Somebody poured an awful lot of it into the whiskey bottle. I'm guessing nobody had poisoned Garnet Devries."

"No, and she didn't seem particularly ill, either, except for the usual morning sickness women in her condition get."

"I don't suppose you learned anything interesting today."

"I did, but not what I expected."

He perked up at this. "What?"

"You told me that Hugh Zeller is Paul's . . . What do you call it when they're both men?"

"Friend," Malloy said.

She raised her eyebrows. "That can't be right."

"I don't know any nice words for it, Sarah. Men like that aren't treated with much respect, and you don't need to know what the cops call them."

He was probably right. "At any rate, I guess I expected Mr. Zeller would be jealous of Garnet or at least that he wouldn't like her very much, but quite the contrary, he actually seemed fond of her and genuinely concerned about her health."

"What about Paul?"

"I didn't see much of him. His mother kept him occupied, but when he was finally able to break away, he was just as kind to Garnet. Not like a lover would be, but like a brother, perhaps. He does care for her, at least, so whoever told you that was right."

"Fond enough to kill for her?"

Sarah shook her head. "I don't know. Something Mrs. Richmond said made me—"

"Who?"

"Mrs. Richmond. I almost forgot, she was with Garnet when I got there."

"That was brave of her. Mrs. Devries doesn't want her in the house."

"I'm sure she knew her daughter would need her, and braving the wrath of Mrs. Devries would be a small price to pay."

"She was probably counting on the fact that Mrs. Devries wouldn't make a scene at her husband's funeral."

"She also managed to keep out of her sight, too."

"You started to say something about her."

"Oh, yes. She remarked that a woman would do whatever was necessary for those she loved, and it made me wonder. Would a man do that, too?"

Malloy frowned. "You mean would a man commit murder?"

"Not exactly. I know men commit murder for many reasons

that don't have anything to do with love. I guess I mean would a man sacrifice for someone he loves, whatever that entails."

"For someone he *loves*, yes. The question is, does Paul Devries love Garnet—or his mother—enough?"

"I guess you'll have to ask him that tomorrow."

"Maybe you could ask Garnet, too."

"What do you mean?"

"I mean I'd like for you to go see Garnet at the same time I'm seeing Paul tomorrow."

"To ask her if Paul loves her?"

"No, to ask her if Chilton Devries fathered her child."

"Oh, my."

"It's not a question *I* can ask her."

"I know. I suppose I should also find out if she is the one who stabbed him with . . . What was it? A nut pick?"

"Yes, a nut pick. And if you could find it in her room with blood still on it, that would be even better."

"And suppose I do? Suppose she tells me Devries was raping her and she stuck him with the nut pick. Then what?"

"Then we find out who poisoned Roderick."

"And why."

"We already know why."

"Do we?"

"Yes. He knew who stabbed Devries."

"Are you sure of that?"

Malloy frowned. "I *was* sure of that. Why shouldn't I be?"

"Maybe you should be, but you're always telling me not to jump to conclusions. We think he knew who stabbed Devries and that person poisoned him to keep him quiet."

"Or someone who wants to protect that person poisoned him to keep him quiet."

"But maybe he didn't really know."

"I don't think it matters," Malloy said. "If the killer thought he knew and killed him because of it, then that's what matters."

Sarah rubbed her forehead. "I hope I can remember all this tomorrow."

THE NEXT MORNING, THE MAID INSISTED ON ANNOUNCING Sarah before escorting her upstairs to Garnet's bedroom. To her relief, Garnet had chosen to be at home to her, even though it was much too early for a formal call.

She found her hostess still in her dressing gown, an untouched breakfast tray on the table next to her chair.

"How are you feeling?" Sarah asked.

"I'm growing bored with everyone being so concerned about my health. Imagine what will happen when my condition becomes apparent to everyone."

"I hope that means you've given up your hope of finding a *remedy* for it."

"Not entirely."

Sarah frowned. "What does your husband say?"

"I haven't told him yet."

Sarah blinked. "But you said everyone is concerned about your health."

"Only because I claimed to be ill yesterday so I wouldn't have to go to the church. My mother-in-law has promised never to forgive me for that, by the way. If that meant she'd never speak to me again, I'd be ecstatic, but apparently, it just means she's going to remind me of my thoughtlessness every day for the rest of my life."

"She would probably forgive you if she knew you were expecting her grandchild."

Garnet sighed and looked away. Her gaze fell on the tray of food. "Can I offer you some tea? Or coffee?"

"No, thank you, but you need to eat something yourself."

She considered that for a moment. "Actually, I was thinking I could starve the child."

"It doesn't work like that. The baby will take what he needs from you, and you'll be the worse for it, not him. I've seen women in the tenements who give birth year after year. They grow thinner and weaker and lose all their teeth, but the babies are still fat and healthy."

"How unfair."

"Not to the babies."

Garnet closed her eyes, and Sarah had the distinct impression she was fighting tears. Malloy would have told her to exploit this moment of weakness.

Hating herself for it, she said, "Garnet, why haven't you told Paul about the baby?"

Her eyes flew open. "That's none of your business."

"You're right, it's not, but I think I know why you haven't told Paul about the baby."

"You don't know anything about it."

"Yes, I do. I know about Paul and his friend, Mr. Zeller. And I know about your father-in-law and what he did."

"I don't know what you're talking about!"

"You tried that before, but I know you do. I also think Paul will be very surprised to find out you're with child, won't he?"

She lifted a trembling hand to her throat. "Why are you doing this to me?"

"Because two people are dead, and at least one of them doesn't deserve to be."

"Who are you talking about? Roderick? That's no one's fault. He killed himself."

"Who told you that?"

"Paul did. No, wait, his mother. She told everyone. He was distraught because Paul told him he had to leave."

"And you believe that?"

"What else could it have been? You can't think someone poisoned him."

"Yes, I can. In fact, I'm sure of it."

"But why? What had he ever done to anyone?"

"He knew who stabbed Mr. Devries."

"How could he know that?"

"He knew everyone who had been with Mr. Devries that morning, Garnet. And he knew everything that had happened."

Garnet uttered a strangled cry, bolted to her feet, and ran across the room. Dropping to her knees, she began to wretch into the chamber pot that had been beneath her bed.

Sarah hurried over, grabbing a towel from the washstand, and knelt down beside her. When Garnet had finished, Sarah handed her the towel and helped her to her feet and back to the chair, where she slumped wearily. Sarah rang for the maid, then went to get the chamber pot so she could set it outside the door, but when she knelt down again to pick it up, something shiny lying under the bed caught her eye.

A nut pick.

FRANK HAD BEEN DREADING THIS CONFRONTATION, BUT he'd given Sarah enough time to get in to see Garnet Devries, and he could put it off no longer. The maid who answered the door didn't bother to conceal her concern when he asked to see Paul Devries alone. To his credit, Paul didn't keep him waiting.

The maid showed him into the formal parlor, where Paul

stood stiffly in the center of the room, his face pale and his hands clenched at his sides.

"Have you discovered who attacked my father?" he asked when the maid was gone.

"Not yet. I need to ask you some questions, Mr. Devries. Could we sit down?"

"Yes, yes, of course." He cast about and chose a pair of chairs near the fireplace.

Frank cleared his throat. "I understand that you met with Roderick after supper on the night he died."

Paul seemed momentarily confused, but he recovered quickly. "Yes, I did."

"Can you tell me what you talked to him about?"

"I had to tell him we were dismissing him. He was my father's valet, you know, and with Father dead . . ."

"Why didn't you keep him on as your valet?"

"I already have a valet."

"But wasn't Roderick more experienced?"

"I'm perfectly satisfied with Winston."

"Does that mean you weren't satisfied with Roderick?"

Paul frowned. "I don't like to speak ill of the dead, you understand, but I never cared for Roderick."

"Why not?"

He shifted in his chair. "I always thought he was a bit . . . sneaky."

"Sneaky? You mean he stole things?"

"Oh, no, at least not that I ever knew, but he was a sly one. In fact . . ."

"In fact what?"

"Well, I hadn't thought of it until this moment, but that last time we spoke, he seemed to think I should be afraid of him for some reason."

"Afraid of him? Why?"

"I'm not sure, but he was quite shocked when I told him we were letting him go. He could stay until the end of the month, I told him, and I would give him an excellent reference. He should have been expecting it, but he tried to argue with me."

"What did he say?"

Paul frowned as he tried to remember. "He said I was making a mistake because he knew what had happened."

"What did he mean by that?"

"I had no idea, and I told him so. That seemed to surprise him, too."

"What did he do then?"

"Nothing. I mean, he didn't argue anymore. He seemed very . . . This sounds odd, but he seemed disappointed. He'd obviously thought he could convince me to keep him on."

"Is that why you gave him the whiskey? To cheer him up?"

"What?"

"The decanter of whiskey from your father's room. You gave it to him and told him to drown his sorrows."

"I most certainly did not! I would never encourage a servant to drink alcohol." His outrage seemed genuine.

"But you knew he would."

"Knew he would what?"

"You knew he liked a nip now and then, and he'd need one that night, after you told him you were letting him go. You knew he'd go to your father's room and take the whiskey and drink it."

"That's ridiculous. How could I know a thing like that?"

"You said yourself he was sneaky."

"I also said I'd never known him to steal. Besides, what harm would it do if he did take it?"

"Because you'd put arsenic in the decanter."

Paul jumped to his feet. *"What?"*

"You put rat poison in the decanter of whiskey—"

"Rat poison?"

"—and you told Roderick he was losing his job, and maybe you even suggested he help himself to the decanter because you felt so bad about having to dismiss him and—"

"Are you insane? Where did you get an idea like this!"

"Because that's how Roderick died, Mr. Devries. He said you gave him the decanter of whiskey, and it was full of rat poison, and that's what killed him."

Paul was scarlet with fury. "Why would he say I gave it to him when I didn't? No one encourages their servants to drink! That would ruin your staff."

To door burst open and Mrs. Devries came charging in. "What on earth is going on in here?"

13

Sᴀʀᴀʜ's ʜᴇᴀʀᴛ ᴡᴀs ᴘᴏᴜɴᴅɪɴɢ ᴀs sʜᴇ ʀᴏsᴇ ᴀɴᴅ ᴄᴀʀʀɪᴇᴅ the chamber pot to the door and set it outside for the maid to get. Schooling her expression to reveal nothing of what she was feeling, she returned to Garnet and sat down beside her.

"Are you all right?"

"What do you care?"

"I care very much. I know what Devries did to you, Garnet. No one would blame you for stabbing him."

Her head jerked up. "What do you mean?"

"I know he came in here that morning. Did he try to rape you again?"

Garnet simply stared back at her with hate-filled eyes.

"No one would blame you for trying to protect yourself. We know you didn't mean to kill him."

"What do you mean, *we know*? Who are you talking about?"

"Mr. Malloy and I. Roderick knew what had happened,

and Paul had to protect you, so he put the poison in the whiskey and gave it to him—"

"No! Paul would never do such a thing!"

"Are you sure?"

Plainly, she was not. She jumped up and ran to the door in the far wall that must lead to his bedroom and threw it open. "Paul!"

"He's not there. He's with Mr. Malloy."

FRANK BIT BACK A CURSE. THE LAST THING HE WANTED was Mrs. Devries's interference.

"This doesn't concern you, Mother," Paul said.

"If it's happening in my house, it concerns me. What are you doing to my son?"

"I was only asking him some questions."

"Then why were you shouting?"

"*I* was shouting, Mother. I'm sorry I disturbed you."

Mrs. Devries glared at Frank. "I want you to leave my house this instant."

"I believe it's your son's house now," Frank said.

She turned to Paul. "Are you going to allow him to speak to me like that?"

"If you leave, he won't be able to speak to you at all."

She gasped in outrage. "Is this the way you treat your mother after all I've done for you?"

"Mother, please, this is between me and Mr. Malloy."

"I won't have it, I tell you. I won't have him coming here and upsetting you."

"I'm not trying to upset him," Frank said, hoping if he remained calm, she would calm down as well. "I just needed to ask him some questions about Roderick."

"Roderick? What could he possibly know about Roderick?"

"He was the last person to speak with him before he died."

"Of course he was! I told him to dismiss the worthless idiot. I was tired of paying him a salary for sitting around and doing nothing."

"Mr. Malloy thinks someone poisoned Roderick because he knew who stabbed Father."

"That's absurd! I told you before, Roderick committed suicide."

"Why would he do a thing like that?"

"How should I know? And why should anyone care? He was just a servant."

"Mother, please!"

Frank didn't know how much longer he could be civil to this horrible woman, but before he could completely lose his temper, Garnet appeared in the open doorway.

"Paul! Don't say anything to him!" she cried and ran to him.

"Garnet, what . . . ?" He looked up and said, "Sarah?"

Sarah had followed Garnet into the room. She cast Frank an apologetic look.

"Garnet, what are you thinking?" Mrs. Devries said. "You aren't even dressed. Go back to your room at once!"

Garnet seemed not to have heard. She had grabbed Paul by the lapels. "Don't say anything to them!"

"Don't say anything about what?" Paul asked in exasperation.

"About Roderick," Sarah said. "We know what you did."

Frank stepped over to her and said very quietly, "I'm not sure we do."

She looked at him in surprise, but no one was paying any attention to them.

"I didn't do anything to Roderick, as I was just explaining to Mr. Malloy," Paul said.

"Of course you didn't. The man killed himself," Mrs. Devries said.

"That seems unlikely," Frank said, "since he knew who had stabbed Mr. Devries."

Everyone turned to him in surprise.

"If he did, why didn't he say so?" Mrs. Devries scoffed.

"I think he was hoping to blackmail Paul into keeping him on," Frank said.

"But now *we* know who did it, too," Sarah said.

Frank blinked. "We do?"

"Yes," she told him. "I found it under her bed." Sarah looked at Garnet. "I know you stabbed Mr. Devries."

Garnet stared back at her blankly, but Paul said, "No! She didn't! I'm the one who stabbed him!"

Garnet and his mother both cried, "Paul!" but he ignored them.

"I did it. He was saying awful things to me, and I stabbed him. I didn't mean to kill him, and he hardly flinched. In fact, he laughed at me. Yes, that's right, he laughed at me, and called me a . . . Well, he called me a terrible name, and I ran out of the room. I had no idea how badly he was hurt."

"Paul!" his mother screamed in anguish, clapping her hands to her ears as if trying to block out his words.

"He's lying!" Garnet said. "He's trying to protect me. I'm the one who stabbed him. You were right," she told Sarah. "Devries came into my room to attack me, and I fought him off!"

"You lying little tart!" Mrs. Devries cried. "How dare you accuse my husband of such a thing!"

"I dare because it's true!"

"It *is* true, Mother. He as much as admitted it to me. That's why I stabbed him."

Mrs. Devries glared at him, breathless in her fury. "Well, he's dead now, so what does it matter? What matters is you, and you're not going to take the blame for stabbing your father, not after all I've done to protect you!"

"What have you done?" he asked.

"I think I know," Frank said, as the picture suddenly became clear to him. All of them turned to him. "You poisoned Roderick, didn't you?"

She glared murderously at him. "Get out of my house, you worthless scum!"

"I think I already reminded you that this isn't your house anymore. You're the one who poisoned Roderick, though. Now it all makes sense. You must've known how he liked to sample his master's whiskey. Maybe your husband had complained about it to you, or one of the servants had mentioned it."

"They did no such thing!"

"He'd already emptied the decanter in Devries's bedroom, so you refilled it for him. You knew he'd be upset after his conversation with your son, the conversation you ordered your son to have with him. Maybe you even called out to him as he was going up to his room and suggested he take the decanter with him."

"I never!"

"Oh, yes," Frank continued, warming to the tale. "That's why he said someone had given it to him."

"I thought he said *I'd* given it to him," Paul said.

"I lied to you," Frank said. "He didn't actually say who it was."

"There, you see," Mrs. Devries said. "He lied to you. None of this is true!"

But Paul was looking at his mother as if he'd never seen her before, and Garnet's lips had curled into a smile of triumph.

"*You* killed Roderick," she said.

"Don't be absurd!" Mrs. Devries tried, looking a little desperate now.

"And for nothing," Frank said.

Once again they all turned to him.

"That's right," Frank said to Mrs. Devries. "You didn't need to kill him at all."

She opened her mouth, but no sound came out. She turned to Paul in silent appeal.

"She thinks you stabbed your father," Frank told him.

"I did!" Paul insisted.

"What did you stab him with?"

"Stop torturing him!" Garnet cried. "I already told you, I did it."

Frank was willing to play along. "And what did *you* stab him with?" Sarah would have spoken, but he silenced her with a gesture. "Mrs. Brandt thinks she found the weapon you used under your bed. All you have to do is tell us what it is."

"It's a knife," Garnet said.

"Where did you get a knife?"

"I . . . I . . . From my breakfast tray."

"She's lying!" Paul said. "I stabbed him."

"With what?" Frank asked, pretending to be very interested.

"A knife, of course."

"And where did you get a knife?"

"From *his* breakfast tray."

"Which didn't arrive until after you left him."

"That's not true!"

"Yes, it is. The maid will confirm it."

Sarah was staring at him with a gratifying amount of admiration. "Neither one of them did it," she marveled.

"What?" Paul said.

"I know you're trying to protect each other," Frank said, "but it's not necessary, because neither of you did it. I was sure one of you had, so I was glad when you started arguing about it. I figured the guilty one would be only too willing to confess, but neither one of you knows what he was stabbed with."

"What *was* he stabbed with, if not a knife?" Garnet asked.

Frank deferred to Sarah.

"Something the size and shape of an ice pick. We thought it was a nut pick."

"Those things Father was always using on his walnuts?" Paul asked.

"Yes. One is missing from the set in his room."

"He had one when he came into my room that morning," Garnet said. "He was eating one of his cursed walnuts and grinning at me—" She clamped a hand over her mouth as if she was going to be sick again, and Sarah rushed to her side.

"She needs to sit down," Sarah told Paul.

"You aren't going to fall for that again, are you?" his mother said. "She's just pretending she's ill to get your sympathy."

"She's not pretending. She's with child," Sarah said, as she and Paul helped Garnet to a chair.

"Good God!" Paul cried in horror. "Why didn't you tell me?"

"Because she's a devious little trollop, that's why. What other reason could she have for not telling you about your own child?"

"Because your son isn't the father," Frank said, watching for her reaction. "Your husband is."

Frank had the satisfaction of seeing the blood drain from her face as she realized the truth.

"Then that wasn't the first time," Paul was saying to his wife. "You should have told me."

"Why?" she asked with a sad smile. "So we could both be miserable? You couldn't have stopped him."

He took her hand. "I'm so sorry."

"He's dead now. That's all that matters."

Sarah discreetly moved away from them and said to Frank, "Except we still don't know who killed him."

"No, but the list of possible killers has gotten much shorter."

"You don't think she did it?" Sarah nodded at Mrs. Devries.

"No, she was too anxious to protect Paul. If she'd done it, she would've known he didn't."

"Paul?" Mrs. Devries said. "I'm feeling very unwell."

She looked it, too.

"Ring for the maid, Mother. I have to look after Garnet." Paul turned to Frank. "If it's true that she killed Roderick, what will you do with her?"

Frank honestly didn't know. He couldn't imagine the New York City justice system bringing a wealthy woman to trial for poisoning a servant. Money would change hands, and the case would simply go away. "I'll talk to you about it later. You need to take care of your wife now."

Sarah followed him out into the hallway. "What will you do now?"

"I need to pay Miss English a visit. Devries had a set of nut picks at his mistress's house, too."

THE HOUSE ON MERCER STREET LOOKED MORE FORLORN than ever. Frank wouldn't have been surprised to find Norah English and her stepmother gone, but Lizzie answered the door with her usual reluctance.

"Can't you leave us alone?"

"No." Frank didn't have to push his way inside. She stepped back, resigned. "Is Miss English receiving visitors?"

"Don't you go scaring her now. She's been nervous as a cat since you come around with the news about Mr. Devries."

"Has anyone from his company been to see you?"

"Not yet, but we ain't waiting to get kicked out."

Frank noticed immediately that most of the furniture was gone. A sagging sofa was the only thing left in the parlor. "I see you took my advice."

"We didn't hardly get nothing for that stuff, either. Everybody's out to cheat you."

Frank had to agree with that. "Did you contact her uncle?"

"Yeah, but we haven't heard back from him."

"You might need to encourage him a bit. Try telling him if he doesn't help, you'll have to go back and live with him again. That should get him moving. And don't let him know you've got any money."

"I do know better than that."

"I'll wait in here while you go get Miss English."

Frank strolled around the nearly empty parlor while Lizzie clomped up the stairs and did whatever was necessary to get Miss English prepared for his visit. She only kept him waiting a few minutes this time.

Today she looked like a schoolgirl in her simple shirtwaist and skirt with her hair in a plain bun. Lizzie hovered protectively, but Frank had no wish to harm or frighten her, unless it was absolutely necessary.

"Let's sit down," he said, indicating the sofa.

She took one end, and he lowered himself carefully onto the other, hoping he'd be able to get back up from its sagging depths without losing too much of his dignity. Lizzie stood at Miss English's elbow.

"I see you've sold the nut bowl," he said.

"You told us to," Miss English reminded him.

"Yes, I did."

"It wasn't solid silver. Nothing he had here was solid silver."

Frank figured Devries was a careful man who wouldn't leave anything valuable where someone else might get it. "He had another bowl of nuts upstairs, didn't he?"

"What difference does that make?" Lizzie asked.

Frank shot her a look, but she didn't seem intimidated.

"He liked walnuts," Miss English said. "He ate them all the time."

"I don't think I told you how Mr. Devries died."

"Did he choke on a walnut?" Lizzie asked with a smirk.

Miss English started to giggle, then caught herself. "Oh, my, did he?"

"No, he didn't. He was stabbed."

"Oh, well, then."

"Didn't you say he died at his club?" Lizzie asked.

"That's right."

"Do you mean to say somebody there stabbed him?"

"No. It's kind of funny how it happened. See, he got to his club and sat down to read the newspapers or something, and they thought he fell asleep in his chair, but it turns out he was dead."

"Oh, dear!" Miss English said.

"They thought he had a heart attack, but when the undertaker comes for him, he finds out he'd been stabbed, but it happened before he got to the club."

"How could that be?" Lizzie asked. "If he got himself stabbed, wouldn't he go to a doctor or something?"

"That's just it. The way it happened, he probably didn't know, or at least he didn't know how bad it was."

Miss English stared at him with her big, brown eyes. "How did it happen?"

"We think somebody close to him got angry and accidentally stuck him with something."

"Nobody gets accidentally stuck with a knife," Lizzie said.

"I didn't say it was a knife."

"What was it then?"

"Something long and thin, like an ice pick."

"You don't get accidentally stabbed with no ice pick, neither," Lizzie said.

"And wouldn't it bleed?" Miss English asked.

"It was on his back, and it didn't bleed much. His clothes soaked up most of it."

"This don't make sense. If it was just a little stick like you say, how could he die from it?"

"It was small, but it went deep. It hit his kidney." Frank reached around his own back to indicate the spot. "It didn't bleed much on the outside, but it did on the inside, and it killed him."

"Didn't it hurt?"

"Maybe, but I figure he thought whoever did it had punched him or something. Maybe he thought it was a bruise."

"Even if somebody hit him, Devries wasn't one to let it pass," Lizzie said.

Frank nodded. "Unless it was a woman who did it."

Miss English's puzzled expression didn't change, but Lizzie's did. "What're you saying?"

"I'm not saying anything. I'm asking. If it was an accident, and Devries didn't report it—"

"He didn't report it because it never happened!" Lizzie said.

"Why are you getting so mad, Lizzie?" Miss English asked.

"Because he thinks you stuck something in the old bugger, that's why!"

Miss English gaped at him. "Do you?"

"I'm asking if you maybe got mad at him and picked up something that was laying around and—"

"Oh, no, I never! I'd never raise a hand to him. I'd be afraid to, you see."

"She learned that pretty quick," Lizzie said, outraged. "First time she tried to complain about something, he hit her good, with a closed fist. What kind of a man does that, I ask you?"

The kind of man who deserves to get stabbed in the back.

"I couldn't chew anything for a week," Miss English said, touching her jaw. "If I'd hit him or *stabbed* him, he would've killed me, I'll bet."

"No doubt about it," Lizzie said.

Just like with a servant, Frank thought. He wouldn't have tolerated anything from anyone over whom he held power.

"Oh, I see now why you wanted his clothes," Lizzie said. "You wanted to know did he get stuck while he was here."

"How would his clothes tell him that?" Miss English asked.

"If there was a hole or some blood, I'd guess."

"That's right, but it's possible he wasn't wearing any clothes when he got stuck."

"Oh! That's why you thought it might be me," Miss English said. Lizzie gave her a poke. "I'm sorry. Wasn't that a proper thing to say?"

Frank wasn't going to reply to that. "Devries's son knows about you, Miss English. I don't know how long it will be until he thinks about doing something about you living here, but you should know."

"I don't suppose he'd like Miss English for himself, would he?" Lizzie asked.

"No, he wouldn't." Frank suddenly recalled something

Sarah had said. "There's a settlement house on Mulberry Street that takes young women. It's near Police Headquarters. They'd take you in." He glanced at Lizzie. "They might even have a job for you there."

"What's a settlement house?" Miss English asked.

"It's a place where they give you charity," Lizzie said. "We'll wait to hear from your uncle."

"At least think about it." He pushed himself up off the sofa, thinking he'd accomplished all he could here. He was just going to take his leave when he remembered a suspicion he'd had the first time he'd visited here. "You might also ask Mr. Angotti for help if your uncle doesn't reply."

"Oh, Lizzie, I never thought of him," Miss English said. "He was so polite, too."

Frank managed not to let her see how pleased he was to discover that she did know the mysterious Italian. "How did you meet him?"

Lizzie glared at him much as Mrs. Devries had when he'd accused her of murder, but Miss English was blissfully unaware of her disapproval. "He called on me one day, didn't he, Lizzie?" When she looked up, she realized her error. "Oh, dear, I wasn't supposed to talk about him, was I?"

"I'm sure Mr. Angotti told you not to mention his visit to Mr. Devries, but there's no harm in telling me. What did he talk about when he visited you?"

Chastened now, Miss English looked to Lizzie in silent appeal. "He wanted to warn her," Lizzie said. "He told her a wild tale of how Mr. Devries wanted to do away with some woman, and he didn't know but what it might be Lizzie."

"Was that what he meant?" Miss English asked, frowning prettily. "He talked so strange, never really saying anything outright. Seemed like he thought I should know what he meant without him really saying it. I thought he was just worried because I live here alone. You should've told me!"

"And scare you to death? Not likely. I didn't trust him anyways. I never do trust foreigners."

"What did he want you to do?" Frank asked.

"He said I should protect myself," Miss English said.

"How were you supposed to do that?"

"He said I should carry a knife, of all things, but I told him I couldn't do that. I'd be afraid I'd cut myself."

"And she wouldn't never use it on anybody anyway, no matter what they done to her," Lizzie said.

"Oh, my, did you know he tried to give me a knife? Is that why you thought I stabbed Mr. Devries?" Miss English asked.

"No, I didn't know."

"But did you really mean I should ask him for help?" Miss English asked.

Frank thought about how perplexed Angotti would probably be by a plea from Norah English. "Yes, I did."

SARAH HADN'T BEEN HOME LONG WHEN HER FRONT DOOR-bell rang. She'd been expecting a summons to a birth. One of her patients was very near her time, but she was surprised to find Malloy on her doorstep instead.

"Was it Miss English?" she asked as she ushered him in.

"No."

"Her maid?"

"No." He looked as discouraged as she'd ever seen him.

"We must have missed something, then."

"I've been going over everything in my head all the way over here, and I can't think of anybody else who had the chance to do it."

"Are you sure about Miss English and . . . What's the other woman's name?"

"Lizzie. Yes. Miss English is just too simple to lie very well. If she knew anything at all, she would've told me."

"What are you going to do now?"

"Mr. Malloy!" Catherine cried, clattering down the stairs, with Maeve on her heels. She ran to him for a hug, and Maeve greeted him happily.

The commotion drew Mrs. Decker from the kitchen, where Sarah had been telling her about the events of the morning.

"Are you here to celebrate the successful completion of your case, Mr. Malloy?" she asked.

"Mrs. Decker, I didn't expect to find you here," he said, a little dismayed.

"How could I stay away when I knew you were questioning Paul this morning? Was it a nut pick, as you suspected?"

"What's a nut pick?" Catherine asked.

"It's a thing you use to eat nuts with," Maeve said. "You come along now. The grown-ups need to talk in private."

Catherine tried a pout, but Maeve was unmoved. She took Catherine from Malloy's arms.

"When we're finished talking, you can visit with Mr. Malloy, darling," Mrs. Decker said. "Run along and play with Maeve now."

Sarah took Malloy's coat, and the three of them returned to the kitchen, where she poured him some coffee and they settled themselves around the table.

"I have to tell you, I'm horrified to discover that Lucretia poisoned that poor man," her mother said.

"I'm sorry," Malloy said. "I know she's a friend of yours."

"Not a friend any longer, I assure you. How could I ever

speak to her again, knowing what she's done? Are you going to arrest her?"

Malloy hesitated for a long moment, then said, "That's up to your husband."

"Why on earth would it be up to Felix?"

"Mother, have you ever known any of your friends to be arrested for anything?"

"No, but none of them have ever committed a murder, either."

"Mrs. Decker, it's very difficult to bring a rich person to trial."

"Why?"

Malloy gave Sarah a pleading glance.

"Because," she said, "many judges and others in authority are willing to accept bribes to lose the paperwork or drop the charges."

"That's outrageous!"

"But it's true."

"What will become of her, then?" her mother asked.

"That may actually be up to you," Sarah said.

"Me? What can I do?"

"You can tell your other friends what she did. She may not go to prison, but you can make sure she never goes anywhere else, either."

"Oh!"

"Unless your husband has a better idea," Malloy said.

Sarah's mother considered this for a few minutes before she said, "But we still don't know who killed Chilton. Did the mistress do it, Mr. Malloy?"

Malloy glanced at Sarah. "No, and her maid didn't either. I'm afraid I came here to tell Mrs. Brandt that I was wrong about everybody, and I'm on my way to report to your husband that I failed, Mrs. Decker."

"You can't give up!" her mother said. "There has to be a solution."

"Mother is right," Sarah said. "And if you were really ready to give up, why did you stop here first?"

"For some coffee and some sympathy," he said with a small smile.

"You're welcome to my coffee, but I'm not ready to give you any sympathy yet."

"Heavens, no," her mother said. "But I would be more than happy to help if you'll just tell me what I could do."

"Could you convince your husband he really doesn't want to know who stabbed Chilton Devries?" Malloy asked.

"This is no time for joking, Mr. Malloy. We must put our heads together and figure out who the guilty party is."

Malloy turned to Sarah. "I wasn't joking."

Sarah rolled her eyes. "Just tell us what Miss English said to convince you she's innocent."

"It wasn't what she said so much as how she answered my questions. I hadn't ever told them how Devries died, and I pretended I thought she'd accidentally stuck him with something."

"A nut pick?" her mother said.

"I didn't come right out and say it. I wanted her to tell me what she used."

"And she denied it?" her mother said.

"She denied stabbing him or doing anything to anger him. Seems Devries punched her once when she talked back to him—"

"*Punched* her? You can't be serious."

"I'm perfectly serious, Mrs. Decker. He punched her in the face so hard she couldn't chew for a week, she said."

For the first time Sarah could remember, her mother was speechless.

"I can see why she wouldn't have dared to stab him," Sarah said.

"And if she did, she would've had to do some real damage or else risk him hurting her even worse than he did before."

"Oh, I see," her mother said. "She couldn't just hurt him enough to make him angry. She'd have to kill him or disable him because he'd turn on her if she didn't."

"And whatever actually injured him was too small to disable him and took a long time to actually kill him."

"So whoever attacked him risked his anger," her mother said.

"His anger and his retribution," Sarah said.

Her mother gave her a small smile. "Now I believe you when you say you don't enjoy this. How frustrating!"

They sipped their coffee, each lost in thought for a few moments. Then Sarah said, "What else did you find out from Miss English?"

"She's sold off most of the furniture in the house, including all the nut picks."

Sarah grinned. "Did you ask her that?"

"I asked about the nut *bowls*. They were silver, but not solid silver, she informed me, so she didn't get much when she sold them. I told her Paul Devries knows about her. I figure sooner or later, he'll get around to evicting her. She's trying to find a new protector." For some reason he smiled at this.

"What's so funny?" she asked.

"I just remembered, I told her to ask Salvatore Angotti for help."

"Why would she go to him?"

"Because he'd called on her."

"Angotti? Whatever for?"

"To warn her that Devries wanted some woman killed."

"Why would he do that when he knew Mrs. Richmond was the one he wanted killed?" Mrs. Decker asked.

"I'm not sure. I think maybe Devries didn't tell him who the woman was at first. Angotti has a lot of people working for him, and he knows some of the men who work for Devries's business, so maybe he found out Devries had a mistress and assumed she was the one. Whatever his reason, he warned Miss English."

"What a curious man," her mother said.

"He certainly is," Sarah said. "He warned Mrs. Richmond, too."

"He's very gentlemanly," Malloy agreed, only a little sarcastically.

"And how nice he didn't actually kill her," Sarah said.

"He's even nicer than that. Not only did he tell Miss English that Devries might want her dead, he tried to give her a knife to protect herself with."

Something stirred in Sarah's memory. "What kind of knife?"

"I don't know. She didn't say."

Her mother leaned forward. "Sarah, what are you thinking?"

"I'm thinking that we originally thought Devries had been stabbed with a stiletto, the kind of knife Italians use."

"Miss English didn't accept the knife," Malloy said. "And if she had, she probably would've stabbed herself by accident."

"But also Angotti went to see Terry Richmond. What if he offered to give her a knife, too?"

14

"THE MEDICAL EXAMINER SAID A STILETTO WOULD'VE MADE a bigger wound," Frank said.

"What if it was smaller than a stiletto?" Sarah said. "If you were giving a woman a knife to protect herself with, she'd need to carry it around. It would have to be pretty small."

"And you think he gave a knife like that to Mrs. Richmond?" her mother said.

"I don't know, but he could have. If he offered it to Miss English, he probably offered it to Mrs. Richmond, since by then he was sure she was the one Devries wanted killed."

"And Mrs. Richmond certainly had good reason to hate Devries," Malloy said.

"But when could she have done it?" Sarah asked. "I thought you'd accounted for everyone Devries saw that day."

"Let's figure it out. He got home from Miss English's house around nine o'clock. He left there around eleven, went to see

Angotti, and left there around noon. He got to his club in the middle of the afternoon. Nobody really noticed the exact time, but let's say two thirty."

"Was that enough time for him to visit Mrs. Richmond in between?"

"I don't know, but it's enough time for him to have visited *someone* and gotten himself stabbed."

"You're forgetting that Chilton was undressed when he was stabbed," her mother said.

"That does complicate matters," Sarah said. "I can't imagine Mrs. Richmond being in a situation like that with Devries."

"Especially because Mrs. Richmond lives in a boarding-house where gentleman callers are only allowed in the parlor under the watchful eye of the landlady," Malloy said. "Besides, I asked the landlady if Devries had ever been there, and she said no."

"Maybe the landlady was out when he called," her mother said.

"Mrs. Richmond would have feared for her life, seeing Devries after what Angotti had told her," Sarah said.

Malloy was thinking. "If she'd stabbed him when he was trying to kill her, he wasn't likely to tell anybody about it, either." Malloy rose.

"Where are you going?" Sarah asked.

"To talk to Mrs. Richmond."

"Oh, my," her mother said. "You aren't going to arrest her, are you?"

"Not if she stabbed him in self-defense."

"Then why even ask her?" Sarah said.

Malloy looked down at her, his expression as solemn as she'd ever seen him. "I have to find out who stabbed Devries and how, so I can tell your father what happened."

Sarah would have protested, but her mother grabbed her arm as Malloy left the kitchen.

"He does have to tell your father," she said. "He has to prove himself."

"He doesn't have to prove himself to me!"

"I told you this was some kind of a test," her mother said fiercely. "I don't pretend to understand what goes on in men's minds. They're so very different from us. They're so very unreasonable and strange, and they always think the wrong things are important, but we aren't going to change them. We just have to take them as they are, and Mr. Malloy believes he must prove something to your father. Perhaps you'd best go with him. Mrs. Richmond might not tell him the truth of what happened between her and Chilton, especially if Chilton was naked at the time."

"But—"

"Hurry, before he leaves without you."

Sarah needed only another moment to decide her mother was right. She jumped up and hurried out to find Malloy buttoning his coat.

"I'm going with you."

"Why?"

She gave him a pitying look. "Terry Richmond isn't going to tell *you* how she came to stab Chilton Devries in his naked back. She might not tell me, either, but at least I have a chance with her. Now go upstairs and tell Catherine you have to break your promise to visit with her while I change my clothes."

By the time Malloy came back downstairs, Sarah was ready. They set off into the afternoon chill. Walking was the fastest way to Mrs. Richmond's boardinghouse, and they traveled most of the way in silence.

Sarah's heart ached when she saw the house where Garnet's

mother had taken refuge. How humiliating it must have been for her to receive her daughter in so humble a place, and how infuriating to know Chilton Devries had put her there.

Malloy knocked on the door, and they waited for what seemed a long time for someone to answer. The slatternly woman who opened the door looked Sarah up and down with cautious approval before glancing at Malloy. She didn't approve of him at all.

"What are *you* doing here? And who's this you've brought with you?"

"Mrs. Brandt, I'd like to introduce the landlady, Mrs. Higgins," Malloy said with a trace of irony.

"I'm very pleased to meet you, Mrs. Higgins," Sarah said with her best smile.

Mrs. Higgins glared at them both. "She ain't here."

"Mrs. Richmond?" Sarah asked.

"If that's who you've come to see."

"Yes, it is, but perhaps you could help us. We just need a little information."

"I ain't in the business of giving out information."

"I know, but it's so important. We're concerned that Mrs. Richmond might be in danger."

"It's nothing to me if she is."

"It will be if the trouble comes to your house," Sarah said with what she hoped was a convincingly worried frown.

"I don't want no trouble!"

"Then answer the questions," Malloy said, earning another glare.

"Mrs. Higgins, we just need to know if, by any chance, you were out of the house last Tuesday afternoon."

"On a Tuesday? Not likely. That's the day I iron. I'm here and on my feet all day."

"Then no one could have visited Mrs. Richmond that day without you knowing it," Sarah said.

"No, they couldn't, but even if they had, she wasn't at home herself that afternoon."

Sarah glanced at Malloy and saw her own surprise mirrored on his face. "She wasn't? Do you know where she was?"

"She don't consult with me, you understand, but I remember particular because she acted so funny."

"What do you mean, funny?"

"I mean strange and upset and maybe a little scared, and in an all-fired hurry, too. It started when she got the telegram."

"A telegram? Who was it from?"

"She didn't say, but I guess she thought it was from her daughter. We ain't on the telephone, so when her daughter wanted to send her a message, she'd send a telegram. Waste of money, if you ask me, but I seen how her daughter dressed, so I guess she don't care about wasting money."

"But you don't think this telegram was from her daughter?"

"Not unless it was real bad news. She got all white and went running upstairs, and in a few minutes she came back down with her coat on and ran out."

"What time was this?"

"How should I know? Early afternoon, I guess. I was ironing, not watching the clock."

"After lunch?" Sarah prodded.

"Maybe, but not long after."

"How long was she gone?"

"Most of the afternoon. She was back for supper, but she hadn't been here long." The woman gave Sarah a considering look. "Say, do you know where she went? Or what was in the telegram? I been wondering."

"No, I don't. Do you happen to know where Mrs. Richmond is now?"

"Went to see her daughter. She got a telegram, as a matter of fact, asking her to come. They had the funeral for that Devries fellow yesterday. She went to that, too. I guess she's trying to worm her way in over there now. Who wouldn't?"

"I don't suppose you happened to see the telegram in the trash," Malloy said. "The one she got last week, I mean."

Mrs. Higgins looked at him in surprise, as if she'd forgotten he was there. "No, she burned it."

Sarah chose not to remark on Mrs. Higgins' very complete knowledge of the history of the mystery telegram. "Thank you so much for your help, Mrs. Higgins," Sarah said. "We're very grateful."

"I don't know what for," Mrs. Higgins said, preening a little.

"I guess we'd better be going, Mrs. Brandt," Malloy said, taking Sarah's arm, but then he looked back at the landlady again. "I wonder if you ever noticed Mrs. Richmond having a knife."

Her eyes widened. "How'd you know about that?"

Sarah's heart lurched in her chest. "Did you see it?"

"Well, she didn't exactly have it hid, did she? Of course I saw it, when I went in to clean the room. Such a pretty little thing, like something out of a museum."

"A museum?" Sarah asked.

"Yeah, it looked like one of them swords the knights used to carry in the fairy-tale books. All fancy in a little case it slipped into, only it was real small." She held out her two forefingers about six inches apart.

Sarah exchanged a glance with Malloy, and this time *he*

thanked Mrs. Higgins for her help. She stood in her open doorway, heedless of the cold, and watched them go.

"Do we dare go back to the Devrieses' house?" Malloy asked.

"I can go alone and just ask to see Mrs. Richmond. If she's not there, I can leave without bothering anyone."

"I don't like the idea of you going alone with Mrs. Devries in the house."

"I promise I won't drink any whiskey while I'm there."

Malloy ignored her jibe. "What do you think your father will want me to do about the old woman?"

"I don't know. I've already instructed my mother she must tell all her friends what she did so they'll drop her."

"Are you sure about that? What about Paul and Garnet? Won't they suffer just as much if people like your parents shun her?"

"Oh, dear, I hadn't thought of that. Charging her with murder wouldn't be much better, though. The scandal would taint the whole family forever."

"And I can't think of any other choices. I hope your father is wiser than I am about how to handle this."

By mutual consent, they headed to the Third Avenue Elevated Train for the trip uptown to the Devrieses' house. The unheated cars weren't exactly comfortable, but at least they were out of the wind, and the duration of the trip was shortened considerably. They got off just a few blocks from the Devrieses' house and walked over as quickly as the crowded sidewalks and clogged streets would allow.

The maid who answered the door recognized them, but she didn't seem pleased to see them. She probably thought they'd already caused enough trouble.

"Is Mrs. Richmond here?" Sarah asked when the girl had ushered them inside.

"Mrs. Richmond?" she echoed in surprise.

"Yes, Mrs. Paul's mother."

"Yes, I know, but . . ."

"It's a little strange to be calling on Mrs. Richmond here, I know, but we need to speak with her, and when we called at her house, they told us she was here. You don't need to bother Mrs. Paul."

"I wouldn't. I mean, I thought maybe you was here to see *her*. She's not feeling at all well. She went right to bed after you left this morning, Mrs. Brandt. Had us send for her mother right off."

"Maybe I should see her after all. I'm a midwife, and—"

"Yes, ma'am, I remember. You brought her a remedy once before. Shall I tell her you're here?"

"Yes, and tell her I'd be happy to see what I can do to ease her discomfort."

The girl left them in the small receiving room, and the moment she was gone, Malloy was on his knees in front of the hearth.

"What are you doing?"

"I'm going to light the fire." Within a few minutes, he'd struck a match to the kindling beneath the logs that had been laid at some past time but never used, and he coaxed the meager flames until they caught the wood.

Sarah hadn't realized how chilled she was until she felt the warmth. By the time the maid returned, she was finally beginning to thaw. The girl glanced at the fire with disapproval, but she knew better than to chasten guests.

"Mrs. Paul said you can come up, Mrs. Brandt." She glanced

at Malloy, who certainly wouldn't be welcome in Garnet's bedroom.

"I'll just wait here for Mrs. Brandt," he said.

"Perhaps you could bring Mr. Malloy some coffee," Sarah said.

The maid took Sarah upstairs and announced her. Garnet really was in her bed. Sarah hurried over to her. "What's wrong?"

"I can't seem to keep anything down, but that's normal, isn't it?"

"Not really. Morning sickness—which is what they call it, even though it can happen any time of the day or night—will happen once or twice, but after you've thrown up, you usually feel better. Oh, no!"

"What?" Garnet pushed herself up on one elbow.

"Could Mrs. Devries have poisoned you?" Sarah could think of many reasons why the old woman might want to get rid of Garnet. "Have you eaten or drunk anything she might have put something in?"

Garnet eased herself back down and smiled slightly. "There's no fooling you, is there? I thought I could convince you this was normal."

"What do you mean?"

"I mean I did take something, but not from the old woman."

"Something to get rid of the baby?" Sarah asked.

Garnet turned her head away. "That's what it was supposed to do. So far, it's just made me sick."

"When did you take it?"

"This morning. I didn't know you and Mr. Malloy were going to turn our world upside down today."

"I don't know of anything you can drink that will really be

effective, but most things they sell for that purpose can make you very sick. If you aren't feeling better by tomorrow, you should probably see a doctor."

Garnet sighed. "I can't bear the thought of having his child. How could I ever love it or care for it? How could I even stand the sight of it?"

"I'm sorry, I don't know."

"Of course you don't. Nobody does."

Sarah ached for her. At least she had her mother to help her through it. She looked around, half expecting to find Mrs. Richmond sitting in a corner, but she wasn't there. "I thought your mother was visiting you."

"I almost forgot the maid said you came to see Mother. She wasn't very happy at the prospect of a visit with you, I'm sorry to say. She went downstairs to make me some tea to settle my stomach. She'll be back in a moment. What did you want to see her about?"

"Nothing important."

"You're a terrible liar, Mrs. Brandt. You'd never last a day in this house. Obviously, it's something *very* important or you wouldn't have come back here so soon. But what could it be? My mother couldn't be with child, so it can't be a professional visit. Besides, Mr. Malloy wouldn't have come with you to visit an expectant mother. No, she was especially distressed when she heard he was with you. How does my mother know him?"

"I believe he visited her."

"Oh, yes, he was the one who told her about the child. But I don't think I know why he went to see her in the first place."

"Didn't she tell you?"

"She doesn't like to distress me," Garnet said with a small smile. "But you've never seemed to mind, so tell me."

In spite of what Garnet thought, Sarah didn't want to distress her either. "I'd rather wait until she comes."

"Ring for the maid to fetch her, then. She might stay downstairs until she thinks you've left. I told you she really did not want to see you."

Sarah pulled the bell rope and in a few moments, the maid came in.

"Would you ask my mother to come back up?" Garnet asked.

"Mrs. Richmond left, ma'am."

"What do you mean, she left?"

"She left the house."

"When?"

"Right after she came downstairs."

"How strange." Garnet dismissed the maid and turned back to Sarah. "I didn't want to tell you, but she actually seemed afraid when she heard you were here to see her. Why would she be afraid?"

Sarah still didn't want to tell her, but Garnet would find out soon anyway. "We believe your mother is the one who stabbed Devries."

"You can't be serious!"

"I'm perfectly serious."

"Why would she do a thing like that? And how? She hasn't seen him in years!"

"We believe she saw him on the day he died, and she had a very good reason to stab him. He was trying to kill her."

"Dear God!" Garnet clamped her eyes shut and covered her mouth with both hands.

Sarah grabbed a bowl sitting on the bedside table and held it ready in case Garnet was sick, but after a moment, she opened her eyes and lowered her hands. "Why on earth would he try to kill her?"

"We suspect he was afraid she would encourage you to leave Paul. He was desperate to keep Paul's secret, which is why he arranged your marriage in the first place. If you left him, people would want to know why."

"I didn't want to leave Paul, you know. I just wanted to leave this house, to get away from *him*."

"I know that now, and maybe that was another reason he wanted your mother out of the way. You couldn't leave if you didn't have a place to go."

"Which explains why he wanted her dead, but it doesn't explain how she could have stabbed him."

"We don't know for sure, but we believe that after Devries visited Angotti—"

"Who's Angotti?"

"He's an Italian gentleman who . . . uh . . . arranges things for people. Devries tried to hire him to murder your mother."

"Dear God," she murmured again.

"Mr. Angotti doesn't do these things himself, you understand, but even so, he didn't have much stomach for having a woman killed, so he went to see your mother. When he heard her story, he decided not to accept Devries's offer, and he apparently gave your mother a small knife to use in case Devries decided to try to do the job himself."

Garnet groaned. "Why didn't she tell me?"

"I'm sure she didn't want to distress you," Sarah said without irony.

"You still haven't told me how it happened."

"As I said, we don't know for sure, but on the day he died, Devries went to see Angotti, and Mr. Angotti told him he wouldn't accept his offer. Devries was angry and he went someplace for a few hours before eventually turning up at his club, where he died."

"What makes you think he saw my mother?"

"The fact that Mr. Angotti probably gave your mother a knife that could have killed him, and the fact that she received a telegram shortly after Devries left Angotti."

"I send her telegrams all the time."

"Did you send her one that day?"

Garnet had no reply.

"This telegram upset her very much, and she went out and didn't come back for a long time. We think Devries arranged to meet her someplace, intending to kill her himself perhaps."

"Or force himself on her."

Sarah blinked in surprise. "Do you really think . . . ?"

"Of course I think he'd do something like that! He'd done it to me, and that morning . . . Well, he didn't expect me to fight back, but I just couldn't let him use me again, so I screamed. I'd never done that before, and of course Paul came rushing in, and . . . Well, he left without getting what he'd come for. He was angry, and if he did want to kill Mother, he'd want to humiliate her first. Oh, no, do you think he raped her? I couldn't stand the thought of that! Poor Mother!"

Garnet started to weep.

"She stabbed him, Garnet. I'm sure she stabbed him to prevent him from hurting her."

"Do you really think so?" she asked brokenly.

"Yes, I do. I'm sure of it."

Garnet dashed the tears from her eyes. "And now Mr. Malloy has come to arrest her."

"He just wants to find out what happened. If Devries was going to harm her, it was self-defense. She won't be arrested for that."

Garnet stared back at her for a long moment, absorbing the truth of Sarah's words, but then her eyes widened. "Dear heaven, she's going to kill herself!"

"What?"

"Kill herself! That's what she meant! When the maid came and told us you wanted to see her, she got very maudlin, and she started talking about my father and how she'd missed him so much and how much she loved me, but she had to do the right thing and not cause me any scandal and I was hardly listening because I felt so sick, and then she kissed me. She *kissed* me! She was only going down to the kitchen, but she kissed me good-bye! Oh, Mrs. Brandt, that must be why she left. You have to stop her!"

"Of course I will. We'll go right back to her boarding-house—"

"No, that's not where she'll go. She was talking about Father and how much she missed him. She'll go to the bridge like he did. He jumped off the Brooklyn Bridge. Did I tell you that? They never found his body. She'll just disappear like he did, so there won't be a scandal over a suicide and no one will ever know what became of her. Please, you must stop her!"

Garnet was frantic now, nearly hysterical, and Sarah rang for the maid.

"Go!" Garnet said. "Find her! Stop her!"

Sarah ran out into the hall. The maid was coming, and Sarah shouted at her to look after Garnet before racing down the stairs. When she reached the bottom of the first flight, Paul Devries and Hugh Zeller had come out of the parlor to see what the commotion was about.

"Mrs. Brandt, what's going on?" Paul asked.

"I don't have time to explain it all, but we think Mrs. Richmond has gone to the Brooklyn Bridge to kill herself."

Sarah didn't stop. She was running down the second flight of stairs, now with Paul and Hugh in her wake.

"Why would she do a thing like that?" Paul asked.

"She's the one who stabbed your father, and she thinks Malloy is here to arrest her for it."

"Dear God," Paul said. "Did she know what he'd done to Garnet? Is that why?"

Sarah didn't have time to explain. Malloy had met her at the bottom of the stairs.

"Did you hear?" she asked him.

"Yes, but why the bridge?"

"That's where her husband killed himself."

"We'll go with you," Paul said.

Malloy was pulling their coats from the rack by the front door.

"Someone should probably go to her boardinghouse, just in case," Sarah said. "And ask Garnet if there's someplace else she might go, too. We need to find her and let her know she won't go to prison."

"I won't let her be punished for it," Malloy told them. "Tell her that, if you find her."

Malloy pulled on his coat while Paul helped Sarah with hers.

"I will," Paul promised. "Do you need the carriage?"

Zeller pulled open the front door for them.

"No, the El will be faster," Malloy said.

"Tell Garnet we'll bring her back here if we find her," Sarah said.

Then they were outside, fairly running down the walk in the direction of the Third Avenue Elevated Train.

They didn't waste breath on conversation until they'd reached the train platform two stories above the street. They had to wait for what seemed an eternity for the next train. Sarah wanted to run back down the stairs and keep running, but she forced herself to stay there. They had a long way to go, and the train would get them there faster than any other mode of transportation.

"You're sure about this?" Malloy asked as she paced in a circle.

"Garnet is sure. Mrs. Richmond was talking about her husband and how she didn't want to cause a scandal. She even kissed Garnet good-bye."

"But to kill herself . . ."

"She's a proud woman. Remember what she said about doing what she must for those she loved? All she wanted was for Garnet to be happy. With Devries dead, she would have a chance at that, but not if her mother was tried and convicted for his murder."

"I should've refused when your father asked me to find out what happened to Devries," he said.

"You couldn't know. What if he'd been a saintly man whose greedy heir had decided he wanted his inheritance sooner?"

"But he wasn't, and your father must have known that."

"Well, we'll take that up with Father at a later time."

"We?" he asked with interest.

Sarah smiled at him. "You can't think I'd let you have all the fun."

The slight vibration in the floor told them the train was coming. They hurried to the edge of the platform, craning and watching and willing it to hurry. They could hardly wait for the doors to be opened once it finally stopped.

At last the train was moving again, carrying them down and down to almost the very tip of Manhattan Island to where the majestic bridge stretched out across the water to Brooklyn.

"What if we're too late?" Sarah said.

"What if this is a wild-goose chase, and Mrs. Richmond is just on a train back to Virginia?"

"Oh, Malloy, do you really think that?"

"No, and I don't think Paul's going to find her at the boardinghouse, either. I wish I did, but I keep thinking how Mrs. Richmond looked that first time I met her, sitting there in that shabby parlor. Devries had taken almost everything from her, but she still had her pride. She'd killed him to keep it, and she'll never let him take it now that he's dead."

"What a horrible man. I wish he was still alive. I'd like to kill him myself."

Malloy widened his eyes at her but she refused to relent.

They rode on in silence for a while, Sarah staring unseeing at the windows they passed where ordinary people lived their lives in full view of the passengers who rode the trains that ran down several of the main streets of the city. Finally, she said, "I can't figure out how she could jump from the bridge when the walkway is in the middle."

Unlike most bridges, where pedestrians walked along the sides, the Brooklyn Bridge had been built with an elevated walkway down the center. A jump from there would only land a person on the tracks of the train that ran along the inside traffic lanes on either side.

"You said her husband managed to jump off of it. She must know how he did it."

"I guess that's possible."

"Even if she tries, she might not be able to go through with it. Lots of people think they want to jump until they get up there and see how high it is and how cold the water looks. They're happy when the authorities come and get them down."

Sarah remembered Mrs. Richmond's pride and prayed they'd get there in time.

When they reached the stop closest to the bridge, they hurried off and clattered down the station stairs to the street.

"Don't wait for me," Sarah said, knowing Malloy could move faster than she, hampered as she was by her long skirts. "I'll catch up."

Grim-faced, he pushed his way through the pedestrians clogging the sidewalk and disappeared. Sarah followed as best she could, pushing and shoving as necessary and paying no heed to the shouted curses she left in her wake.

The wind on the bridge nearly took her breath as she finally made her way out onto the walkway. Below her, one of the elevated trains rumbled along, returning to Manhattan. She scanned both sides of the bridge, looking for anyone who might be Terry Richmond. How would she find her? How would she get to her? And how would she stop her from jumping?

Sarah took heart at the way the people around her were calmly going about their business. She was the only one who seemed upset or harried. Surely, if someone had jumped from the bridge, someone would have seen, and the horror of it would have caused the hundreds of people nearby to react. But nothing seemed out of the ordinary, at least not yet.

Sarah walked slowly, hugging the rail and straining to see a place down below, along the side of the bridge, where a person might get to the edge and climb up over the rails and cables and . . .

"Sarah!"

She turned and saw Malloy. He was on the other side of the walkway. She darted and dodged among the other pedestrians to reach him.

"Do you see her?' she asked.

"No, but I can see how you could get out there." He pointed to a narrow strip of pavement at the edge of the outer traffic lane, which was probably for workmen to use. They could see for a long way down the length of the bridge and saw no sign of her.

"How far would she go?" Sarah asked.

"I doubt she'd walk out very far onto the bridge. Too much chance of someone seeing her and stopping her."

"Where is she, then?" Sarah looked again in all directions. "I'll go back to the other side and watch from there."

Once again she was buffeted and bumped by the heedless individuals intent on getting where they were going. When she reached the rail, she saw the same narrow access area on this side as well. The only difference was that on this side, a solitary figure hunched against the wind was making her way gingerly along it.

15

"MALLOY!" SARAH SCREAMED AS SHE FRANTICALLY SCANNED the area below, trying to figure out how to get down to where Terry Richmond was. "Mrs. Richmond! Terry!" she called, waving.

Someone grabbed her hand and pulled it down. "Don't," Malloy said. "If she sees us up here, she might panic and jump."

"What can we do, then?"

"We need to get down there so you can tell her she doesn't have anything to be afraid of. Come on."

He took her arm and propelled her into the streaming mass of pedestrians heading for the Manhattan side of the bridge. Sarah had to resist the urge to knock people over in her desperation to reach the end of the bridge again. Fortunately, many of them were also in a hurry, and they were soon back where they had started.

Sarah had no idea how to get onto the walkway Mrs. Richmond was using, but fortunately, Malloy did. They had to cross through the line of vehicles entering the traffic lanes, but after only a couple close calls as they darted in front of skittish horses controlled by impatient drivers, they reached the point at which Mrs. Richmond must have entered the bridge.

"Hey, where're you going?" a young workman yelled at them as Malloy helped Sarah up the steep steps to reach the narrow walkway that ran along the edge of the bridge.

Malloy identified himself. "There's a woman out there who's planning to jump."

The young man swore, and Malloy cuffed him on the ear.

"Watch your language, and get some help. We're going out to stop her, so don't make a lot of noise when you come up. Let us talk to her."

The fellow nodded and ran off.

Sarah had reached the top of the steps, and she could see Mrs. Richmond. She was maybe a hundred feet out. She'd stopped and was looking down over the side, probably judging the distance as Malloy had predicted.

"I'm going to hang back," Malloy said. "If she sees me, she might jump before we get a chance to say anything to her. Are you going to be able to do this?"

Sarah had no idea. Her heart pounded in her chest, and she felt as if she couldn't draw enough air into her lungs, but she looked deep into Malloy's dark eyes and nodded.

"Go on, then," he said.

Sarah wanted to run, but the path was narrow and the wind buffeted her, bringing tears to her eyes and forcing her to clutch at the railing as she moved forward. Remembering Malloy's warning, she resisted the urge to call out. Finally, she was close enough that Mrs. Richmond sensed her presence. Her head jerked up, and she took a step back.

"Don't come any closer!"

Sarah raised both her hands in a gesture of surrender. "Don't do this. You don't have anything to be afraid of."

She laughed at that, an ugly, bitter sound. "What do you know?"

"I know everything. I know you stabbed Devries with the knife you got from Mr. Angotti, but it was self-defense. You won't be punished for that."

"You're lying. I know Mr. Malloy came with you this morning. He's going to arrest me. I won't put Garnet through that, not after what's already happened to her."

She reached up and grabbed one of the thousands of cables that supported the bridge, stuck her foot into the grillwork, and began to hoist herself up.

"No!" Sarah cried, sprinting toward her. "Stop! Listen to me!"

From the pedestrian walkway above, a voice shouted, "Somebody's jumping!"

Mrs. Richmond froze, instinctively looking up to see who had spoken. The foot traffic on the walkway had stopped, and dozens of faces were peering down at them.

"Jump! Jump!"

"What're you waiting for!"

A cacophony of voices showered down on them, jeering and urging her on. Nearer, the wagon drivers were stopping their horses, wanting to see the show.

"Don't listen to them!" Sarah said, stopping just short of touching distance. "Listen to me! You can't do this to Garnet, not after what she's been through. Your daughter needs you."

"She doesn't need me to shame her!"

"You won't, I swear it. Mr. Malloy is here. He'll tell you himself. He just wanted to make sure you were the one who did it so he could stop the investigation."

"But your father won't stop it. Devries was his friend."

She hoisted herself higher, ready to swing her leg over the edge when a gust of wind rattled the cables and threw her backward, dislodging her other foot so for a heart-stopping moment she swung free, clinging to the cable with both hands.

With a cry, Sarah threw herself forward and wrapped her arms around Mrs. Richmond's flailing legs. The force of her struggles slammed Sarah against the side of the bridge.

"Let me go!" Mrs. Richmond bucked and squirmed, but Sarah held on, refusing to let go, refusing to fail.

Locked in a desperate embrace, they seemed frozen there for a brief eternity as a roar of voices above protested Sarah's heroics. Then the shouts were closer and followed by the pounding of running feet, and Malloy was there with his minions.

He took Mrs. Richmond's weight and others pried her hands from their death grip on the cable, and then she was down, standing on the pavement, except her knees buckled, and Malloy had to lift her into his arms.

Sarah was vaguely aware of the shouts still raining down on them from the frustrated gawkers who had been cheated out of a spectacle, but she didn't care. She was too busy thanking the grim-faced bridge workers who had assisted Malloy as they escorted them back off the bridge.

Trotting along behind Malloy, Sarah heard Mrs. Richmond ask, "Where are you taking me?"

"To your daughter," he said.

* * *

WHEN FRANK ARRIVED AT THE DECKER HOUSE SEVERAL hours later, he wasn't surprised to be immediately escorted into the family parlor. First of all, he was accompanied by the Deckers' daughter, which would have guaranteed him admittance. Even more important, though, the phone call he had made to Decker from the Devrieses' house had announced that he would be delivering the solution to Chilton Devries's death, which made him just as welcome as Sarah.

Both of the Deckers rose when they were ushered into the family parlor, and Mrs. Decker came forward to greet them. She took Sarah's hands and raised her cheek for a kiss, but then turned her full attention to Frank, giving him her hand and then covering his with her other one so he wouldn't release it immediately.

"Mr. Malloy, you've found the truth at last."

Frank stared back at her in surprise, not sure what sort of response would be appropriate to this odd remark.

Mr. Decker saved him the trouble. "I don't need your subtle reminders, Elizabeth. I am well aware of Mr. Malloy's accomplishments."

Mrs. Decker flashed Frank a conspiratorial smile before releasing his hand. "Of course you are, my dear. Let's sit down so he can tell us everything."

The Deckers sat together on the sofa and Frank and Sarah took the chairs opposite.

"I'm not sure how much you already know," Frank said.

"I haven't told him anything," Mrs. Decker said, earning a frown from her husband that she ignored. "I wasn't sure what was fact and what was theory, so I decided to wait until you had an opportunity to confirm everything."

"All right, then," Frank said, pretending not to notice Sarah's grin. "You know the story of how Devries tricked Mr. Richmond into an investment scheme that ruined him in order to pressure Garnet to marry Paul."

"Yes, so he could conceal Paul's . . . uh, proclivities from the world," Decker said.

"Is that what it's called? Proclivities?" Mrs. Decker asked.

"No," Decker said. "I'm simply trying to pretend you are too refined to wish to hear anything indelicate."

Frank studiously avoided meeting Sarah's gaze.

"In the past few months, however, Mrs. Richmond began to sense from Garnet's letters that something was very wrong with her daughter, so she came to the city to find out what it was."

"Garnet was thinking of leaving Paul," Sarah said.

"Which would be understandable, under the circumstances," Mrs. Decker said.

Mr. Decker sighed. "Mr. Malloy?"

"We have discovered that the reason Garnet was unhappy was because Mr. Devries had forced himself on her."

"Good God!" Decker said.

"More than once," Mrs. Decker said. "And she is with child by him."

Decker covered his eyes for a long moment while he came to terms with this horror. "Why didn't Paul stop him?" he asked hoarsely.

"He didn't know," Sarah said. "Garnet finally admitted that she didn't tell him because Devries had already threatened to claim *she* had seduced *him* out of frustration over her husband's neglect. Paul might not have believed him, but he would have been powerless to stop his father without causing a scandal that would have ruined Garnet."

"And Lucretia would certainly have taken Chilton's side," Mrs. Decker said.

"So I assume Garnet is the one who stabbed him," Decker said.

"That's what we thought at first. The morning Devries died, he'd gone to Garnet's room again, but this time she fought him off, and Paul heard her and came in."

"Paul thought it was the first time Devries had tried this, and he had a terrible row with his father," Sarah said.

"So Paul stabbed him," her father said.

Frank began to feel sorry for him. "I figured it was one or the other, and when I confronted them, they both confessed."

"What?"

"They were trying to protect each other," Sarah said.

"So one or the other of them did it," Decker said.

Frank shook his head. "Neither one of them knew what kind of a weapon Devries had been stabbed with. The medical examiner had told me it was something the size and shape of an ice pick, but when I asked them what they'd used, they both said a knife, so I knew neither of them had done it."

Frank could tell Decker was holding his temper with difficulty, but Mrs. Decker didn't seem to care.

"They did find out who killed the valet, though," she said.

"Not Paul or Garnet, surely," Decker said as if it were a prayer.

"No," she said smugly. "Lucretia did."

"*Lucretia?*"

"She thought Paul had stabbed his father," Frank hastily explained. "And she thought Roderick knew it."

"But he couldn't have known it because it wasn't true," Decker said.

"No," Sarah said, "but Roderick apparently *thought* Paul

had done it. He actually tried to blackmail Paul, but he failed because Paul didn't know what he was talking about."

Malloy took pity on Decker and finished the tale. "Because Mrs. Devries thought Paul had killed his father and Roderick knew it, she told Paul to dismiss him, then she put poison in the decanter of whiskey and gave it to Roderick to console him."

"You're sure of this?" Decker asked.

"Positive," Sarah said. "She practically admitted it."

They gave him a moment to absorb this shock. "I don't suppose she could have stabbed Chilton, not if she thought Paul had done it."

"No," Malloy said.

"Then who did?" Decker asked, at the end of his patience. "I'm assuming you wouldn't have come if you didn't know."

"I told you Devries wanted Angotti to have Mrs. Richmond killed," Malloy reminded him. "We thought it was just because she might help Garnet leave Paul, but now we know Devries had his own reasons for wanting to keep Garnet in his house."

"I can see that, yes."

"What Angotti didn't tell me—and Mrs. Richmond didn't mention when I visited her—was that when Angotti had warned her Devries might try to kill her himself, he gave her a small dagger that she could use to protect herself."

"A stiletto with a very thin blade," Sarah added.

Frank reached in his pocket, and both the Deckers gasped when he pulled out the beautiful instrument of death. Made like a tiny sword in a yellow enameled scabbard, it looked almost like a lovely toy.

Frank handed it to Decker to examine. He turned it over in his hand, then pulled the blade from its sheath. The soft *clink* made Malloy wonder if Devries had recognized that sound as his doom when he'd heard it. "So Chilton had gone to murder her that day?"

"We knew he'd met with Angotti after he left his house, and Angotti told him he was not going to have Mrs. Richmond killed. After that, he disappeared for a couple hours, and when he arrived at the Knickerbocker, he'd been stabbed. Mrs. Richmond didn't want to talk about it, but your daughter was finally able to coax the story out of her." Frank turned to Sarah, happy to give her the credit for this.

She told the rest of it. "Shortly after he left Mr. Angotti, Devries sent Mrs. Richmond a telegram ordering her to meet him at a disreputable hotel. He promised he would have good news about Garnet, but she wasn't fooled. She knew he was planning to murder her, so she took the knife Angotti had given her and she went to meet him."

"But why did she go at all if she knew what he was planning?" Decker asked.

"Because she was afraid he would come after her if she didn't. At least this way, she had the advantage of surprise because he didn't know Angotti had told her."

Decker considered this for a moment. "Wait, didn't you tell me Devries was undressed when he was stabbed?" he asked Frank.

"That's why Mrs. Richmond was so reluctant to tell her story," he said.

"When she arrived at the hotel room," Sarah said, "she found him waiting for her with just a towel wrapped around him. He was going to make her submit to him, and then he was going to murder her."

Mrs. Decker made a small sound of distress, and Decker automatically reached over and touched her hand, but he never took his gaze from Sarah. "I hope you will believe me when I tell you I had no idea he was capable of these . . . these *abominations.*"

"Of course, Father. We know he kept that side of himself hidden from those he considered his friends."

"I hope she stabbed him before he could . . . do anything," Mrs. Decker said in a near whisper.

"She told me she had the knife in her hand when he opened the door. Mr. Angotti had told her to stab him in the throat or the eye—it's such a small blade, it wouldn't do much damage otherwise—but she couldn't bring herself to do that. The instant he turned his back, she stuck it in him."

"Good for her!" Mrs. Decker said.

"He roared, she said, but he didn't seem to be hurt at all, just angry. She said something in warning, like she'd kill him if he tried to hurt her again or words to that effect. She couldn't remember exactly. Then she ran out. She walked around the city for hours, fully expecting the police to be waiting for her when she got back to her boardinghouse. When they weren't, she thought Devries must have been too embarrassed to report her."

"When I went to question her, she didn't know he was dead," Frank said, "and she thought I was going to arrest her for stabbing him. When I told her he was dead, she realized nobody knew who'd stabbed him, so she thought she would get away with it."

"How on earth did you ever get her to tell you all this, Sarah?" her mother asked.

"After Mrs. Brandt saved her life, she felt obligated," Frank said, earning a scowl from Sarah.

Her parents gaped at her. "How did you save her life?" her mother asked.

"Malloy and I went to see her at the Devrieses' house, after we'd figured out she must have been the one who did it. When she heard we were there to see her, she realized we must know. She thought Malloy was going to arrest her, and she decided she would kill herself to spare Garnet the scandal."

"Oh, no!" her mother said.

"Her husband had jumped off the Brooklyn Bridge, and something she said made Garnet think she was going to do the same thing," Frank said. "That's where we found her, and your daughter kept her from jumping."

Both her parents seemed impressed, although Mr. Decker was more surprised.

"But you aren't really going to arrest her, are you?" Mrs. Decker asked.

Frank looked at Decker, meeting his gaze squarely and unflinchingly. He had no idea what Felix Decker would consider justice in this case, but he said, "No, I'm not. She was protecting herself. There's no crime in that."

The women were watching Decker, too, waiting for his reply. After another moment he said, "No, there isn't."

THE FOLLOWING SUNDAY, THE WEATHER BROKE, BRINGING an unseasonably warm and sunny day that hinted at the change of season still weeks away. Winter-weary city residents flocked to the parks where children could release some of the energy they'd been storing all winter. Malloy and Brian had arrived on Sarah's doorstep, and the five of them had walked to Washington Square so the children could enjoy the spring-like weather.

Sarah and Malloy found a bench where they could talk while watching Catherine and Brian playing tag with Maeve.

"I visited Garnet yesterday," Sarah said.

"How is she?"

"She isn't expecting a baby anymore."

Malloy raised his eyebrows in a silent question.

"I didn't ask and she didn't say, so I don't know how it happened, but she's apparently recovering nicely. Paul is taking her to Italy to recuperate."

"That's romantic."

"Hugh Zeller and Terry Richmond are going with them."

"Ah, not so romantic, then. Is she planning to stay married to him?"

"I know you noticed how fond they are of each other. After what she endured with Devries, she isn't interested in men that way, so her marriage to Paul suits her fine. He and Hugh dote on her and keep her entertained, too. She told me that Paul has promised to divorce her immediately if she falls in love with someone else, but in the meantime, they are perfectly content with things as they are."

"And what about Mrs. Richmond?"

"When Paul found out what happened between her and his father, he was appalled and very anxious to make it up to her. He inherited everything, you know, so he set Mrs. Richmond up with an independent income that is adequate to her needs, although she is also going to live with Paul and Garnet for the time being."

"What does Mrs. Devries think about that?"

Sarah had been saving the most interesting news until last. "Do you remember you asked my father what he wanted you to do about her?"

"Yes, and he said he would speak with Paul about it. Don't tell me she's going to prison?"

"Of course not! At least not the kind of prison you mean. Paul has put her in a sanitarium."

"You mean an asylum? For crazy people?"

"Not the kind of place you're thinking of. This is more like a nice hotel, except the locks are on the outside of the doors. It's where rich people send the relatives they don't want other people to see anymore."

"I just remembered, Hugh or Paul, one of them mentioned that Devries had threatened his wife with that once."

"It's no secret that men have sometimes rid themselves of unwanted wives by doing that, but in this case, I believe Father argued that no woman in her right mind would have poisoned a servant the way she did."

"He was right about that."

"And then Garnet remembered that when she was ill, my first thought was that her mother-in-law had poisoned her. When Paul realized she might harm someone else, he didn't need any more encouragement."

"And her daughters didn't object?"

"Not after Paul told them what she'd done. Apparently, after he told them, he asked if either of them would like to have her. That was enough to convince them it was the right decision."

They watched the children playing for a while. Here in the park the air smelled almost clean, and the laughter of children could help her forget the evil she knew was never far away. Here, with Malloy beside her, she felt safe and content, as if the world were a better place than she knew it to be.

Then she remembered a message she was supposed to deliver.

"Mrs. Richmond wanted me to thank you."

"What for?"

"For not arresting her."

"She didn't commit a crime."

Sarah smiled at him. "Not all men would see it that way. If you'd arrested her, they could have said she was meeting Devries voluntarily. They would have accused her of being a wanton woman who had stabbed her lover out of jealousy when she found out he had another mistress or something."

"That's ridiculous."

"Of course it is, but you've seen it before. When a woman kills a man, other men get nervous. If mistreated women started fighting back, their lives might be in danger, too."

"So it's best not to let one of them get away with murder."

"Exactly," she said.

"I wonder if that's what your father wants to talk to me about."

Sarah blinked. "What?"

"Your father. He sent me a message. He wants to see me at his office tomorrow."

"He does? Why?"

"He didn't say. Men like your father don't have to give reasons."

Sarah's mind was racing. It could be nothing. Perhaps he had another matter he wanted Frank to look into. Perhaps he just wanted to commend him for the way he had handled the Devrieses' situation.

But she kept remembering what her mother had said about the case being some kind of a test. If so, she thought Malloy had passed it, but would her father agree? And if he did, what would that mean?

Her father didn't control her life, of course. He couldn't tell her what to do and expect her to obey. But, she realized with a sudden shocking clarity, he could expect Malloy to obey him. He had power and influence, and he could destroy Frank's life with a word in the right ear.

Or he could make it infinitely better.

Which would it be?

"Look," Malloy said, pointing at a pushcart nearby. "They're selling hot gingerbread. Let's get some."

Although his eyes still held the wariness he might always feel around her, he smiled in the way that made her feel warm to her bones. Warm and safe and cherished. She tucked her arm through his. "Yes, let's. The children will love it."

Author's Note

WHILE I WAS WRITING THIS BOOK, TWO VERY INTERESTING and apparently unconnected things happened. First of all, I read the biography of Consuelo Vanderbilt, the heiress who was married off, at the age of eighteen, to a penniless English duke who needed her ten-million-dollar dowry to fix up his ancestral home. It was in such disrepair that the young couple had to take a yearlong honeymoon to allow time for repairs before they could actually take up residence. Their marriage eventually ended in divorce, and Consuelo and the duke both married for love the second time.

The second thing that happened while I was writing this book was that two scandals broke in the news in which powerful men were caught engaging in behavior toward women that was at best reprehensible and at worst criminal. I won't bother to mention the specifics. By the time you read this, we will have probably heard of several more. The sad fact is that I started out to write a story that showed how poorly women were treated by powerful men back at the turn of the last century, only to be reminded that the more things change, the more they stay the same.

I shouldn't be surprised. I often find that the theme of the latest Gaslight Mystery is one that still resonates with modern readers. At least today, people are outraged by this behavior, so we're making progress.

Please let me know how you liked this book. Find me at my website, www.victoriathompson.com.